ALSO BY CATHERINE MULVANY

Something Wicked

Shadows All Around Her

Run No More

I'll Be Home for Christmas
A Short Story Anthology

Wicked Is the Night

CATHERINE MULVANY

POCKET **STAR** BOOKS

New York   London   Toronto   Sydney

Pocket Star Books
A Division of Simon & Schuster, Inc.
1230 Avenue of the Americas
New York, NY 10020

This book is a work of fiction. Names, characters, places, and incidents either are products of the author's imagination or are used fictitiously. Any resemblance to actual events or locales or persons, living or dead, is entirely coincidental.

Copyright © 2008 by Catherine Mulvany

All rights reserved, including the right to reproduce this book or portions thereof in any form whatsoever. For information address Pocket Books Subsidiary Rights Department, 1230 Avenue of the Americas, New York, NY 10020

First Pocket Star Books paperback edition December 2008

POCKET STAR BOOKS and colophon are registered trademarks of Simon & Schuster, Inc.

For information about special discounts for bulk purchases, please contact Simon & Schuster Special Sales at 1-800-456-6798 or business@simonandschuster.com

Cover art by Chris Cocozza
Design by Min Choi

Manufactured in the United States of America

10 9 8 7 6 5 4 3 2 1

ISBN-13: 978-1-4165-2558-5
ISBN-10:   1-4165-2558-0

ACKNOWLEDGMENTS

A special thanks to Liz Jennings for her help with Italian, to Shelley Bates for sharing her knowledge of San Francisco, and to the members of jCW for their insightful critiques.

"Mirror, mirror on the wall,
Who's the fairest of them all?"

—"Snow White,"
The Brothers Grimm

ONE

"Marcello, my friend, you drive like a woman." Patrick Granger scowled at the taillights of the logging truck they'd been stuck behind for the last three miles. "Lean on the horn and get the hell around that bozo." Admittedly a challenge that fell into the easier-said-than-done category. The truck's driver hugged the center line like a long-lost friend and slowed to twenty every time he came to one of the hairpin turns that made this stretch of road between Tahoe and Placerville such a challenge.

"*Testa di cazzo*," Marcello muttered.

"Dickhead?" Trick said. "That's a little harsh. The guy's not much of a driver, but—"

"I was not referring to the truck driver."

Trick raised an eyebrow. "Okay, I'm acting like a jerk. I admit it. But there are extenuating circumstances. If I don't get some aspirin soon, my head's going to explode. Of course," he couldn't resist adding,

"I realize you have limited experience driving mountain roads . . ."

Marcello vented his spleen in a torrent of Italian invective. "I am entirely competent, and you know it. If you must place blame, blame this gutless piece of garbage I am driving."

In reality, the Jeep Wrangler Trick had bought shortly after they'd arrived in the U.S. a month ago was far from gutless, but then, it wasn't Italian-built, and from Marcello's perspective that automatically qualified it as an inferior vehicle.

Marcello hit a pothole dead center.

On purpose, Trick suspected. He groaned as the jolt triggered a fresh burst of pain. "Damn it, watch where you're going!"

"Stiff suspension," Marcello said. "In a Lamborghini, one would scarcely—"

"When in Rome, blah-blah-blah, but this isn't Rome, my friend. Keep your eyes on the road. My head won't survive another thump like that last one." Not to mention his queasy stomach.

"If you did not drink so much . . ."

To which Trick had no snappy comeback. Marcello was right. But if he didn't muddle his brain with alcohol, he might have to think about what he was going to do with the rest of his life. And that was too damned depressing to contemplate. Not many career choices open to a guy with a limp and an eye patch, pirates being in short demand these days.

Neither man spoke a word for a full two minutes. Then, "Straight stretch dead ahead," Trick said. "Get ready to punch it. The driver of the BMW behind us just turned on his signal. No way he's getting around until we do."

"What is that quaint American saying?" Marcello frowned as if he were scouring his memory. "Ah, yes. 'Nobody likes a backseat driver.' " But he punched it as instructed.

"I'm not *in* the backseat, so technically . . ." Trick let his comment trail off as headlights seemed to materialize out of nowhere, heading straight for them. "Oh, shit! Back off! Back off!"

Marcello hit the brakes and pulled back in behind the truck. Either the driver of the BMW didn't see the oncoming car or didn't care. The logging truck's brake lights lit up as the guy in the BMW blew around both them and the truck.

Swearing under his breath, Marcello hit the Jeep's brakes again as they nearly kissed the truck's rear end.

The driver of the oncoming car, an older-model Cadillac, laid on his horn. Swerving to miss the Beemer, he swung too wide and slid half off the pavement to churn through the gravel on the shoulder, almost but not quite scraping the guardrail.

The BMW whipped back into its own lane, avoiding disaster by inches before continuing blithely on its way.

Crisis past, the truck ahead began to pick up speed. Marcello didn't. Too busy tracking the Caddie's erratic progress in the rearview mirror, Trick suspected.

A girl suddenly catapulted out of passenger-side door of the truck's cab and tumbled down the embankment.

"Stop!" Trick yelled, then grabbed his head to keep his brains from spilling out his ears.

Marcello slammed on the brakes.

Trick's head whipped forward, then snapped back against the headrest. He swore softly and steadily under his breath as Marcello eased the Jeep off the highway into a small turnout. Still swearing, Trick released his shoulder harness and opened his door.

"What is wrong?" Marcello asked. "Is it your stomach? Do you feel as if you are about to—"

"No! I'm going back to help the girl."

Marcello frowned in confusion. "What girl?"

"Right after that near collision between the Beemer and the Caddie, a girl either fell or was thrown from the truck ahead of us."

"I did not see a girl," Marcello said.

"Because you were focused on the Cadillac."

"Would the truck driver not have stopped if he had lost his passenger?"

"Not if he dumped her on purpose," Trick said, thinking maybe the girl had been dead before she'd been tossed from the truck. "Anyway"—he dragged his cane out of the back end—"I'm going to go check it out."

"Absurd," Marcello said. "You stay here. I will go take a look. Perhaps you were mistaken. Perhaps it was only a bag of trash." He didn't wait for a response, just jumped out of the Jeep and took off at a lope.

Trick, whose loping days were over for a while, banged his bad leg on the edge of the door as he struggled awkwardly from the vehicle. For a few moments, the throbbing in his knee rivaled the throbbing in his head. He turned the chill mountain air blue with his epithets, but swearing didn't help any more than drinking did. One clumsy, lame-ass gimp was what he was. Worthless as a flat tire.

Frustrated, he propped himself on his cane, leaned against the Jeep's door, and tracked Marcello's progress along the moonlit highway with his one good eye.

Before the Italian had gone twenty yards, a small figure clambered up the embankment and staggered onto the shoulder. A young woman in dark clothing. Slender, fragile-looking with shoulder-length dark hair and pale skin, she limped a little as she accompanied Marcello back to the Jeep.

"Are you all right?" he meant to ask as soon as she drew close enough, but then he got a good look at her face—a perfect oval with huge dark eyes, a straight, narrow nose, a sweet, soft mouth—and the words clogged up in his throat. He knew that face. It belonged to the Gypsy girl who'd haunted the Granger mansion since the 1850s.

The young woman stared at him, her face completely expressionless.

Not Blanche, he realized belatedly. Not his ghost made flesh. This woman was smaller and paler, her mouth fuller, her cheekbones less prominent. Still, at first glance the resemblance had been startling. "What's your name?" he demanded, sounding more abrupt than he'd intended.

"Jane Doe. Or at least it would have been if that truck driver had had his way."

Trick frowned. "You're saying the man tried to kill you?"

"I'm saying he shoved me out of a truck going thirty miles an hour." Her face still betrayed no emotion, but strain had frayed the edges of her voice. "Apparently, that's the way it plays out when some sicko orders you to give him a blow job and you refuse."

Marcello frowned. "What is this blow job?"

Trick translated for him and Marcello's frown deepened. "We must call the police."

"No!" the woman said quickly. "I mean, nothing actually happened. I'm not hurt. Not seriously. It would be my word against his, and . . ."

"And?" Trick prompted.

"I'd rather not get involved with the police right now."

"I see," he said, wondering if he did. She looked so young, so frail, so innocent, and yet her reluctance to involve the authorities seemed to argue that she was—or recently had been—involved in something illegal.

"You may see, Trick, but I do not," Marcello objected. "Miss, you must try to bring this man to justice. He should not be allowed to—"

"To what?" she said. "Proposition females stupid or reckless enough to hitchhike?"

"I'm guessing you're neither stupid nor reckless," Trick said.

"No? Then what am I?" She faced him squarely.

"Desperate?" he said softly.

She went very still, and for a brief moment, he caught a glimpse of the vulnerability she was working so hard to hide. Then it was as if shutters slammed down to mask her emotions once again. "*Desperate*'s a strong word," she said. "I prefer . . . *cautious*."

Marcello shifted his gaze back and forth from Trick to the girl. "Yes, but the authorities—" he started, then stopped abruptly when he saw Trick's warning scowl.

Trick stepped toward the girl, extending his hand. "I'm Trick Granger. Patrick Donatelli Granger."

"The race-car driver," most people responded, placing the name if not the face, but this woman's expression remained stuck in neutral. Not the faintest flicker of recognition sparked in her eyes.

She gave his hand a hesitant shake. "Nevada White."

"Unusual name," he said.

"Not when your mother's a hippie-turned-blackjack dealer. I count myself lucky that she didn't call me Vegas."

"Or Roulette," Marcello said.

Both Trick and Nevada turned to him in surprise.

He shrugged. "I once had a cat named Roulette."

Trick turned back to the woman. "Nevada White, meet former cat owner Marcello Bellini."

"How do you do?" she said formally.

Marcello nodded. "Very well, thank you." As if they were in a receiving line, not standing at the edge of a mountain road at four in the morning.

If Trick hadn't felt so lousy, he'd have laughed. "Well, Nevada White," he said, "if you don't mind riding in the backseat, you're welcome to a lift. Midas Lake is the nearest town. About five miles that way." He pointed down the road with his cane.

A faint frown rippled across her face, there and gone so fast he might have imagined it. She said nothing.

"We can drop you off at Buzz's Stop 'N Go. Should be easy enough to hitch another ride there." He paused. When she didn't respond, he added, "Or we can take you to the bus station. Your choice."

She searched his face but still said nothing.

"Do not worry." Marcello gave her an earnest look. "We are neither rapists nor serial killers."

"Definitely not," Trick said.

"Which, considering that there are two of us, would be most unlikely in any case. Ninety-nine-point-nine percent of all rapists and serial killers work alone," Marcello pointed out.

"Very reassuring," Trick said, "that you'd have that statistic on the tip of your tongue."

Marcello ignored him. "Besides, after all the media coverage that followed Trick's near-fatal crash at Le Mans, everyone knows who he is."

Nevada White gave Marcello a blank look. "I don't."

"Trick Granger, world-famous race-car driver?"

"*Former* world-famous race-car driver," Trick said, not without a twinge of bitterness.

Nevada White shook her head. "I don't follow sports."

"But the accident was front-page news," Marcello protested.

Not to mention, Trick thought, that the Granger curse angle had made it major tabloid fodder.

The woman's eyes widened, as if they'd accused her of some heinous crime. "I don't pay much attention to the news," she said, then added slowly, "but now that you mention it, I guess the name does ring a bell."

Nevada White didn't know him from Adam. Which was no big deal. What Trick couldn't understand was why she was pretending she did. He searched her face, but no hidden motives revealed themselves. Maybe she was just being polite. "So," he said. "Do you want a ride or not?"

"I . . ." Nevada White studied him long and hard, then shifted her gaze to Marcello, submitting him to the same intense scrutiny.

"Yes or no?" Trick said.

She turned to search his face once again. "Yes," she said at length. "I would. Thanks."

"Then let's move it. I'd like to reach Midas Lake before my brain goes ballistic."

She shot him a questioning look as he shifted aside to let her climb into the backseat.

"Headache," he explained.

Marcello snorted. "Of the self-inflicted variety."

Trick hoisted himself awkwardly into the passenger seat. "I had a little too much to drink." Okay, a lot too much. He scowled at Marcello, who grinned back, thoroughly unrepentant. "*Sei un rompicazzo, Marcello.*"

The Italian slid behind the steering wheel and turned the key in the ignition. "*Vai all'inferno.*" He punched the accelerator, pulling back onto the road with a jerk.

Trick groaned as jolts of pain zigzagged through his head. "Hell? Already there, my friend."

They weren't serial killers. Or so they said. And they definitely weren't cops—federal, state, or local—which should have been reassuring. So why was her gut still tied in knots?

The driver glanced back at her. "How are you doing?" he asked in his heavily accented English.

"Fine," she said because she knew that's what he wanted to hear, and even if he didn't, she couldn't exactly tell him the truth: *I have two killers on my tail, and I'm scared out of my mind.*

"You sure?" Granger, the ex-race-car driver, peered at her around the edge of his headrest.

Had something in her voice sounded a false note? Did she look as desperate as she felt? *Chill,* she told herself. *No red flags.* Slowly, deliberately, she unclenched her fists and forced herself to relax. Above all, she needed to avoid raising any suspicion.

"Maybe we should take you to the ER, have you checked out."

"I'm fine. Really. A few bruises maybe. Nothing serious." She mustered a smile but couldn't prevent herself from reaching as she always did in times of stress for her amulet.

It wasn't there.

Fortunately, Granger had turned back around by then and didn't see the panic she knew must be reflected in her face. She reached behind her to check the hood of her sweatshirt, thinking maybe the amulet was stuck in the folds, but no such luck. She unzipped the hoodie, hoping to find the pendant caught between her sweatshirt and the T-shirt she wore underneath. Not there, either. She must have lost it in the struggle with the truck driver. Or maybe during the roll down the embankment.

Damn it. Tears prickled her eyes.

She no longer remembered where the gold amulet had come from or who had given it to her, but she treasured it anyway, her only tie to her old life, to the person she'd once been. Gone now just like her memories of her preinstitutional life.

A second wave of panic suddenly constricted her chest. What if the pendant wasn't the only thing she'd lost in her unplanned dive from the truck?

She jammed her hands deep in the pockets of her hoodie, relieved to find that she still had her two dog-eared twenty-dollar bills, most of her change, the scrap of paper that held the only clue to her real identity, and, thank God, the plastic bag full of little peach-colored pills. "As long as you take one first thing every morning, you'll be fine," Yelena had promised, though she'd never explained exactly what the pills did. Suppressed Nevada's "gift" maybe? She hadn't had an episode in a while now.

As for her counterfeit social security card, the foundation of her new identity, it was safely hidden inside her right shoe.

In the front seat, the two men were engaged in a

low-voiced argument, possibly about her, though she couldn't be sure since they were speaking Italian, not a language she understood.

"Where are you headed, Ms. White?" Granger asked suddenly in English.

"Nowhere in particular," she lied, unwilling to confide in a stranger. The truth was, San Francisco was her ultimate destination. Written on that scrap of paper in her pocket was the anonymous Pacific Heights address Yelena had copied from Nevada's file at the Appleton Institute.

He turned around to face her. "On the run, huh?"

"No," she said quickly. Could he tell she was lying? "I took a year off between college and grad school. I've been bumming around, trying to see as much of the country as I can." She'd used that story several times in the last week.

"Oh, really?"

Definitely suspicious, she thought, despite that bland expression.

"The Sierra Nevadas are well worth an extended visit," Granger said. "Bountiful wildlife, breathtaking scenery. Plus, the area's rich in history."

The Italian snorted. "You have been reading the Fodor's again."

"But hitchhiking's not the safest way to travel through the mountains," Trick Granger continued, ignoring the Italian's interruption. "Or anywhere else for that matter."

"I know that," she said. "The thing is, I'm running low on cash. I suppose I could call home, but I really don't want to listen to all the I-told-you-sos. What I need is a job."

Granger turned back to Marcello, rattling off some more Italian.

Marcello answered sharply in the same language.

"Do you know of any hotels that might have an opening on the housekeeping staff?" A waitressing job would do in a pinch, though she preferred a position with less public exposure.

"I doubt it," Granger said. "Business is slow right now. Ski season's over, and it's a little early for the usual influx of warm-weather tourists."

Disappointing but not totally unexpected. Nothing was ever easy.

Granger turned back to face her again, studying her for a moment in silence before saying, "I do know of one job opening that might interest you."

"No," Marcello protested.

"Yes," Granger said.

"What are you talking about?" she asked.

"A job," Granger said.

"In his brothel," Marcello added.

Nevada's stomach clenched.

"Marcello's joking," Granger said, though the Italian had sounded perfectly serious, even grim, and Granger didn't seem particularly amused, either. "I recently inherited a mansion, a three-story Victorian that formerly housed a brothel—emphasis on the *formerly,* but—"

"No real estate agent will touch it, buried as it is under a century's worth of grime," Marcello said.

Granger scowled at the other man. "*Century's worth*

is a gross exaggeration. The mansion's only been empty for fifty years." He angled around to make eye contact with her again. "Marcello's right about the grime, though."

The Italian grunted. "Filth. Layers of it."

"I need someone to clean the place up so I can put it on the market. I've had a help wanted ad running in the *Nugget*—that's the local paper—for three weeks now, but no one's applied for the job."

"Because everyone believes the house is haunted." Marcello met her gaze momentarily in the rearview mirror, his expression unreadable.

"Which is, of course, ridiculous," Granger said.

"I—" Nevada started.

"Ghost stories are inevitable, I suppose," he continued, "considering how long it's been since the mansion was occupied."

"Unless you count mice and spiders," Marcello put in.

No doubt some of that abundant wildlife Granger'd been touting earlier.

"The place has been abandoned for years," Granger said. "You have to expect—"

"I feel certain the curse has also discouraged job applicants," Marcello said.

"Curse?" she repeated.

"Superstitious nonsense." Granger's laugh seemed more forced than convincing. "But in the interest of full disclosure . . ." He paused. "In the early 1850s one of my less illustrious ancestors, brothel owner Silas Granger, ran afoul of a Gypsy, grandmother of a young woman who died in his employ, and got himself and his family cursed. Ever since, male Grangers have been dropping like flies."

"I thought you said the curse was nonsense."

"It is." Granger nodded. "The body count's merely coincidence. Or maybe genetics." He shrugged. "But curses make for better headlines. The mansion, Silas Granger's former brothel, is filthy beyond description but one hundred percent curse-free. I admit it's a dirty job, but—"

"Somebody's got to do it," she finished.

"You'd be well compensated."

"How well?"

"Five hundred dollars a week."

"I don't know. . . ."

"All right. Seven hundred fifty. That's assuming you know one end of a broom from the other."

"I've killed a few dust bunnies in my time."

"Bunnies?" Confusion clouded Marcello's voice. "These are rabbits, yes? And you kill them?"

"It's slang," she said, "meaning I know how to clean."

"Is that a yes?" Granger asked.

"More like a maybe. The prospect of spiders doesn't bother me, but I'm not crazy about mice."

"Good," Granger said, "because I'm not, either."

"Nor I," Marcello chimed in.

"Marcello works for me," Granger explained.

"The Bellinis have served the Donatelli family for generations," the Italian added.

"How charmingly feudal," she said dryly.

"Unfortunately, the tradition of service doesn't include windows," Granger muttered.

"I am a personal assistant," Marcello said with exaggerated patience, as if this were a distinction he'd explained many times in the past. "I will cook. I will garden. But I draw the line at cleaning."

"We could really use your help, but if you're concerned about propriety—"

Marcello launched into an impassioned flood of Italian as they entered Midas Lake, a charming little resort town, heavy on log construction and retail shops aimed at the tourist trade—handmade quilts, chainsaw sculptures of bears and eagles.

She needed the money and was tempted to take the job. But since her escape, every time she'd stopped for more than a few hours, her pursuers had caught up with her. She'd already survived two close calls, one in Chicago, the second, two nights ago in Nowheresville, Nebraska. She was afraid she might not be so lucky a third time.

On the other hand, the job sounded very low profile.

Marcello hit the red at the first of three stoplights on the main drag. Directly ahead of them, also stopped at the light, a police cruiser idled. A scruffy-looking man in the backseat repeatedly slammed his handcuffed wrists against the grillwork separating him from the officer in the driver's seat. Blood splattered, but the prisoner was apparently too worked up to feel any pain. Under the influence, Nevada guessed.

The cop spoke into his radio, then glanced in the side mirror.

A searing pain pierced Nevada's eyes and buried itself in her brain. "He beats his wife," she blurted.

The babble of Italian in the front seat came to an abrupt halt. Marcello twisted around to look at her. "I beg your pardon?"

She clenched her fists so hard that her nails dug into her palms. Squeezing her eyes shut, she fought to clear her mind of the ugly images.

"She said she thought that guy in the back of the cop car was a wife-beater. Wouldn't surprise me any. He sure as hell looks the part."

No! She could feel the anguished denial trying to escape, but she kept her lips tightly sealed. The prisoner wasn't a wife-beater. At least she had no reason to think so. The cop was the one she'd been talking about. The cop was the one she'd seen in a disturbing psychic flash. The cop was the one who beat his wife.

Love taps. That was how Morgan the Orderly described what he did to his spouse. Only way to keep the bitch in line, according to him.

Love taps wasn't really a description, though. It was an excuse. A lying excuse. And Nevada ached to set the record straight, to scream the truth at the top of her lungs the way she'd done with Morgan the Orderly.

Except that hadn't turned out too well, had it? When she'd gone berserk, they'd stuffed her in a strait jacket and tranqued her. So unless she wanted to go back to the Institute to play guinea pig again—experimental drugs and experimental treatments, most of them with undesirable side effects—she would be smart to keep her mouth shut.

Seven hundred fifty a week for however many weeks it would have taken to clean Granger's mansion would have given her a cushion, but it wasn't going to happen. Marcello was already giving her that wary look she'd come to fear. "Drop me at a truck stop," she said. "I'll hitch a ride from there."

TWO

Damn it, Trick thought, what was Nevada White's problem? She needed a job. She'd said so herself. So why turn down the one he'd offered? It didn't make sense.

Of course, the depth of his disappointment didn't make sense either. No, he couldn't sell the mansion in its current condition, and yes, he'd had a hard time finding someone to whip the place into shape, but Nevada White's rejection of his job offer was hardly the end of the world.

So she bore a passing resemblance to his ghost. Big deal. So he found her attractive. Again, big deal. Physical attraction was hardly proof positive that he'd found the perfect person to clean the mansion. More like proof positive that he hadn't been getting any lately.

Nevertheless, he twisted around in his seat, intending to convince her to change her mind. But the second he saw her face—cheeks pale, eyes haunted, lips pressed tightly together—he jettisoned his plan. Could she have sustained internal injuries in her fall from the logging truck? "You okay?"

She nodded, but she didn't look okay. In fact, she looked about twice as bad as he felt, and that was saying something.

"Hungry perhaps," Marcello suggested in his native tongue.

"When did you last eat?" Trick asked.

"I don't know," she said. "Just drop me at the Stop 'N Go, and I'll take it from there. Feeding me isn't your responsibility."

So why did he feel that her well-being rested squarely on his shoulders? Why this fierce desire to protect her? It didn't make sense. None of it made sense. He hesitated as instinct warred with common sense. For once, common sense won out. "Head for the Stop 'N Go," he told Marcello.

"And already he forgets our little discussion about backseat drivers," Marcello muttered under his breath.

Trick flipped him the bird, then closed his eyes and leaned his aching head against the headrest.

Trick watched Nevada cross the parking lot toward the entrance of the truck stop restaurant. She would be all right, he told himself, but he wasn't convinced. "Maybe we should wait to make sure she gets a ride," he said.

Marcello shot him a sideways glance, the sort of look normally reserved for raving lunatics. "What we really should do is make a police report."

"No," Trick said quickly. Then, "Son of a bitch!" he swore.

"What?" Marcello asked, obviously startled by Trick's vehemence. "What is wrong?"

"That truck." Trick pointed to the far end of the parking lot, the section reserved for big rigs. A logging truck—the same damned logging truck Nevada had come tumbling out of—sat parked between two semis. Trick opened his door and reached for his cane.

"What are you doing?" Marcello asked.

"I intend to have a chat with a certain truck driver," Trick said, *chat* being a euphemism for beating the crap out of the bastard.

"Nevada White is not your responsibility."

"Maybe not, but the thing is, I don't like perverts. Or bullies."

"Then report him to the authorities."

"The girl was right. They wouldn't do anything. It would be her word against his. He'd get a slap on the wrist at best." Trick slid out of his seat, balancing on his good leg as he positioned his cane. Then he slammed his door shut and struck out across the parking lot. A man with a cane could move pretty fast, especially when driven by anger.

Marcello followed, almost running to catch up. "This is crazy," he said. "You do not even know if the girl's story was true."

"It was," Trick said with conviction.

"You cannot be certain of that," Marcello argued.

"Okay, fine," Trick said. "No problem. I'll let the slimy son of a bitch tell his side before I beat the crap out of him."

Marcello ran in front of Trick, forcing him to stop.

"Wait a moment. Calm down. Consider what you are about to do."

"Get out of my way."

"No, not until—" Marcello uttered a grunt of surprise and stumbled aside as Trick whacked him a good one with his cane. *"Testa di cazzo!"*

Nevada paused just inside the front door of the truck stop restaurant. Despite the hour, the place was busy, mostly truckers but some teenagers, too, and a scattering of tourists.

Even if they hadn't been wearing sunglasses, the two big, broad-shouldered men in black suits would have stuck out like sore thumbs. The fluorescents overhead gleamed off the African American's shaved head. The second man, the one with the ramrod-stiff military posture, looked pale by comparison with close-cropped blond hair and a milky complexion. The two sat at the far end of the counter, sipping coffee from oversize mugs and flirting with the waitress.

Praying they wouldn't turn around, Nevada slipped back outside into the relative darkness of the parking lot. Her hands were shaking, her heart racing in reaction to her close call. Pulling up her hood—some disguise was better than none—she scanned the lot for Granger's Jeep. Still parked fifty feet away beneath one of the security lights. No one inside, though, which was odd. Where had the two men gone?

She crossed the cracked pavement at a quick walk. Still no sign of Granger or the Italian. No sign of anyone aside from a couple of diesel customers near the pumps. She glanced back over her shoulder toward the restaurant. No sign of her pursuers either, thank God.

The Jeep was empty, just as she'd thought. Once again she slowly scanned the area, wondering where the two men could have gone. They hadn't followed her into the restaurant and they weren't over by the gas pumps. Which left what? The convenience store? The restrooms? But surely, wherever they'd disappeared to, they wouldn't be gone for long.

She tried the passenger side door, surprised to find they'd left it unlocked. She'd been prepared to crawl underneath the Jeep and hide until the two men returned. Now she wouldn't have to.

Without hesitation, still running on fear and adrenaline, Nevada scrambled into the backseat. She grabbed a fleece blanket from the back end, then curled up on the floorboards, pulling the blanket over herself and praying for invisibility.

How had her pursuers known she'd show up here? It made no sense.

Trick banged his cane against the logging truck's driver's side door. "Open up!" From where he stood, he could see the driver's shadowed profile, but if the man heard him, he gave no indication of it. Trick reached for the door handle.

"Stop!" Marcello said. "What are you doing?"

"Hard to hear the bastard's side of the story if he won't even acknowledge my presence," Trick snapped.

Marcello scowled at him, then banged on the door himself. "Sir, open up. We need to speak with you."

The driver ignored Marcello just as he had Trick.

"Sir?" Marcello tried again.

"To hell with it." Trick yanked the door open.

Without the door's support, the trucker's body slumped over sideways, hanging halfway out of the truck's cab and giving Trick a bird's-eye view of the horrific wounds on the trucker's throat. "Holy shit!" he swore.

"What is it?" Marcello took a step closer to see for himself.

The trucker's eyes stared sightlessly into the night. His stringy gray ponytail stirred in the chill evening breeze, but that was the only movement. His mouth hung slack, revealing tobacco-stained teeth. Blood darkened the front of his faded flannel shirt.

Marcello made a disgusted noise.

Trick didn't blame him.

"Who did this?" Marcello demanded.

"You mean, *what* did this?" Trick corrected him. "If I'm not mistaken, those are bite marks on his neck."

"But how . . . ?"

"Maybe he forgot to feed his pet pit bull. I don't know. Solving gruesome mysteries isn't my job. I think it's time to call the cops."

"Agreed," Marcello said, sounding shaky.

Trick dug in his pocket for his cell phone.

"Wait." Marcello grabbed Trick's arm. "The mansion."

Trick stared at his friend. "What does the mansion have to do with this guy's murder? Surely, you don't believe my ghost is responsible, do you?"

"No," Marcello said, "but that will not stop the tabloids from creating connections. If you report this murder, you might as well forget selling the mansion."

"But we can't pretend we didn't see him. We can't just leave the body here."

Marcello frowned. "What did you touch? Anything besides the door handle?"

"No, but—"

"Good." Marcello used the tail of his shirt to wipe the truck door handle free of fingerprints. "You can report the crime anonymously from a pay phone."

"Don't you think you're being a little paranoid?"

"Do you wish to sell the mansion or not?"

"You know I do."

"I tell you, if you involve yourself in a grisly murder investigation, you will be inviting unwelcome media attention."

Including the tabloid reporters who'd had such a field day when he'd had his accident. "Luck of the Grangers—It's All Bad." "Race-car Driver Sidelined by Ancient Gypsy Curse." "Trick'ed by Fate."

"Why add to the notoriety?" Marcello demanded. "Why diminish your chances for making a sale?"

Trick had to admit what Marcello said made sense.

But it still felt wrong.

The car doors opened and Nevada's heart threatened to punch its way past her breastbone.

"You made the report," Marcello said. "What more could you do?"

Granger groaned. "Damn it, no one deserves to die

like that, not even some sleaze who tried to coerce a girl into going down on him."

What did he mean? Was he talking about the truck driver?

"You fully intended to beat him up yourself."

"Knock him around, yes. Rip his throat out, no."

Rip his throat out? A shudder ran down Nevada's spine. Rip his *throat* out?

Marcello started the engine and the Jeep began to move.

Shuddering uncontrollably now, Nevada tried to think. Had the men who were following her killed the truck driver? She knew that the two were capable of violence, but ripping someone's throat out? Why go to such extremes?

"What if the girl's in danger, too?" Granger asked.

"Why would she be?" Marcello asked.

"Maybe," Granger suggested, "whoever killed the truck driver was trying to get information about Nevada White."

"How could the murderer know there was a connection between the girl and the driver?" Marcello demanded.

Granger didn't answer.

"The answer is," Marcello continued, "he could not. Therefore, Nevada White is in no danger. Quit worrying."

"I can't help it," Granger said.

Marcello muttered something in Italian. Then both men lapsed into silence.

"I do not wish to alarm you," Marcello said quietly a

minute or two later, "but I think we are being followed."

By the men who'd been chasing her ever since she left Boston, Nevada thought with a chilling certainty.

"What the hell . . ." Granger said.

"Two men," Marcello told him.

"Cops, you think? Could someone have seen us hanging around the logging truck and reported it?"

"There are no lights mounted on the roof of the car," Marcello said.

"Looks like a Crown Vic, though." Granger sounded worried. "Cops are big on Crown Vics."

Her pursuers drove a black Crown Victoria. Nevada curled herself into a tight little ball and concentrated on breathing.

"Lose them," Granger ordered.

"But would that not make us appear as if we had something to hide?" Marcello objected.

"Maybe so, but what if the men in the Crown Vic are responsible for the truck driver's death?"

"Most unlikely," Marcello said. "His throat was savaged. No human was responsible for that."

"They could have a trained attack dog."

"I do not see a dog in the car. Just the two men." Marcello must have flipped on a turn signal because Nevada heard a clicking sound, followed by a sharp left turn onto a bumpy surface.

Marcello swore softly. "They just pulled into the drive behind us." The car rolled to a stop, and Marcello turned off the engine.

"Stay cool," Granger said. "Maybe they're only looking for directions."

Someone knocked on a window. "Excuse me, gentle-men, I'm Detective Branson, and this is Sergeant Col-lier."

It could have been one of her pursuers. Nevada wasn't sure. She wasn't familiar enough with their voices to make a positive ID.

A window rolled down, and the same voice con-tinued, sounding much louder now. "We're looking for a woman who escaped six days ago from a facility for the criminally insane. Would you mind having a look at this photograph?" A pause ensued. Presumably Granger and Marcello were studying the photograph.

A photograph of her?

"Do you recognize the woman?" A different voice this time. "We have reason to believe she hitched a ride this evening with a truck driver."

Definitely her.

"I do," Granger said. "We gave her a lift into town earlier after she was thrown from the truck driv-ing ahead of us on the road from Tahoe." He paused. "Criminally insane, you say?"

"Murdered her own father," the first voice said.

Not true. Oh, please God, not true. She couldn't have done something like that.

"Didn't seem crazy," Granger said. "Or dangerous, either."

"Looks can be deceiving," the man said. "Where is she now?"

"She was pretty bruised and battered," Granger said. "I tried to talk her into getting checked out at the ER."

"But she refused," Marcello said.

"Then you won't object if we search your vehicle."

Nevada's blood ran cold.

"Knock yourself out, detective," Granger said. "We've got nothing to hide. The girl asked us to drop her at the truck stop on the edge of town, and that's what we did. I assume she planned to hitch a ride from there. For some reason, she seemed pretty anxious to get to Sacramento."

"Sacramento?" the first man asked sharply.

"Is there a problem, detective?" Marcello asked.

"No problem. None at all. You've been very helpful."

"You're not going to search?" Granger asked, sounding surprised.

"No, we have all we need."

A few seconds later, a car engine started up. Her pursuers were leaving.

"Sacramento?" Marcello asked.

"First thing that came into my mind," Granger said.

"Seemed to mean something to them." Marcello hesitated a second, then asked, "Why did you lie? If the girl really is criminally insane—"

"She's not."

"You cannot know that for certain."

"The hell I can't! That was not the face of a murderer."

"But—"

"Look, those two only followed us in the first place because they knew we'd picked her up."

"But how could they—"

"Exactly. How could they? The only possibility that

makes sense is that the truck driver told them," Granger said, "sometime before they ripped his throat out."

Nevada waited until she was sure Granger and Marcello were gone before crawling from the relative safety of her hiding place. She closed the Jeep's door quietly, then moved quickly into the shadows under the pines that edged the rutted gravel drive.

The night was cold enough for her to see her breath. She shivered in her sweatshirt, wondering what to do next, where to go. She glanced wistfully toward the lights of the mansion, a large Victorian, elegant despite its shabbiness. She was sorely tempted to knock on the door and ask for a bed for the night . . . or what was left of it, an idea she rejected almost as soon as it occurred to her.

She could curl up in the backseat of the Jeep, wrapped in the same fleece blanket she'd used earlier for camouflage. Only what if her pursuers came back?

She shuddered at the thought.

She should leave, walk until she came to a highway and hitch a ride in the first car that stopped. Only again, what if the first car belonged to the men who were chasing her?

The Jeep was parked in front of a square outbuilding with a trio of dormer windows sprouting from the attic roof. Garage? Former stables? As possible refuges went, it didn't look especially promising, but maybe if she borrowed the blanket from the Wrangler, she could hole up inside and stay warm. And safe.

She had just opened the Jeep's passenger side door and started to reach for the blanket when someone grabbed her arm.

Instinctively, she fought to free herself, but her captor was strong, much stronger than she was.

"What are you doing here?" he asked suspiciously, his thick Italian accent betraying his identity. "Trying to steal the Jeep?"

"No!"

"Not that it would be a great loss, you understand, but still . . ."

"I wasn't stealing the Jeep. I wasn't stealing anything. I was . . . borrowing . . . the blanket. I was planning to sleep in the stables."

"The building is locked," Marcello informed her. "How were you planning to get in? Break a window perhaps? That is vandalism, you know. I told Trick we should have turned you over to the authorities. But no, he would not hear of it. We shall see what he has to say now that I have caught you red-handed."

"I didn't do anything illegal. I'm not a criminal."

"That is not what those detectives said."

"They weren't detectives. Not police detectives at any rate."

"How do you know?" he challenged.

"I just do," she said, admittedly not the most convincing of arguments.

Marcello dragged her toward the back door of the house, moving so quickly it was all she could do to maintain her balance. He wrenched open the door and shoved her inside ahead of him. "Trick!" he yelled as he manhandled her through the back entry into an enormous old-fashioned kitchen. "Come see who I found riffling through the Jeep." He gave her one last shove that sent her staggering into the middle of the room.

"I wasn't riffling through anything," she protested, rubbing her arm where Marcello had clamped down so hard, he'd nearly stopped her circulation.

"Sit down," Marcello said in a voice that brooked no disobedience, "and hold your tongue."

Nevada sat on a spindle-backed oak chair, one of eight that surrounded a large oval table.

"What's all the yelling about?" Trick Granger appeared in the doorway, balancing on his cane, carrying an aspirin bottle and a whiskey decanter in his free hand. When he noticed her sitting at the table, his face went totally blank for a second. "Where did you come from?" He frowned. "Or am I dreaming again?"

"She was trying to steal the Jeep."

She scowled at Marcello. "You keep saying that, but it's not true."

"I saw the overhead light go on when I was upstairs," Marcello told Trick. "When I went down to investigate, I caught her."

"I wasn't stealing anything," she told Trick, then turned to Marcello. "As I told you once already, I was *borrowing* a blanket from the back end. That's all. I was going to use it, not keep it."

Trick set the whiskey bottle down on the countertop, shook a handful of aspirin into his palm, downed them in a single gulp, then followed the pills with a chug from the whiskey bottle. "But how did you get here?" he asked. "We left you at the Stop 'N Go."

Nevada felt her cheeks grow warm. "No," she said. "Actually, you didn't. The minute I went inside the restaurant, I spotted the two men, and—"

"Who?" Trick asked, taking another long swallow from the whiskey bottle.

"The two men," she said. "The two men who're following me."

"The detective and the sergeant," Marcello translated.

"They aren't cops," she protested. "I don't know who they are or who they're working for, but one thing I'm certain of—they're not cops. I saw the one who calls himself Sergeant Collier hit an elderly woman on the El in Chicago. A cop wouldn't do that."

Trick seemed to consider that for a second. "Probably not," he agreed. "But then again, how do we know you're telling the truth? According to 'them,' you're criminally insane, recently escaped from a mental institution."

"I was institutionalized," she admitted, "but it wasn't a mental hospital or a prison, either. I'm not a criminal, and I'm not insane. I'm . . ."

"What?" Trick demanded. "You're what?"

"Psychic," she said.

Both men stared at her.

"Meaning what?" Trick asked. "You read minds?"

"Not exactly," she said. "It doesn't work like that . . .

at least not for me. My gift is unpredictable, totally random. Sometimes, often when I least expect it, I'll catch a glimpse of someone's reflection and—"

"The guy in the back of the squad car," Trick said suddenly. "That's why you said he beat his wife."

"Not the man in custody," she said. "The cop. I saw his reflection for a second in the side mirror of the squad car, and I just knew. I blurted it out before I could stop myself. Unfortunately, that's usually the way it works. I don't have much control over my so-called gift. People tend to think I'm crazy."

"*Crazy* gets my vote," Marcello said.

Trick frowned at him, then turned to her. "When did you last eat?" he asked in a seeming non sequitur.

She tried to remember. She didn't feel hungry. She didn't feel much of anything aside from scared out of her mind. If they turned her over to the police, she'd end up back at the Appleton Institute for sure. And if they turned her over to her pursuers, she'd end up dead. Neither prospect held much appeal. "I'm not sure," she said finally. "I remember grabbing a cheeseburger at a fast-food place, though I couldn't tell you when or where."

"Heat up some of that minestrone you made yesterday," Trick said to his assistant.

Marcello's nostrils flared. "She tries to steal your car, so now you are going to feed her?"

"She'll need her strength if she's going to clean this filthy house." He turned to Nevada. "You *are* going to clean this filthy house, aren't you? You'll take the job?"

"But—" Marcello sputtered.

"Yes," she said. With her pursuers halfway to Sacramento, Midas Lake was as safe a place to hide for a while as anywhere else.

Upon Trick's orders, Marcello had given Nevada White a stack of clean linens and escorted her over to the former caretaker's quarters above the stables, but he was not happy about the situation. Yes, they needed someone to give the place a thorough cleaning, but in Marcello's opinion, Nevada White was less a solution than a potential problem. She had made a good case proving her allegation that the two men following her were not police, but she had not explained what they really were or why they were after her. She could be criminally insane as they claimed. She could be a murderer, a thief, a terrorist. All right, probably not a terrorist, but . . . He slammed in through the back door, muttering under his breath.

"What's the problem, my friend?" Trick said softly. He sat at the kitchen table, working his way through a bowl of minestrone.

"You are eating," Marcello said in surprise.

"I was hungry." Trick spooned up another mouthful of soup.

When was the last time Trick had eaten anything without being coaxed? Lately all he seemed to want to do was drown his sorrows, food be damned.

Marcello took a seat across from Trick. "How is your headache?"

"Better," Trick said, "thanks to some aspirin plus a little hair of the dog."

"You ate dog hair?" Marcello asked, certain he must have misunderstood.

Trick grinned.

Marcello tried to remember the last time he had seen Trick grin. Not since before the accident.

"It's an expression," Trick explained. "To take a hair of the dog that bit you means if you're suffering the effects of a hangover, you should knock back a medicinal shot of whatever it was you got drunk on in the first place."

"Hair of the dog. Dust bunnies. English is a most illogical language."

Trick grinned again. "I'm sure Mr. Spock would agree with you."

"Who?"

"Never mind," Trick said. "Did you get our new housekeeper settled in?"

"Yes," Marcello said. "That is what I wanted to speak to you about."

"I suspected as much," Trick said. "Quite the little enigma, isn't she? Her eyes are green. Did you notice that? They're so dark, I thought they must be brown, but when I saw her in the light, I realized my mistake. Her eyes are green, a deep, secretive forest green."

"I did not pay attention. What concerns me is—"

"I wonder who the two thugs are working for. You don't think she's a runaway, do you? A victim of abuse? Maybe a Mafia wife?"

"I had not considered the matter. I simply assumed the two men who were tracking her told the truth."

"Really?" Trick glanced up in surprise. "Why would

you assume that? They were responsible for that truck driver's death. They must have been. Who else could have told them we picked up the girl?"

"I could not say."

"And since when"—Trick emphasized his point by poking the air with his soup spoon—"can you believe anything a murderer tells you?"

"I suppose you cannot," Marcello admitted, "but still, we know next to nothing about this Nevada White. We do not even know if that is her real name. She could be anyone, anything. A psychopath, a murderer."

"She's neither," Trick said flatly. "Trust me."

"You, I trust. She is the one I have concerns about."

"Our running into Nevada White was fate, my friend. The moment I saw her, I knew it was no chance meeting."

"You had a great deal to drink tonight—" Marcello started, but Trick cut him off.

"She looks like Blanche."

"The Granger ghost?"

"Not exactly, of course, but the resemblance is undeniable."

"A coincidence surely."

And again Trick's mouth curved in a grin. "I don't believe in coincidence."

"But you *do* believe in ghosts," Marcello said dryly.

"Not until I moved into this mansion. Look, you may not have seen Blanche or heard her sobs the way I have, but admit it, you've felt her presence."

Marcello shrugged. "The atmosphere of this place is depressing, yes, but I fear the manifestations are figments of your imagination. If you did not drink so much . . ." This was touchy ground. Marcello expected his words to trigger anger and defensiveness.

Instead Trick shot him a rueful smile. "Really been feeling sorry for myself, haven't I? Poor Trick. Wrecked his race car and his dreams all in one fell swoop. But honest to God, Marcello, those sobs are no drunken fantasy. They're real, though I admit I've been using the alcohol to try to drown them out."

Trick believed what he was saying, but Marcello wasn't convinced. "And Nevada White," he said. "How does opening your home to a woman with a dubious past aid the situation?"

"She's not the villain. She's the victim, and she needs my help," Trick said as if that were the ultimate in unassailable arguments.

Marcello wasn't sure he trusted the woman, but he had to admit she had the helpless waif act down pat. Or maybe Trick was right. Maybe it wasn't an act. And even if it was, did it really matter? Regardless of her motives, Nevada White was having a positive effect on Trick. For the first time in a long time, he was acting neither angry nor depressed. Nor was he wallowing in self-pity. For the first time in a long time, Trick Granger was thinking about someone besides himself.

THREE

A little after nine, Trick was awakened by the sounds of scraping and thumping overhead. He smiled grimly to himself. Marcello had no doubt thought it amusing to set Nevada White loose on the rooms directly above his bedroom. Alarm clock and cleaning lady all in one.

He showered in lukewarm water—apparently Ms. White's cleaning orgy had already taxed the mansion's ancient hot water heater to its limits—then shaved, dressed, and made his way downstairs to the kitchen, where Marcello sat at the table, systematically working his way through a stack of paperwork.

"You are up early," Marcello remarked, feigning surprise.

"Think you're quite the comedian, don't you, Bellini?"

Marcello frowned. "I do not understand."

"Of course, you don't. What's for breakfast?"

"We have plenty of cold cereal. Unfortunately, Ms. White used the last of the milk."

"Any croissants left?"

"No, I finished them off earlier. We have eggs, though, and bread."

"Bacon? Cheese?"

"No bacon. I think there might be a piece of cheddar."

"Omelet," Trick decided. Omelets and steaks on the grill defined the parameters of his cooking prowess. And since they didn't have any steak . . .

He was grating cheese when someone knocked twice on the back door.

"Come in," he and Marcello chorused in unison.

The door swung open and former Olympic skier Britt Petersen rode in on a stiff spring breeze. With her wind-tossed blond hair and elegant, long-limbed body, she could have made a fortune as a runway model. Instead, she owned and managed the Lakeshore Lodge, a high-end resort that bordered Trick's property. "Your pine boughs washed up on my beach," she told Marcello by way of greeting. "I told you not to pile them so close to the water."

"Consider them a gift," Marcello said without looking up.

"I'm making an omelet," Trick said. "Are you hungry, Britt?"

"No, thanks." She turned back to Marcello. "You're an ass. You know that, right?"

A smile twitched at the corners of Marcello's mouth. "She wants me," he said in Italian.

"Wants to kill you maybe," Trick answered in the same language.

Britt scowled. "Speak English already!"

"He said he'll be over to clean up your beach as soon as he finishes paying bills."

Britt studied Trick's face. "I suspect that's a rather loose translation."

He grinned. "I may have taken a liberty or two."

A loud thump sounded overhead. Britt gave a start. "What was that?"

"The ghost," Marcello said—in English this time.

"Ghost?" Britt shot him a funny look. "You must be joking."

"He is," Trick told her. "We hired a woman to clean the place. I suspect she's moving furniture."

"So you took my advice and found someone in Tahoe."

"Actually—" Marcello started, but Trick cut him off.

"Yes," Trick said. "Thanks for the tip. Sure I can't interest you in some breakfast?"

"I've got to get back to the lodge," she said. "I'm scheduled to take a group on a hike up to Midas Falls in about fifteen minutes, that is if they don't cancel on me after last night's wolf scare."

Trick glanced quickly at Marcello, who kept his nose buried in his paperwork. "Wolves? Around here? Seriously?"

"That's the buzz," Britt said. "The story's been all over the radio this morning. I'm betting it'll make the front page of today's *Nugget*, too."

"So what happened?" Trick asked.

"An anonymous caller contacted the cops last night to report some truck driver who'd been mauled to death. Then maybe ten minutes later, one of the cooks at the Stop 'N Go discovered a second body behind a Dumpster. Denise Jackson. One of the waitresses."

A *second* victim? *What the hell?*

"Had her throat ripped out. The speculation is that wolves were responsible."

"But wolves in the Sierras? Since when?"

"Ridiculous, huh?" Britt said. "I figure it must have been wild dogs . . . or maybe coyotes. I know they've had problems with coyote attacks around Lake Tahoe."

Nevada waited until the tall blond woman left before entering the kitchen. "Two bodies with their throats ripped out?" she said. "Maybe it wasn't the men who've been following me after all."

"Maybe not," Trick Granger said, "but despite the bite marks, I don't see how the trucker could have been killed by a wild animal. When Marcello and I found him, he was inside the cab of his truck with the windows rolled up. How would an animal have gotten to him?"

"And it is reasonable to assume the two men talked to the truck driver sometime shortly before his death," Marcello said. "Otherwise, how would they have known we picked you up?"

"Ripping someone's throat out is a pretty strange way to shut them up," she said.

"Not if you're a vampire." Trick laughed at his own joke, then smiled directly at Nevada.

And it was a great smile that made her feel warm

and tingly but . . . "Two murders in one night is not a joking matter," Nevada said.

"No," Marcello agreed. "It is not. But if the men tracking Nevada were, indeed, responsible for the trucker's death, why would they have murdered Denise Jackson? Her death makes no sense."

"Denise Jackson," Trick repeated. "That's the blonde who always flirts with you."

"She likes my accent," Marcello admitted.

"Liked your accent," Nevada said. "Past tense. The woman's dead. Someone murdered her."

"But made it look like a wild animal attack to disguise the fact it was murder." Trick smacked his hand on the counter for emphasis.

"Only why kill the waitress?" Nevada frowned. Could they be talking about the same waitress she'd seen flirting with her pursuers? "Tell me. What did Denise Jackson look like? Was she a blonde in her forties, thin, average height?"

Trick frowned. "How did you know?"

"When I stepped inside the truck stop restaurant, I saw the two men who've been following me talking to a woman who fits that description."

"Maybe they were asking if she knew anyone who drove a Jeep Wrangler," Trick suggested.

"And they killed her so she couldn't point a finger at them later," Nevada guessed, "in case they had to dispose of you and Marcello, too."

Marcello looked thoughtful. "If that is, indeed, what happened, then it is most fortunate, Trick, that your mention of Sacramento distracted them."

• • •

"You're positive she's here in Sacramento?" State representative and gubernatorial hopeful Daniel Snowden scowled at the two men he'd sent to track down his half sister, Whitney.

Sarge Collier chewed on his lower lip. "Now that she's no longer wearing the tracking device, we can't be positive, no, but that's what we believe."

Billy Branson nodded agreement.

"So Appleton screwed up. He swore she doesn't know who she is, that she wouldn't remember the past, but if she doesn't remember, why was she so determined to come here?"

The two hired guns made no reply, no doubt figuring—rightly—that his question was rhetorical.

Sarge stepped forward. "We were able to retrieve the tracking device. Found it on the floorboards of the logging truck's cab. My guess is, she lost it in a tussle with the truck driver." He handed Daniel the gold amulet that hid the bug.

Daniel cradled the antique pendant in his palm. A Gypsy charm, according to his first stepmother, Whitney's real mother. She'd claimed it had come down through her family from a distant forebear. A good luck charm, she'd called it, though it hadn't prevented her from dying in childbirth. Hadn't done much to protect her daughter, either, during the years she'd been institutionalized.

His forethought in planting the tracking device had served him well, though. His men had had little trouble following Whitney, at least until she'd lost the amulet.

He frowned. Was Sarge right? Had she lost the amulet in a struggle with the truck driver? Or had she deliberately gotten rid of it, somehow having discovered that he was using it to track her?

"How much did you tell the truck driver? I don't want him putting two and two together."

Sarge and Billy exchanged a look that raised the hairs along Daniel's neck.

"What did you do?" he demanded.

"Took care of it," Sarge said. "You don't need to worry about the truck driver."

"What did you do?" Daniel repeated.

"It was night. No one around. We were hungry. What do you think we did?" Sarge shrugged.

Billy laughed.

"Fools," Daniel said. "I'm surrounded by fools."

Sarge bristled. "Who are you calling a fool?"

"What's going to happen if the media pick up the story? Did you give that a moment's thought? You might as well send out an SOS to every demon hunter in the country. Of course, chances are a single body with bite marks on its throat will fly under the radar." Glancing up, Daniel caught the look that passed between Sarge and Billy. "What?" he demanded.

Billy did his best to avoid Daniel's gaze.

Daniel narrowed his eyes. "Don't tell me you left more than one body."

"The truck driver told us someone in a red Jeep Wrangler had picked up the girl, but there's a hell of a lot of red Wranglers in California. Got lucky while we were talking with this waitress at the truck stop. Turned out one of locals owns a red Jeep. She identified him for us, told us where he lives," Sarge said. "But if we'd had to take out the Jeep's owner, she'd have been a liability. We couldn't risk her talking to the cops."

"So why not just shoot her?"

Billy gave him a reproachful look. "And waste all that blood. We were still hungry."

"You couldn't have found a stray dog or two?"

Billy muttered something Daniel didn't catch.

"What was that, Branson?"

"I said stray dogs have fleas."

Daniel glared at the pair of them. "You two morons have no self-control whatsoever. I should stake you here and now."

Sarge's nostrils flared, but he held his tongue.

A wise decision. Daniel hadn't been joking about staking them. He tamped down his anger and marshaled his thoughts. "I doubt Whitney has much cash at her disposal. She won't be able to afford anything too pricey, so you'll probably have the best shot at tracking her down if you hit every cheap motel in town. Keep the body count down this time, though. Understood?" He glared at the two incompetents. "Just concentrate on your primary goal. Find her."

"And when we do?" Billy asked.

Daniel smiled. "Then she's all yours. Play with her to your heart's content. Suck her dry if that's what makes you happy. I want her out of the picture. Permanently. All I ask is that you don't leave the body lying around to be identified. I don't need that kind of publicity."

"No problem," Sarge said. "We won't let her screw up your campaign."

The campaign was the least of Daniel's worries, but he didn't bother to set Sarge straight. The fewer people who knew the truth, the better.

Nevada stood in the shabby dining room, eyeing a wall of framed photographs, dozens of them, maybe hundreds. And every single one needed to be cleaned. Grubby gilt-trimmed frames draped in cobwebs surrounded faded images nearly obscured by a heavy layer of dust. Cleaning the wall of photographs promised to be both time-consuming and tedious. Not to mention creepy.

She'd never believed in ghosts, but she had to admit the Granger mansion had very bad vibes. No matter which room she worked in, she always felt as if she were under observation. In fact, right this minute she could almost swear hostile eyes were lasering the back of her neck. A nasty sensation. Almost like being back at the Institute.

She gave an involuntary shudder.

"Problem?" Trick Granger said from behind her.

Nevada jumped, nearly dropping her rags and bucket of soapy water. "Don't sneak up on a person like that!"

"Sorry." He gave her a questioning look. "You're shaking."

"Not much." She frowned, angry at having betrayed weakness.

"Any more and you'd be registering on seismographs

all over the state. Why so jumpy? Did you think the Granger ghost was about to trail chilly fingers down your spine?"

"No."

He raised an eyebrow.

"Okay, maybe. The atmosphere in this house . . ." She shrugged.

"Tell me about it. Two parts eerie to one part creepy as hell. And that's hell in the literal sense. All except for the kitchen. No weirdness there, probably because that part of the house was remodeled back in the thirties. Marcello just brewed a fresh pot of coffee, by the way. Why not take a ten-minute break in the ghost-free zone?"

She shook her head. "I really need to get started on this wall of photographs."

"The stable, you mean."

"What?" She hadn't even made a dent in the mansion, and already he wanted her to tackle the stable? "I thought I'd leave the outbuildings until last."

Trick laughed. "Not that kind of stable," he explained. "Silas's girls. That wall you're about to attack is a pictorial record of every whore who ever worked for Silas Granger back when the house was a brothel."

"Really? All these women were . . ." Whores seemed harsh. ". . . prostitutes?" She examined the photographs more closely. "No wonder none of them are smiling."

He laughed again. "People seldom smile in old photographs. Didn't you ever notice that? Back in those days, the cameras took a while to capture an image, and it's hard to hold a smile for any length of time."

Nevada set her bucket down, wondering if it would be more efficient just to take down all the photographs first, scrub the wall, then clean each frame before re-hanging it. She probably wouldn't get every picture back on its original hook, but did that really matter? The girls were long dead. No one knew one girl from the other anyway, let alone the proper order of the pho-tographs.

"Why were those two men so determined to catch up with you?" Trick asked suddenly.

Caught off balance, she glanced up in surprise. "I don't know," she said honestly. "I wish I did. The truth is, I'm not sure who they are or who they're working for. I don't even know who *I* am." Drug-induced amnesia. That's what Yelena had called it. "They experimented on me at the Institute." She stared fixedly at the rag in her fist.

"Experimented?"

"With various drug regimens and other . . . treat-ments. They erased my memories, destroyed all my links to the past." She frowned at him. "And the scary part is, I don't even know if the memory loss was the point or merely a side effect."

"I'm sorry," he said, sounding as if he meant it.

"Yeah, me, too." Tears sprang to her eyes, but she blinked them away.

Trick Granger moved a step closer. He didn't touch her. Even so, his sympathy wrapped itself around her, as warm and soothing as a quilt on a cold, winter night.

Neither of them spoke for ten long heartbeats.

Then, "So your mother wasn't really a hippie-turned-blackjack dealer?" he said.

"I doubt it, but who knows?" She shrugged.

"And your name's not really Nevada White?"

Her smile faded. "Subject 111," she said bitterly. "That's the only name I remember. It's what they called me at the Institute. All except . . ." She fell silent.

"Except?"

Nevada met his gaze, and her heart gave a little jolt. Why did he have to be so understanding? Cruelty, she could endure. Viciousness, heartlessness, even indifference, but the tenderness in his gaze stripped away all her defenses. *I will not cry. I will not cry.*

"Except?" he said again.

She shifted her gaze so he couldn't see the glassiness of her eyes. "Except Yelena," she muttered.

"A fellow inmate?"

Nevada shook her head. "A member of the cleaning staff. My only friend. She's the one who christened me Nevada White."

"An odd choice of names."

"Yelena's idea of a joke. Nevada means snowy. So Nevada White is a twisted variation on Snow White, fitting since she referred to the head of the Institute as Dr. Poison Apple."

"Because he put you to sleep," Trick guessed.

"In a manner of speaking." She frowned.

"Dr. Poison Apple put you to sleep, but the prince never showed, and you finally got tired of waiting for him," he said.

"I got tired of playing lab rat."

"So you took matters into your own hands."

"With Yelena's help," Nevada said. "She was the one who showed me how to avoid swallowing the pills that kept me in a zombielike state, the one who bought me a fake ID, then conveniently 'lost' her keys, the same keys I used to escape."

"Sounds like she was a good friend to you, kind and generous." He cocked his head to one side. "So why do you look so sad every time you mention her name?"

Nevada didn't respond for a second. She couldn't trust her voice not to crack. "They killed her," she finally managed to say. "The men who're following me killed her. That was the reward for her kindness. They tracked me somehow to her town house, showed up at the door. I managed to escape out the bathroom window. Yelena wasn't so lucky." Nevada began removing framed photographs from the wall, hoping to bury her guilt in a flurry of activity.

"It wasn't your fault," Trick said quietly.

"She was like a mother to me," she said.

He gave her shoulder an encouraging squeeze. "She cared for you. I'm guessing you filled an empty spot in her heart."

"Maybe, but I can't help thinking she'd have been better off if she'd never met me." *I will not cry. I will not cry.*

A vow that would have been easier to keep if Trick's expression hadn't been so full of kindness and sympathy. "You didn't kill her," he said softly.

She tore her gaze from his. "I didn't kill the truck driver or the waitress, either, but the truth is, they're both dead because of me. In fact, if you were smart, you'd send me packing before you end up on the hit list."

Trick shrugged. "I'm living on borrowed time anyway."

She glanced back up at him in surprise. "I thought you didn't believe in the Granger curse."

"I don't"—he smiled a crooked smile—"but that's no guarantee the curse doesn't believe in me."

She turned back to the wall of photographs, trying to hide her response to his smile. He didn't mean anything by it. He was only trying to comfort her. He hadn't meant to trigger that weird, shuddery sensation in her stomach.

What was her problem anyway? One second she was on the verge of tears, the next she was having a major lust attack. So what if Trick Granger was sweet and charming and devilishly good-looking? She didn't have room in her life at the moment for any of those things.

Studiously ignoring him, Nevada forced herself to concentrate on the wall of photographs. She gazed unseeingly for several seconds. Then, "Oh!" she said, too surprised to control her reaction.

"What?" Trick moved up behind her, so close she could feel the warmth radiating from his body, so close she could smell the citrusy tang of his shaving gel, so close her traitorous body reacted in a number of inappropriate ways. As he leaned closer yet, peering at the wall, she forced herself to edge sideways, out of range of all that potent masculinity.

"Ah, that explains it." He tapped a photograph, the same photograph that had elicited her startled oh. "You found Blanche."

"Blanche?" What was he talking about?

Her puzzlement must have been obvious in her expression. "Blanche," he repeated. "My ghost. Your double."

"Your what? My who?"

He lifted the framed photo from its hook and passed it to her. "Blanche Smith was the girl my ancestor murdered. She's the ghost who haunts the place."

"Yesterday you called the haunted house rumors nonsense."

"Yesterday I was doing my best to talk you into taking the job."

"You lied." Nevada wasn't sure why that hurt so much. After all, she'd told her share of lies in the past week.

Trick nudged the photograph with the tip of one finger. "Blanche isn't dangerous. You probably won't even see her. She only manifests at night and then all she does is cry."

Nevada met his gaze full on, surprised anew at the almost electric jolt of attraction. What would happen if he touched her? Kissed her? Her throat suddenly felt dry as dust. She swallowed hard. "You called her my double. Why?"

"Blanche looks like you. Or rather you look like her. Not exactly, but there's a resemblance."

"There is?" Nevada hadn't really noticed the girl's face. She'd been too focused on the amulet that hung around the girl's neck, an amulet identical to the one

Nevada had lost in her struggle with the truck driver. But now that she paid closer attention, she could definitely see what Trick was talking about. She and the dead girl could have been sisters. "Weird," she murmured.

"You think?" Trick laughed sharply. "Welcome to my life."

There had to be a connection, Trick decided, between the long-dead girl in the photograph and the girl standing next to him, a stunned and mildly wary expression on her face. Such a marked resemblance couldn't be coincidence. But he didn't buy the everyone-has-a-double theory, and reincarnation didn't fit the facts, either. Wasn't the whole point of reincarnation that the reincarnated person came back in a *different* body? "May I see that picture again?" he asked.

Nevada passed him the photograph, and he examined it closely. Even with the old-fashioned clothing and hairstyle, Blanche Smith bore noticeable similarities to his new housekeeper. Idly, he turned over the framed photograph. The cardboard backing was stained and faded with age. Along the bottom edge, spidery, old-fashioned cursive spelled out four words: All my love, Blanche.

An odd thing, surely, for a whore to write on the back of her official stable photo. Had there been more than a business relationship between Silas Granger and the young prostitute? A tiny frisson of alarm shivered down Trick's spine, and for a second or two, he could almost swear he heard the echo of a sob.

He made eye contact with Nevada. "Like I told Marcello, this can't be coincidence. You're here for a reason. We're being maneuvered like pieces on a chessboard, you and I."

"Manipulated," Nevada said, her expression unreadable. "Welcome to *my* life."

Nevada worked on the ground floor rooms until Marcello announced that dinner was ready—spinach salad, hard rolls with garlic butter, and chicken cacciatore. Marcello and Trick ate their meal in front of the television where a soccer game—Italy versus Brazil—was going strong. Nevada, no big soccer fan, opted to enjoy her dinner in the peace of the kitchen.

Afterward, she migrated into the study, a room at the back of the house that Trick had told her had once been the brothel's business office. Nevada hoped to find records that offered insight into the life—and death— of Blanche Smith, the woman who'd looked so much like her.

But if there were records in the study, Nevada decided after a forty-minute search, they must be locked away in the safe. Of course, she hadn't even realized there *was* a safe at first. It wasn't until she'd examined the portrait behind the desk that she'd discovered what it hid.

The man in the portrait, presumably Trick's villainous or at least somewhat morally reprehensible ancestor, Silas Granger, gazed solemnly down from his ornate frame. A dark-haired man with pale, piercing eyes, long sideburns, and a handlebar mustache, Silas had been undeniably handsome.

Trick was good-looking, too, but aside from the dark hair, there was no family resemblance. Trick's face was harshly attractive rather than classically handsome, his cheekbones too wide, his nose too long, too aquiline, his chin too square. Only the fullness of his lower lip offered a hint of softness. Silas, on the other hand, was almost too handsome. Too perfect. Too Hollywood.

With some difficulty—the frame was heavier than it looked—she removed the portrait from the wall and wasted fifteen minutes or so trying various combinations on the safe before finally giving it up as a waste of time. Maybe the correct combination was written down somewhere, perhaps tucked away in the big rolltop desk.

But the desk was empty. Someone had cleaned it out long ago. All that remained in the many drawers and pigeonholes was a thick layer of dust and a few desiccated insect corpses.

Frustrated, she worked her way through the leatherbound volumes in the bookcase, hoping at least some of them would be business ledgers, but none were. There were books of sentimental poetry, a well-worn first edition of Nathaniel Hawthorne's *The Scarlet Letter,* two books on ornithology, and several devoted to practical medicine, with hints on everything from how best to treat a fever—willow bark tea and cold compresses—to how to set a broken arm—splints and bandages.

But no ledgers. No records of any sort.

This time when the prickling sensation on the back of her neck told her someone had her under surveillance, she didn't panic. "You move very quietly for a man with a cane," she said as she turned to find Trick standing in the doorway.

"Rubber," he said, which made her blink in surprise until she figured out he was talking about the tip of his cane, not a condom. "You're still cleaning?" he asked. "It's almost ten."

"Not cleaning. Playing Nancy Drew."

A startled expression flickered across his face.

Score one for her team. "In an effort to dig up more information on my 'double,'" she explained. "I didn't mention this earlier, but the truth is, Blanche Smith and I have more in common than our looks."

"Oh?"

"In her official stable photograph, Blanche is wearing an amulet."

"I hadn't noticed," he said.

"Well, I did." Nevada frowned. "And the strange part is, I had one just like it."

Trick raised an eyebrow. "Had?"

"I lost it in my wrestling match with the truck driver."

"And you say your amulet was just like Blanche's?"

"Identical."

"Interesting," he said.

"More like frustrating. I follow the clues, but all I find are brick walls." She sighed. "Who was Blanche Smith, and why do I resemble her so closely? I thought there might be some useful information in here—old records, something. I don't suppose you know the combination to the safe."

He crossed the room without a word, worked the combination, then swung the door open. "Empty," he said. "After the brothel went out of business, the family donated all the records to the Midas Lake Historical Society. My guess is, they didn't want any reminders of the house's dubious past hanging around."

"And yet they kept the pictures of the stable," Nevada reminded him.

Trick shrugged. "So they did."

Daniel glanced up as his housekeeper ushered Sarge Collier and Billy Branson into his home office. "Find her?" he asked, even though he knew already from their expressions what the answer was going to be.

"No," Sarge said. "Not yet."

"Did you check all the low-end motels as I suggested?"

"Low end, high end, and everything in between," Sarge reported.

"Homeless shelters?" Daniel said. "Church basements? Vagrant camps beneath freeway overpasses and bridges? Public parks? Alleys?"

"No," Sarge said.

"Then go check, and don't come back until you've exhausted all possibilities."

"If she hadn't lost her tracking device . . ." Billy started.

"But she *did* lose her tracking device," Daniel said, pulling the amulet from his top drawer and dangling it from its broken chain.

"And if we search everywhere you said and we still

can't find her, then what?" Billy asked, his tone edging perilously near rebellious.

"Then I go with Plan B," Daniel told him.

"What's Plan B?"

"That's where I prune back the dead wood and hire a couple of investigators who know what they're doing."

"Dead wood?" Billy echoed blankly.

Daniel smiled. "Emphasis on the *dead*."

FOUR

"Where's Nevada?" Trick asked Marcello, who was busily tapping away at the keys on his laptop. He sat at the kitchen counter, not because the old barstool was a comfortable perch but because that position put him close enough to the phone jack to hook up his slow-as-molasses, landline Internet connection.

"She said she planned to attack the library this morning." Marcello glanced up, apparently took in Trick's less-than-pristine appearance, and frowned. "Bad night?"

Trick nodded without elaborating. Just the memory of the heartbreaking sobs that had gone on half the night was enough to set his teeth on edge. His room still reeked of the whiskey he'd used to dull his senses.

"Taking a sleeping pill would make more sense," Marcello said, as if Trick had given a full explanation.

"Sleeping pills set the dreams free." Nightmares, he meant. He poured himself a cup of coffee. "I want you to check something for me. Do a Google search or whatever." Trick himself was virtually computer illiterate.

"What am I supposed to be searching for?"

"Two names. First, a woman named Yelena something who died recently in a home invasion. Second, a doctor who runs some sort of research facility."

"Does this doctor have a name?"

"Presumably."

Marcello gave him a nasty look. "And it is?"

"Sorry. No clue. No, wait. His nickname's Dr. Poison Apple."

"Most helpful," Marcello said, heavy on the caustic wit. "Do you know what sort of doctor he is?"

Trick shrugged. "A psychiatrist maybe."

"You have given me very little to work with," Marcello complained. "A woman's first name and—"

"An uncommon first name," Trick said.

"In the U.S.? Yes. In Russia? No."

"Which works in our favor since I want you to limit your search to the U.S."

Marcello made a rude hand gesture. "As for this Dr. Poison Apple . . ." He raised both hands in mock surrender, then heaved an exaggerated sigh. "Are there any other miracles I can perform for your amusement?"

"I'll ignore your feeble attempt at sarcasm," Trick said. "And yes, I'd appreciate one more miracle. I'd like you to do a general search for young women recently reported missing from private institutions."

"Mental hospitals, you mean?"

"Possibly." Trick frowned. "Though I doubt it. I

think it will be some sort of research facility, Dr. Poison Apple's research facility, to be precise. I suspect it's a place that specializes in the investigation of psi powers."

"What are psi powers?" Marcello asked.

"Extrasensory perception, telepathy, telekinesis, anything along that line. And you might want to cross-reference that search with the search for the recently deceased Yelena."

"You are trying to find out where Nevada came from," Marcello said.

Trick nodded. "Also who's after her. And why. But I don't want her to know what you're doing, okay?"

"I will exercise the strictest discretion."

Nevada sat on a lichen-covered boulder in the shade of a big pine, staring out across the water. She hadn't realized the Granger mansion stood on the shore of a mountain lake. The water wasn't visible from the house. Trick said they thought it had been originally but that in the years since the mansion was first built, the trees had encroached upon the view. And what a view. Steep, pine-covered slopes rose sharply from a crescent of sparkling water. Cobalt blue. The same color as Trick Granger's good eye.

She sighed. If only her life weren't so unbearably complicated. If only . . .

She remembered the gentle touch of his hand, the raspy rumble of his voice, the heart-melting charm of his smile.

Damn it.

"Damn it!" someone said behind her.

She turned so sharply that she nearly gave herself whiplash, but there was no one in sight. Just trees, trees, and more trees. Silently, she slid from her rocky perch, prepared to run back up to the safety of the house. The only problem with that plan was, the voice had come from the direction of the house.

"Son of a bitch!" the unseen man shouted.

If he was trying to sneak up on her, he was doing a lousy job of it, and that would seem to indicate that he *wasn't* trying to sneak up on her, that, in fact, he wasn't even aware of her. This theory seemed to be borne out when the man finally appeared, crashing through the lower limbs of a young pine, then sliding downhill on a slippery layer of pine needles, stopped only when he crashed into the rock where she'd been sitting. The surprise on his face would have seemed comical if she hadn't been so rattled.

"Well, hello," he said. He glanced back over his shoulder. "You probably heard . . . sorry about that, miss. Didn't mean to sully your ears. Didn't know anyone else was around. Take my advice. Never try to hike in the timber wearing cowboy boots." He raised one foot and tapped his sole. "Slicker than sn—" He stopped abruptly, censoring whatever he'd started to say.

Slicker than what? Nevada wondered. Snail slime? Snowballs? Snake oil? She studied the man. He was tall. Even without the high-heeled cowboy boots he'd have been tall, even taller than Trick and Marcello, who both topped six feet by a good inch. She did a quick inventory: shaggy brown hair, gray eyes, beard stubble, and a smile that showed off perfect teeth. Good-looking and very much aware of it.

"This is private property," she told him.

The smile faded. He blinked twice, perhaps surprised to find himself somewhere he hadn't meant to go or perhaps just surprised to discover that his charm hadn't worked. "Britt said—"

"You're a guest at the lodge."

"I am," he said.

"There's a fence separating the two properties, but it doesn't go all the way down to the lake. You must have come across below that."

"Didn't mean to trespass on your property," he said, and he sounded sincere. Nevada wasn't sure why she didn't believe him. Maybe because he was laying on the charm so thickly. Or maybe because she'd have seen him wandering onto Granger land if he'd crossed at the shoreline any time within the last half hour.

"It's not my property," she said. "I just work for the owner. Nevada White." She leaned forward, extending her hand across the boulder.

He took her chilly fingers into his warm grasp. "Ethan Faraday," he said. "And believe it or not, I'm working, too. Came to Midas Lake to pursue a story. I'm a reporter for the *Inquisitor*—you've heard of the *Inquisitor*?"

"The supermarket tabloid?"

"That's the one." He grinned again. "Thought there

might be a story here when I heard about the two mauling deaths, the truck driver and the waitress. You know what happened, right?"

She nodded warily. "Read about it in the paper. Terrible tragedy."

He shot her a quizzical look. "And yet here you are out in the sticks all by yourself, practically begging to be attacked. I'd think you'd be more cautious."

"Both attacks happened at night," she said. "I suspect it's safe enough in the daytime. Besides, I'm not really alone. Number one, you're here. And number two"—she squinted out across the water—"I'm in plain sight of at least four boaters."

"And number three," Marcello said, emerging from the trees to glare at Ethan Faraday, "the house is a mere fifty meters up the hill." He shifted his attention to her. "Is this gentleman bothering you, Nevada?"

Nevada shrugged. *Yes* sounded too harsh, and *no* would be a lie.

"You must be Marcello Bellini," Faraday said, extending his hand. "Britt told me all about you. I'm Ethan Faraday, a guest at the lodge."

Marcello ignored him. "Lunch is ready," he told Nevada. "You should go eat before it gets cold."

"I'm investigating the two wild animal attacks," Faraday said. "I'd like to do a story for the *Inquisitor* if I can find an angle."

"*Inquisitor?*" Marcello asked.

"One of those cheesy newspapers they sell in grocery stores," she said, "the ones with headlines like

'Aliens Visit Kremlin for Secret Meeting with Putin' or 'Dog-Faced Boy Catches Rabies.' "

"Ah." Marcello nodded. "A tabloid. So this 'angle' you are seeking,"—his voice was heavy with irony—"that would be the rabid dog-faced boy?"

Faraday laughed. "Not bad. Is there any evidence to suggest such a thing? I was thinking maybe wild dogs, figuring something like that would be pretty easy to tweak into a possible werewolf attack."

"Werewolf?" Marcello asked.

"Imaginary creatures," Nevada explained. "Men who change into wolves when the moon is full." She paused. "Come to think of it, the moon *was* full that night."

Marcello stared at her as if she'd lost her mind.

She shrugged. "I'm just saying . . ."

Faraday flashed his grin. "Werewolf, it is then."

"Though, come to think of it," Nevada said, "Trick mentioned vampires."

This time both men stared.

"He was joking," she said.

"I do not trust that Ethan Faraday." Marcello stood at the kitchen window, staring in the direction of the lodge.

Not that he could actually see the lodge through all the trees, but maybe, Trick thought, it wasn't the lodge he was trying to see. Maybe it was Britt. Britt and her new guest.

Marcello scowled. "Faraday is no more a reporter than I am."

But he was handsome in a rugged cowboy sort of way. Britt had brought him over for a short visit after lunch, not short enough to suit Marcello apparently. Though maybe it wasn't the visit that had bothered him as much as the fact that Britt had seemed to hang on the cowboy's every word. Not that Britt was prone to hang on Marcello's every word even when there was no competition, but Trick had always suspected their constant wrangling masked an underlying mutual attraction.

"If Faraday's not a reporter, then why did he say he was?" Trick asked.

"To give himself an excuse to poke and pry and ask impertinent questions."

"Questions like 'Britt, would you like to go out to dinner tonight?'" Trick suggested just to see what sort of response he'd get.

Marcello's nostrils flared, but he said nothing, just did some more scowling out the window.

"Do you think he's working with the men pursuing Nevada?" Trick asked.

Marcello frowned uncertainly. "No," he said slowly.

"Then . . . ?"

Marcello shrugged. "I wish I knew. He smiles with his mouth, but not with his eyes. He is hiding something. I am certain of it."

Marcello had dropped Nevada off at the historical society at five thirty. Trick had tried to talk her into waiting until after dinner, but that really wasn't an option since the Midas Lake Historical Society closed its doors promptly at seven. She figured she could scrounge for leftovers later if she got hungry. Some things were more important than food.

She looked enough like Blanche Smith to be her sister. She'd had—until recently—an antique amulet that appeared to be identical to Blanche's. There must be a connection, a connection that might eventually lead to her more immediate past. To her family.

Nevada tried to imagine her family—father, mother, brothers and sisters, grandparents, aunts, uncles, cousins—but her efforts failed. What sort of family would place a teenager in a hellhole like the Institute and promptly forget she'd ever existed?

One of her pursuers had claimed she'd killed her father. She'd dismissed his words at the time. She didn't feel like a murderer. The idea of taking another's life, let alone her *father's* life, revolted her. But she had to face facts. Anything was possible. She didn't remember life before the Institute. Maybe she *was* a monster and just didn't know it.

Trick had claimed these first weeks of May were part of the off-season, but the picturesque boardwalks of downtown Midas Lake were full of tourists. The visitors moved from shop to shop, museum to museum, restaurant to restaurant, seemingly determined not to miss a thing. A line of people waiting for an underground tour of the original Midas Touch gold mine stretched for half a block. A second line had formed across the street at the train depot, where every hour on the hour the Midas Express departed for a leisurely tour of the surrounding countryside on the same narrow-gauge track once used to haul ore from the outlying mines.

None of the tourists seemed to be interested in the Midas Lake Historical Society, though. Bells jangled above the door as Nevada entered, but the place appeared deserted aside from a gray-muzzled black lab snoozing on a rug in front of the wood stove at the far end of the long, narrow room.

"Hello? Anyone here?"

A thin little old man with sharp black eyes and a shock of unruly white hair popped out from behind a freestanding bookcase. The pink and purple feather duster he flourished in one hand contrasted sharply with his conservative tweeds.

Nevada stifled an exclamation. "You startled me," she said.

"Sorry." A smile twitched at the corners of the little man's mouth. "May I help you?"

"I'm looking for information about a young woman who lived here in Midas Lake during the gold rush. Blanche Smith."

"Common name, Smith."

"Yes, I know, but Midas Lake isn't very big."

"Not now," the man said, "but back in the day, it had a population of almost thirty thousand."

"Maybe the census records?"

"Yes, of course," he said. "I'm Jonathan Calhoun, by the way. And you are?"

"Nevada White."

"You're not a local."

"No," she said.

He studied her closely. "And you're not a tourist. Tourists never come in here. Probably because we don't give out coupons for free sarsaparilla or ten percent off on a tour of the Midas Touch," he added, his voice edged with sarcasm.

"I accepted a short-term job here in Midas Lake," she told him, hoping he'd leave it at that.

But of course, he didn't. "Where? One of the hotels?"

"No, I'm working for a private party, cleaning a house that's been empty for a while."

"Ah, yes." He nodded. "The Granger mansion." Again, he eyed her closely. "The house is rumored to be haunted. Not that I believe in such things."

"Nonsense," she agreed.

"Out of curiosity, though, may I ask if you've noticed anything . . . unusual?"

She shook her head. "Sorry. Not a thing."

"Oh," he said, sounding inordinately disappointed for a self-avowed disbeliever.

"Census records," she reminded him.

"Yes, of course." Jonathan set down his feather duster and made his way to a computer humming away in the back. "We have most of the information online these days. Saves wear and tear on our original source material. What was that name again?"

"Blanche Smith. She . . . worked . . . for Silas Granger."

"Ah," Jonathan said. "A whore. Back in those days, whores accounted for about ninety-eight percent of Midas Lake's female population, you know."

"I didn't, actually."

He nodded. "Conditions were primitive—law and order pretty lax. In 1853, the saloon-to-church ratio in Midas Lake was something like fifty to one." He slotted himself into the black leather computer chair and started punching keys like someone who knew his way around an online data bank.

"Find anything?" she asked, when he suddenly stopped typing.

"Old newspaper article," he said. "Have a look." He swiveled the monitor around so she could see.

Someone had scanned in the original article— yellowed paper, rips, tears, and all. Nevada skimmed the text. Blanche, it seemed, wasn't the only person to die in the brothel under suspicious circumstances. A week after Blanche had been found stabbed to death in her third-floor room, Miss Opal Hinkley, the madam Silas Granger had employed to see to the day-to-day running of the brothel, was discovered dead in her sitting room, an apparent suicide. She'd died of a bullet wound to the head. The murder weapon, Miss Opal's own derringer, had been lying on the floor next to her chair. Though the police had not suspected foul play, the writer of the article, one Harold Hawley Brewster, had obviously disagreed.

He took pains to relate an eyewitness account from someone identified only as Midget Molly. In it, Midget Molly described a heated confrontation between Silas and Opal, a "bitter and acrimonious" dispute that took place the day after Blanche's death. Was Silas Granger responsible for Blanche's vicious murder?

Miss Opal's "suicide"? Midget Molly seemed to think so, and Harold Hawley Brewster apparently agreed.

"If Silas murdered Blanche," Nevada speculated out loud, "and Miss Opal somehow found out, she might have threatened to expose him."

"Yes," agreed Jonathan, getting into the spirit. "So he murdered Opal to shut her up."

"Where's Nevada?" Trick asked Marcello. "It's almost eight. Didn't she say the Midas Lake Historical Society closed at seven?"

Marcello glanced up from his laptop. "Perhaps she decided to go shopping. Most of the stores are open until nine." He paused, not sure how to broach the topic he needed to discuss. "Trick? I did that research you asked me to do."

"Yes?" Trick said.

"I checked a few other things as well." Because he did not believe in coincidences.

"And?" Trick shot him an impatient look.

"Some people . . . rational people . . . believe vampires exist."

Trick stared at him. "Vampires? You've been researching vampires? Why the hell . . . ?"

"You gave me the idea," Marcello said, trying—but failing—to keep the defensiveness out of his voice.

"*I* gave you the . . . ? Oh, right. With my off-the-wall comment the morning after the trucker and the waitress had their throats ripped out. But you can't seriously think that was the work of vampires." Trick gave an incredulous laugh.

"In Europe, many people believe—"

"Uneducated peasants maybe." Trick raised an eyebrow. "But you are neither uneducated nor a peasant."

"Some educated people believe. Dr. Hiram Appleton, for example, holds a doctorate from Harvard."

"Who the hell is Dr. Hiram Appleton? Dr. Poison Apple?"

Marcello nodded. "I think so, yes. And educated as the man undoubtedly is, he still gives credence to all sorts of seemingly unlikely theories. His facility, the Appleton Institute, is dedicated to researching paranormal phenomena."

"Like vampires." Trick eyed him skeptically.

"I found no mention of vampires, per se," Marcello admitted, "but—"

"But what?"

"Yelena, the woman you told me had been killed in a recent home invasion . . ."

"You found her, too?"

"It would seem so. A woman named Yelena Petrov worked at the Appleton Institute."

"I suspected as much."

"She was not, however, murdered in a typical home invasion," Marcello told him.

"No?"

"Someone—or something—gnawed at her neck." Marcello paused. "Gnawed at her neck and drained all her blood."

Trick wasn't buying Marcello's ridiculous vampire theory, but he still didn't like the idea of Nevada wandering around alone after dark. He waited until eight thirty. When she hadn't returned by then, he set off to look for her.

The looking part was easy; the finding part was the challenge. He'd dragged himself in and out of every store on Sutter Street, Midas Lake's main thoroughfare, then checked out half the restaurants before he finally spotted her sitting at the counter in Aunt Bettie's Ice Cream Parlor.

Two teenage girls were leaving as he approached the entrance. Trick swung the door wide, holding it for them. They mumbled their thanks in between fluttering eyelashes and nervous giggles.

Nevada didn't turn around. She was too busy talking to the man on the stool next to hers. No, Trick corrected himself. Not just an anonymous man. A specific man. Ethan Faraday, the oversexed cowboy who was staying at Britt's.

Faraday said something in that low drawl of his, something Trick couldn't quite hear, but something charmingly witty, judging by the way Nevada laughed.

Trick muttered imprecations under his breath.

Or maybe not quite as far under his breath as he'd thought. Nevada whipped around, a spoonful of hot fudge sundae suspended halfway to her mouth. "Trick," she said. "What are you doing here?"

"Faraday." He nodded an acknowledgment at the other man.

"Granger." Faraday looked as if he were teetering on the edge of a smirk.

"What are you doing here?" Nevada asked again, a

little warily this time, as if she'd picked up on the discordant vibes between him and Faraday.

"I thought you might like a ride home."

"How thoughtful!" she said. "But Ethan already offered . . ." Her voice trailed off uncertainly.

"A neighborly gesture." Trick realized he was gripping his cane tightly enough to snap off the head. He forced himself to relax.

"I was going in that direction anyway." Faraday shrugged.

"As I said, a neighborly gesture. But unnecessary," Trick told him, "now that I'm here." He turned to Nevada. "Have you had dinner?"

She held up her sundae. "Does this count?"

"Calorie-wise, yes. Nutrition-wise? That's another question." He took a seat on the stool next to Nevada. "But it does look good. Maybe I should have one."

"Hot fudge sundae for the gentleman, Cindy," Faraday called to the girl behind the counter.

"You've been here . . . what? Two whole days? And already you know the waitress's name?"

Faraday gave a smug smile. "What can I say? I'm a friendly guy."

Right. Friendly. Trick glowered at him. "Dig up anything interesting yet?" he asked, more to prevent himself from saying something he'd regret than because he gave a rat's ass.

Faraday smirked, as if he knew exactly what was running through Trick's head. "Depends on your definition of interesting. Seems a couple of men in suits and sunglasses were spotted hanging around the truck stop the night the waitress and the truck driver were mauled to death."

"And you suspect they have some connection to the maulings?"

Faraday shrugged. "I didn't say that, but it's odd, don't you think, that two men in suits and sunglasses would be hanging around a truck stop in the middle of the night?"

"Lots of strange people hang around truck stops in the middle of the night," Nevada pointed out.

"Strange, yes," Faraday agreed as the waitress set a sundae in front of Trick. "Teenagers amped up on hormones. Truck drivers zoned out on caffeine. Maybe even a hooker or two. But men in suits and sunglasses? Not so common. The night manager at the truck stop told me the two men in question monopolized one of his waitresses that night, the same waitress who was later found dead behind the Dumpster. Coincidence? I don't think so."

"Where does the truck driver fit in?" Trick asked. He picked the cherry off the top of his sundae and dropped it onto the paper doily under his sundae dish.

"Who knows?" Faraday gave another careless shrug. "Maybe he saw what was happening to the waitress and tried to intervene."

"It's a nice theory, but where's the proof?" Trick demanded. "According to the newspaper account I read, both the waitress and the truck driver died as a result of animal attacks. Their throats were ripped out. You're telling me the two men in suits were responsible?"

"I talked to one of the cooks on duty that night.

She told me when she slipped outside for a smoke sometime between four thirty and a quarter to five, she heard growling sounds coming from the direction of the Dumpster, thought it was stray dogs fighting over scraps. Then a few minutes later, she saw two men emerge from the shadows along the back of the building and head across the parking lot." He tilted his head to one side, his expression cocky. "You do the math."

"But she didn't see the truck driver running over to investigate, so where does he figure into the equation?" Trick asked.

"Werewolves are unpredictable," Nevada said, her expression serious, though her eyes were dancing with suppressed mirth.

"Werewolves?" Trick frowned at Faraday. "That's your angle."

"Haven't made my final decision yet," Faraday told him with a lazy grin. "Werewolves, shape-shifters, or vampires. One of the three. Which monster would sell more papers? That's the question."

"I vote for werewolves," Nevada said. "Full moon, right? Seems obvious."

"But werewolves don't morph back and forth that fast. If the two men had gone all hairy by the light of the moon and attacked the waitress and/or the trucker, they wouldn't have been able to resume human form that quickly."

"You talk about this stuff as if it were real," Trick said, reminded uncomfortably of his recent discussion with Marcello.

"It is . . . to my readers." Faraday flashed him a quick smile.

Too quick? Too ingenuous? Trick studied the other man, trying to figure out what he was really after. Could he be in cahoots with the thugs chasing Nevada? Was she in danger from this cowboy?

Nevada scraped the last of the hot fudge from the bottom of her sundae dish. "So vampires then? Was there a significant blood loss associated with either death? The paper didn't say."

"I already asked that question of both the doctor who examined the bodies and my contact in the sheriff's office," Faraday said. "Nobody's talking."

"Then," said Trick, "sounds like you can put whatever spin you want on the story and no one will dispute it."

Faraday met his gaze, his expression unreadable. "Vampires it is then."

FIVE

Trick had hardly said a word the whole way back to the mansion. "Are you angry with me?" Nevada asked as he parked the Jeep in its customary spot in front of the stables.

"Why?" He switched off the ignition, then turned to look at her, the expression on his face hard to define. "Should I be?"

"No."

"Then I must not be."

"Is it because I was with Ethan Faraday?"

"No law against having a sundae with a tabloid reporter."

"You make him sound like a threat." She unfastened her seatbelt and got out of the Jeep.

Trick climbed out on the driver's side, reached into the back end for his cane, then shut the door. "I don't know that Faraday's a threat," he said slowly, "but the thing is, you don't know that he's not. Hanging around with a nosy journalist doesn't seem like the wisest course of action for someone with secrets."

"Meaning me," she said.

"Meaning you."

She studied his face as they made their way to the back door. That scowl didn't look like a worried scowl. In fact, it looked a lot like a jealous scowl. Laughter tickled at the back of her throat, but she clamped down on it. Former world-famous race-car driver Trick Granger getting dog-in-the-mangerish over Subject 111. Wouldn't Dr. Appleton's staff psychologists have a field day with that one?

Trick opened the door, nodding brusquely to indicate that she was to go ahead.

"Look, I didn't trust him at first, either, but the truth is, Faraday has a one-track mind," she said.

He closed the door, then swiveled around to face her. "That so?"

"The charm? The flirtatiousness? An intrinsic part of his personality, yes, but entirely superficial. He's not after me. He's after a story."

"I seriously doubt that." Marcello stood in the doorway to the dining room. "Mr. Faraday aroused my curiosity, so I Googled him. As far as I can tell, he has no connection to the *Inquisitor* or any other tabloid."

"Then what—" Trick started.

"I did, however, discover that until two years ago, he was a deputy sheriff in Mammoth County near the Oregon border."

"A deputy sheriff?" Trick echoed.

"He resigned after solving a case involving a biker

gang accused of kidnapping and murder. Most of the gang vanished without a trace, but Faraday and another deputy did manage to take the head biker's girlfriend into custody. The case never went to trial, though. The woman was struck by lightning as the deputies were escorting her to the squad car."

"Bizarre," Nevada said.

Marcello nodded. "But what is even more bizarre, there were multiple reports of livestock mutilations in the region that summer. And at least three humans were attacked—a young man who was run down prior to having his throat ripped out and two women, only one of whom survived."

Nevada frowned. "The young man had his throat ripped out, you say? Was there any mention of the women's wounds?"

"Bite marks on their necks. Significant blood loss."

"If I believed in vampires . . ." she started.

"Most people thought the attacks were the work of a pack of feral dogs. No one in Mammoth County put forth the vampire theory, although there was talk of chupacabras."

"What are chupacabras?" Trick asked.

Nevada had been wondering that herself.

"Monsters from Central America," Marcello explained with a self-satisfied smirk. "I Googled them, too. Chupacabras, also known as goat suckers, are believed to suck blood the way vampires do, only they are more likely to attack livestock than people."

"So what do you think Faraday is really up to?" Trick asked.

"Either he's after me," Nevada said, "or he's after the men who are chasing me."

Trick frowned at the far wall. "If he were after you, you'd be in custody already. It's your pursuers he's tracking."

"Why doesn't that ease my mind?" Nevada wondered aloud.

Sarge Collier and Billy Branson had arranged to meet Daniel at a fast-food place on the outskirts of Sacramento just off I-5. Not the sort of place Daniel normally patronized, but that was actually a plus. Less chance of running into one of his colleagues or constituents.

The two hired thugs sat at a table overlooking the play area, deserted at this late hour. Both were chowing down on burgers and fries as if they'd hadn't eaten in days. Feeling out of place in Armani—he should have thought to change into something more casual, damn it—Daniel made his way to Collier and Branson's booth.

Collier glanced up at his approach and indicated with a jerk of his head that Branson was to move over to give Daniel room to sit down.

Branson obliged, and Daniel sat, careful not to brush his jacket sleeves across the grease and ketchup residue that marked Branson's original position.

"Not eating?" Sarge dunked a handful of french fries in ketchup, then poked the entire mess in his mouth. For a few seconds, a blob of ketchup smeared his lower lip like blood. Then his tongue snaked out to lap it up.

Daniel averted his eyes. "I already ate."

"So did—" Billy aborted whatever he'd started to say, as if maybe Sarge had kicked him under the table.

Daniel glanced from one thug to the other, wondering if he was missing something. "I assume you didn't drag me all the way down here just to tell me you'd disposed of my . . . problem."

"Could have done that over the phone," Sarge agreed, stuffing another handful of fries in his mouth.

"So," Daniel said briskly, "what have you learned? Have you traced her whereabouts?"

"We think so, yes," Sarge said.

Daniel felt a flutter of anticipation. "Where is she?"

"San Francisco," Billy said.

"If our intel's right," Sarge added quickly.

"Makes sense," Daniel said.

"We thought so," Sarge agreed, "even though our witness couldn't make a positive ID from the photo we showed him."

"She could have changed her appearance," Daniel said.

Sarge nodded agreement. "Guy who owns the franchise on this place hired her last week, but she left after only two days. Told the boss she'd located family in the Bay Area and was going to go stay with them."

"I'd like to talk to him," Daniel said.

Sarge frowned. "I don't think that's a very good idea."

"Why not?" Daniel studied the other man's face. "Damn it, don't tell me you—"

"Couldn't be helped," Billy said. "The guy got suspicious, threatened to check us out with the local cops."

"I hope you had sense enough to take care of the body this time," Daniel snapped.

Sarge nodded. "Chained it to cinder blocks and dumped it in the river."

Where chances were good the body would be sufficiently deteriorated before it was found—if it was found—to disguise the fact the man had had his throat torn out. "So why bring me here, if not to talk to the witness?"

"For the food," Billy said. "Best burgers in town. If you don't believe me, just check the sign outside."

Daniel scowled.

"He's just jerking your chain," Sarge said. "We got you down here to talk to Tara, the girl who works the counter. Thought she might be able to tell you more about your half sister, them working the late shift together and all."

"Have you two lost your minds?" Daniel demanded. "I can't get personally involved. I'm a public figure. Any hint of scandal could ruin me."

"Just trying to be helpful," Sarge mumbled.

"If you want to be helpful, you'll do the job I'm paying you to do. Go to San Francisco, locate Whitney, and eliminate her."

Nevada couldn't sleep. She tried to tell herself that she was worried about Faraday's motives, but that wasn't it. No, what her tired brain kept fixating on was Trick's jealousy. Because the thing was, he wouldn't feel any jealousy toward Ethan Faraday if he didn't care about her . . . at least a little. Only was that a good thing or a bad thing? Nevada wasn't sure. Of course, that didn't mean her brain was about to give up its obsession, say, "Oh, hey, forget about it. Let's get some sleep." No, it just kept replaying that scene in the ice-cream parlor, analyzing and reanalyzing every word spoken, every facial expression, every nuance of body language. No doubt about it, if she wasn't insane before, she was definitely insane now. Insane to the nth power.

Frustrated, she finally got up, dressed, and made her way back to the main house. If she couldn't sleep, well then, she might as well work. Tackle something tedious and time-consuming. Something that would take her mind off Trick.

Gathering her cleaning supplies, she headed up to the library on the second floor. Earlier, she'd dusted the bottom five shelves, but she still had to clean the top two, a task she wasn't looking forward to since it meant she had to work off a ladder. Not that she was afraid of heights. It was wobbly old ladders that worried her.

An hour and a half later, she was halfway along the top shelf, listening to the music on Marcello's iPod, which she'd found abandoned on the kitchen counter and figured, *hey*, he wasn't using it, so why not? And no, his taste wasn't quite the same as hers, but even *Aida* and thirty-year-old Beach Boys hits were better than listening to the house creak in the wind.

Nevada was dusting her heart out and singing along to "Good Vibrations" when Trick said, "What the hell are you doing?" from right behind her. He startled her so badly that she not only lost her dust rag, she lost her grip on the ladder and would have done a belly flop onto the unforgiving hardwood floor if Trick hadn't cushioned her fall. With his body. Not a conscious choice on his part. He just happened to be standing in the wrong place at the right time.

"Are you okay?" she asked, worried about his messed-up knee.

"Remind me again why I hired you," he croaked, but she could tell from the glint of suppressed laughter in his eye that he wasn't hurt. Of course, he'd lost his cane and gotten the wind knocked out of him, but Nevada figured he deserved it. After all, she wouldn't have fallen on him if he hadn't scared the daylights out of her. His fault, the whole thing.

But then, quite suddenly, her initial surprise gave way to a heightened awareness.

She was lying on top of Trick, she realized, in a very suggestive position, her breasts pressed firmly against his chest, her hips against his hips, her legs against his legs. Oddly, she didn't feel at all embarrassed to find herself in such a compromising position. But she did find it a little arousing.

Okay, a lot arousing.

She caught her lower lip between her teeth, studying Trick's face. His features might not be as classically handsome as his ancestor Silas's, but she found him very attractive, very masculine. His lips curved in a faint smile, and that was all it took to push her over the line. Her skin tingled. Her nipples ached. She wanted . . . needed . . .

Gradually, Trick's smile faded. A muscle jumped in his cheek. He drew a long shaky breath. Maybe he'd been hurt after all.

"Are you sure you're all right?" she said, surprised when her voice emerged as a husky whisper.

He stared up at her, not saying a word, his taut expression sending unnerving little jolts of energy zinging through her.

"Trick?"

In lieu of a verbal response, he wrapped his arms around her and pulled her even closer.

She stiffened, but just for a second. Then her resistance dissolved. *She* dissolved. At least that's the way it felt, as if her bones and muscles had suddenly melted.

Trick raised his head and brushed his lips softly across hers in a delicate whisper of sensation.

Nevada found herself shivering, not with cold but with excitement, as his mouth captured hers in a kiss that tasted of whiskey and desire.

She knew she was playing with fire. She knew she should pull away, *run* away, but instead she kissed him back, long and hard and sweet. But it wasn't enough, the kissing. Not even close.

Her skin burned. Did Trick feel it, too? Or was all this lovely searing warmth one-sided?

As if in answer to her unspoken question, he flipped her over on her back and pinned her to the floor with his body. "I want you," he said, his voice rough, his hands gentle.

"I want you, too," was what she intended to say, only her voice refused to cooperate. She opened her mouth, but no words emerged. Nothing but a sigh. So she wrapped her arms around his neck and let her kisses do the talking.

And for about thirty seconds, everything was steamy hot, just-about-to-burst-into-flames perfect. Then Trick ruined it all by pulling away.

"Wh-what's wrong?" she stammered, wondering if she'd done something to turn him off.

"I've been drinking. My judgment's skewed. I shouldn't have started this. I'm sorry."

"Don't be," she said. "I'm not."

"Not yet."

"Not ever." She stroked his cheek, ran her thumb across his lower lip. "Kiss me, Trick. Kiss me again. Please."

He groaned. "Damn it, Nevada."

"I want you."

"No, you don't."

"Yes"—she wrapped her arms around his neck and dragged him back down within kissing range—"I do. So kiss me. Love me."

His blue eye looked black in the dim light of the table lamp. "You don't know what you want."

"Don't I?" she said. "You're not the only one who couldn't sleep. Why do you think I was up here working in the middle of the night? Because I was restless. Because I couldn't settle down. Why? Because of you.

I'm attracted to you, Trick, but I wasn't sure if you felt the same, not until I saw the way you glared at Ethan Faraday earlier. When you spotted us together in the ice-cream parlor, you were jealous, weren't you?"

"No, I—"

"Yes,"—she nipped gently at his lower lip—"you were."

"No, just concerned," he said. "He's a charmer, that Faraday. I don't trust him."

"Concerned? Okay, maybe a little. But jealous, too. Admit it. You want me."

"It's not that simple."

"It's exactly that simple. You want me. I want you. What's the problem?"

He frowned. "The problem is, I've had too much to drink and you're sleep-deprived. What seems like a good idea now may not seem so terrific in the morning."

"You talk too much," she said, and pulling his mouth down within range again, she kissed him.

He didn't resist, but he didn't reciprocate, either.

Frustrated, she released him. "You're really not going to do this, are you?"

He frowned. "I'm really not."

"But why? I don't understand."

He rolled off her and, using his cane for balance, shoved himself to his feet. "You deserve better."

But, damn it, she wanted *him*.

Long after Trick had left the room, she just sat there, hugging her knees to her chest.

• • •

Nevada left the ladder and cleaning supplies where they were. She'd finish in the morning. After retrieving Marcello's iPod from under one of the armchairs that flanked the fireplace, she returned it to the kitchen where she'd found it. Then she let herself out the back door.

The night air raised gooseflesh on her bare arms. Hugging herself, she made a beeline for the exterior stairway at the rear of the stables, but her steps slowed as she mounted the stairs.

Nevada paused uncertainly on the landing outside her apartment, her hand on the doorknob. She didn't remember leaving a light on inside. In fact, she clearly remembered flipping the switch just before she'd pulled the door shut.

So why was the light on now? Who was in her apartment?

Her pursuers?

Shivering uncontrollably, as much from fear as the cold, she carefully eased her hand off the knob, planning to back away, to run to the house for help. But when she released the knob, the mechanism inside made a noise. Not a loud noise, the tiniest of clicks, but it seemed to thunder in her ears—even louder than the deafening thrum of her racing heartbeat.

Run.

An owl hooted in a nearby tree and she nearly jumped out of her skin.

Run.

And then she heard another sound, heavy footsteps crossing the room on the other side of the door.

Run!

And she wanted to, she did. But her feet refused to cooperate. They seemed to be glued to the landing. Or maybe petrified. Solid rock feet.

The door swung open slowly. Light from inside fanned out across the boards of the landing. And then a long shadow emerged. A man's shadow. "Who's there? Nevada, is that you?"

Oh God. Ethan Faraday.

Relief turned her legs to overcooked spaghetti. She would have fallen if she hadn't clutched at the stair railing behind her with both hands. "Ethan. You nearly scared me to death. What are you doing here?"

"Waiting for you, of course."

"Me?" Suspicion nibbled away at her relief and sharpened her voice.

"I need to talk to you."

"And it couldn't wait until morning?"

"Look, it's important. All I need is five minutes of your time."

"Five minutes?"

"That's it. I promise."

"Okay," she said, moving past him into the apartment. Maybe she should have been a little more wary, but something about Ethan Faraday—those direct gray eyes, maybe, or the square, determined jaw—lulled her suspicions. She didn't trust him 100 percent, but neither was she frightened of him. In any case, she doubted he presented a danger. After all, he'd already had numerous opportunities to take her out, and yet, here she was, still breathing, albeit a little irregularly.

"I didn't mean to frighten you," he apologized. "I probably should have waited outside, but the door was unlocked, and I was cold."

She glanced at the wall clock as she took a seat on her lone kitchen chair. "Three thirty-seven in the morning is a weird time to be paying a social call."

"This isn't your typical social call," he said, making himself at home on the lumpy brown sofa.

"No?" She raised her eyebrows.

"I decided I needed to level with you. If I didn't and you got hurt, I'd never forgive myself."

Hurt by whom? she wondered. "So spit it out, whatever it is."

"I lied before. I'm not a reporter."

"I know. Marcello Googled you. You're a deputy sheriff—"

"Former deputy sheriff."

She ignored his interruption. "And you're after whoever killed the waitress and truck driver."

"Yes," he agreed. "Two dangerous psychopaths who also happen to be blood-sucking fiends."

She blinked. "I beg your pardon?"

"Vampires," he said. "Creatures of the night. Dracula wannabes."

She stared at him, speechless. Was he serious? He looked serious, but vampires? Who was he kidding?

"I can tell you think I'm crazy." He heaved a sigh. "It's asking a lot, I know, to expect you to buy into this whole weird bloodsucker scenario, but it's the truth. I swear to God. I didn't believe it the first time I ran face-to-face with one, either. In fact, I didn't become a true believer until I saw one go up in flames. It took two of us—me and another deputy—to drag her—"

"I think this part was in the newspaper account Marcello found."

"A sanitized version of it," he said. "We were arresting the woman for assault. She'd bitten a teenager, coerced him into lying to us."

"With some sort of evil mesmerizing spell?"

"You're enjoying this, aren't you?"

"It's fascinating," she said.

"And true, damn it." He frowned. "But to answer your question, no, she didn't use a spell. She wasn't a witch, for crying out loud. She used threats to keep the boy in line. He'd witnessed his parents' fate. Her friends had bled them to death right in front of him. Then she sank her fangs into his throat to give him a hint of what was in store for him if he didn't cooperate."

His story sounded like complete nonsense, but she found it increasingly difficult to discount what he said. His expression was so earnest, his voice so full of conviction.

"When we tried to arrest her, the vampire fought us every inch of the way. We finally got some cuffs on her and dragged her outside, intending to put her in the back of a squad car, but before we'd gone two steps into the morning light, she burst into flames. Burned the hell out of the hand I had clamped around her arm." He extended his left hand to show her the scars.

"Spontaneous human combustion," she said.

"That's one theory." But the disdainful twist of his

lips demonstrated how little credence he put in it. "The deputy assisting me offered another. He swore she'd been struck by lightning, despite the fact there wasn't a cloud in the sky."

"A bolt from the blue," she said. "I've heard of that."

"Hell, if it had been lightning, I'd have felt the electricity. My hair would have stood on end. My heart would have fluttered. Something."

"So you don't buy the lightning scenario, either. In your world, it's more believable that she was a vampire."

"Within seconds, she was gone. Nothing left but a pile of ashes. A lightning strike might have fried her to a crisp. Ditto spontaneous human combustion, but there'd have been something left. A blackened corpse. Charred remains. But in this case, there was nothing but ash."

"There must be some logical explanation," she protested.

"There is. She was a vampire. When a vampire meets sunlight, the result is ashes on the wind." He scowled, staring at the faded and peeling wallpaper on the far wall, but focused on some grim vision in his head. "There was a whole gang of vampires in Mammoth County that summer. Most of them died one way or another, but two escaped."

"Don't tell me," she said. "Your two psychopaths."

Those clear gray eyes bored into hers. "I wish I knew how to convince you that this isn't a joke."

"Believe me, I don't consider psychopaths a joke. They scare the daylights out of me."

"They should," he said grimly, then frowned. "What I haven't been able to figure out is why they're following you."

"Following me?" She pretended to be shocked. "Where'd you get a crazy idea like that? I suppose you think I'm a vampire, too?"

He shrugged, doing his best to act casual, but his eyes were intent, watching her closely. "Are you?"

"No, of course not." She forced a laugh. "Okay, I realize I'm pale to the point of pallid, but that doesn't make me a vampire. Come back around noon. I'll walk out in the sun, and you can check whether or not I burst into flames."

"I have it on good authority that sunscreen works pretty well short term."

"Okay, so check my mouth for retractable fangs. I dare you. No, wait. I have a better idea. Follow me." She led the way into the bedroom and, edging around the rumpled bed, stopped in front of the old-fashioned burl oak dresser that took up most of one wall. She pointed at the oval mirror attached to it. "See? I have a reflection."

"Sorry," he said. "That whole vampires-not-casting-a-reflection thing is a myth."

Nevada met his gaze in the mirror, then had just a split second to register his mocking expression before the pain of the flash seared her eyes and pierced her head. "My God," she gasped. "All that blood!"

Trick paced restlessly back and forth the length of his bedroom. He couldn't sleep, and for once he couldn't blame it on the ghost. Blanche had been oddly silent ever since he'd returned to his room.

Click, thump. Click, thump. First one direction and then the other. He was an idiot. What was worse, a frustrated idiot.

Click, thump. Click, thump. Back and forth, then back and forth again.

Damn it.

He stopped at the window and shoved back the heavy shutters. From there, he had a perfect view of the rear of the stables, of Nevada's apartment.

Her light was on, meaning she wasn't sleeping, either.

Shit.

Again, he resumed his pacing, moving even faster now, more recklessly. Small wonder he swung too wide and bashed his bad knee into the armoire door. Not hard enough to damage it. Just hard enough to hurt like hell. "Damn it," he muttered.

But damn *him* was more like it. Damn him for a noble, self-sacrificing fool. She'd wanted him. She'd said as much. And God knew he'd wanted her. Still wanted her.

But then, just as he'd been about to take what he wanted, chivalry had reared its ugly head. Yes, Nevada deserved a prince, but if she was willing to settle for a second-rate buccaneer, who was he to deny her?

God, he was such an idiot.

Doubly an idiot. Because the thing was, he wasn't the only game in town. Earlier, in the ice-cream parlor, Faraday had made it pretty damn clear he was interested. Trick hadn't missed those flirtatious sideways glances, the teasing laughter, and he was fairly certain Nevada hadn't, either, despite her protests about Faraday's one-track mind.

Her light was on.

All he had to do was march himself over there and knock on the door. If she wasn't interested anymore, well then, all she had to do was say so. On the other hand, if she was interested . . .

Trick headed downstairs before he could change his mind.

SIX

✦

Whats wrong?" Ethan Faraday's reflection mirrored his concern. "Did you cut yourself on something?" he asked Nevada.

"Cut myself?" Her voice sounded as shaky as her knees felt.

"You said something about blood."

"Because I saw it, a room covered in it." Her voice rose shrilly. "But it was your memory, not mine." Nevada's mind felt numb, her legs weak. She sat down abruptly on the end of the bed. It wasn't just her legs that were quivering now; she was shaking all over. And cold. So cold.

She tugged the quilt free and wrapped it around her shoulders.

Faraday disappeared into the other room and returned a short time later with a glass of apple juice. "Drink this," he ordered, then sat down next to her and draped an arm around her shoulders. "It's okay," he said. "It's going to be okay."

But it wasn't okay. All that blood. She shuddered.

"What the hell did you do to her?" A harsh voice. Demanding, almost threatening.

Nevada glanced up, startled. Trick Granger stood in the doorway, and he didn't look happy. He looked . . . What did you get when you crossed a marauding pirate with an avenging angel?

"Look at her," Trick snapped. "She's practically catatonic. What did you do to her, you bastard?" He advanced on Faraday, jerking the other man to his feet.

Nevada lost her grip on the apple juice. The glass hit the floor and shattered. Juice splattered everywhere.

Trick hauled Faraday's face within inches of his own. "What was your plan? Did you think forcing booze down her throat would make it easier to take advantage of her?"

"Booze?" Faraday said blankly. "It was apple juice."

"Apple juice," she repeated, feeling oddly removed from the scene.

Trick's sharp gaze raked Faraday's face, as if searching for the truth. Slowly the fury faded from his expression. He frowned, looking more confused than angry. "Apple juice?"

"She had a dizzy spell. I thought maybe she'd feel better if she got a little sugar in her system."

Trick released his grip on Faraday's shirt front, and Faraday took a step back out of range. He glanced from Trick to her and then back to Trick, as if he couldn't figure out which one of them was the bigger nutcase.

"I had a psychic flash," she told Trick, "after I dragged him in here—"

"Into your bedroom?" Trick said in a low, dangerous voice.

"—so he'd see my reflection and realize I'm not a vampire."

"He thinks you're a vampire?" Trick said in an oh-please-get-real tone of voice.

"No," Faraday said. "I don't think she's a vampire, but I'm starting to wonder if she's an escaped lunatic."

Nevada's breath caught in her throat. Neither she nor Trick spoke a word for a full five count.

"Chill out," Faraday said. "I'm joking. Why don't we all take a deep breath, then go back into the living room and get this sorted out."

"Good idea," Trick said.

But Nevada wasn't so sure, not if sorting things out meant she'd have to explain to Ethan Faraday, former *lawman* Ethan Faraday, that she was an escapee from a research facility who didn't have a clue who she really was.

Nevada took the wooden chair, leaving the sofa for the two men, who settled at opposite ends, as far from each other as possible. Trick leaned his cane against the arm of the couch and propped his bad leg on the rickety coffee table.

Faraday shot her a searching look. "Explain the blood comment."

"I'm psychic," she said, "but I have no power over my gift. It's totally unpredictable. Sometimes—and I never know when it's going to happen—I'll catch a glimpse of someone's reflection and see something else. Something beyond what's really reflected there."

"Something like blood?" Faraday said. "I don't get it."

"Blood, violence. It's always something traumatic, something from the person's past, a memory."

"So the blood was my memory?" He looked confused, not guilty.

Nevada was pretty sure that was a good thing.

"Was there anything else that you remember? Some indication of time or place maybe?" he asked. "Because this blood thing is pretty generic. I was a cop, remember?"

Nevada didn't want to think about the flash, though every detail was burned into her brain in digital high-def. "I'm not sure where it was geographically because all I saw was an interior, a cheap motel room, I think, very ugly and generic even if it hadn't been for all the gore. There was blood everywhere—the bed, the carpet, the walls. An ocean of blood." She shivered.

"A motel room. An ocean of blood." He looked a little sick. "The Oasis. Unit seven. I thought at first the blood was just splashed around for shock value, to make us worry about the hostage's safety." He frowned. "Later it turned out the blood had belonged to the couple who owned the motel. The vampire gang slaughtered them, literally ripped them to pieces."

"Again with the vampires," Trick said. "Just so we're clear on this, you didn't participate in the slaughter, right? You're not a mass murderer."

"Hell no!" Faraday said, but he seemed more startled than angry.

"Okay, then." Trick nodded. "That explains why Nevada looked so pale and upset, why you brought her a glass of juice, even why you had your fricking arm around her, but it still doesn't explain what the hell you're doing in her apartment in the middle of the night."

"Jealous?" Faraday asked.

Taunting Trick was not a smart move. Nevada didn't miss the tightening of his jaw, the dangerous narrowing of his eye, even if Faraday did.

"Jealous?" Trick said. "Of you?"

"Because that's how you're acting."

"Stop!" she said. "Both of you, just stop."

"Okay," Trick said through gritted teeth. "So what are you doing here?"

"Confessing that I'm not really a tabloid reporter."

"Yeah, we had that one figured."

"I'm a demon hunter," Faraday said.

The ensuing silence was thick enough to cut with a chainsaw.

A full minute passed before Trick said, "Excuse me?"

"Like Buffy," Nevada said.

"Not like Buffy." Faraday shot her a disgusted look. "First of all, Buffy was a fictional character. Second, she was a girl. And third, she was a slayer. I'm a hunter. It's a whole different thing."

"You just track them down. You don't kill them," Nevada said.

"Well . . ." Faraday looked uncomfortable.

"You *do* kill them," Trick said.

"Sometimes I have no choice," Faraday explained. "I

staked one back in February, yes, but only because he attacked me. It was self-defense."

"I don't believe this," Trick said. "Vampires? Blood-soaked motel rooms? Staking? None of this is real. I'm dreaming, aren't I?"

"I wish," Faraday said. "But it's the absolute truth—all of it. I came here to warn Nevada. I think the two vamps I'm pursuing have been following her. I'm not sure why, though you probably know, don't you, Nevada?"

She didn't say anything, but she suspected her flushed cheeks were a dead giveaway.

Two vertical lines appeared between Trick's eyebrows. "What makes you think they're looking for Nevada?"

Faraday shrugged. "Fairly obvious deduction. They showed up here in Midas Lake the same day she did."

"Yes, but that could be purely coincidental," Trick pointed out.

"They spoke to several people at the truck stop—not just the waitress who turned up dead. And everyone I interviewed told the same story. The two vamps asked if anyone had seen a girl. They had a photograph. Now I didn't see the photograph, but I'm betting if we take Nevada over to the Stop 'N Go and talk to those same witnesses, they'll recognize her from the picture. What do you think?"

"I think you're smarter than you look," Trick said.

Faraday grinned. "I'll take that as a compliment." He angled toward Nevada and his expression turned grim. "I don't know where Sarge and Billy have gone—"

"Sacramento," Trick said. "Marcello and I told them she'd hitched a ride to Sacramento."

"And they bought that?" Faraday asked, sounding skeptical.

"Sacramento was like a magic word," Trick said. "They didn't question it for a second, just took off."

"Sacramento?" Faraday said. "What's so special about Sacramento?"

"I don't know. Maybe you should go check it out," Trick suggested.

"Maybe I will," Faraday said.

"Faraday's gone," Marcello announced at lunch the next day, and for someone who wasn't interested in Britt Petersen, Trick thought, he seemed pretty damned pleased to be rid of the competition.

"He left for Sacramento this morning," Nevada said. "I talked with him down on the beach before he took off," she added in response to Trick's questioning look, then turned to Marcello. "Saw Britt, too. She told me more of your brush pile washed up on her beach last night, and she didn't sound happy about it."

Marcello muttered something extremely rude in Italian. "I do not understand how this keeps happening. I am very careful to pile everything well above the high-water mark." In his free time, Marcello was trying to clear away enough trees and brush to provide a view of the lake from the mansion. Every Realtor they'd talked to had promised that a lake view would up the selling price by thousands.

"Beavers?" Nevada suggested.

Trick fought a smile as Marcello turned to her with an incredulous, "What? What are these beavers?"

"Large rodents with flat tails?"

Frowning, Marcello looked at Trick. "She is making a joke at my expense, no?"

"No." Nevada said. "Beavers gnaw down trees and build dams."

"In streams, not lakes," Trick pointed out.

Nevada shrugged. "It was only a suggestion." She took a bite of her tuna sandwich.

"Maybe it's a bunch of kids," Trick said. "They drag the branches down to the lake, intending to tie them together to make a raft."

"I have not seen any children on the property."

"Maybe it's the ghost," Nevada said, a remark Marcello didn't even dignify with a response.

Trick was reaching for some grapes when he remembered the message. "You got a call earlier," he told Nevada. "A Jonathan Calhoun from the Midas Lake Historical Society. He said he'd found more information for you on Blanche Smith."

After lunch, Nevada hitched a ride downtown with Marcello, who was headed for the grocery store. Even though Trick hadn't asked, she'd made a point of promising to make up her lost hours that evening after dinner. That way, if he wanted to avoid her, he could. And if he didn't . . . even better.

"Drop me at the mercantile," Nevada said when Marcello was stopped at the first traffic light.

"You told Trick you were going to the Midas Lake

Historical Society." He made it sound like an accusation.

"And so I am," she said, "but in case you hadn't noticed, my clothes are getting shabbier and more threadbare by the day. I need a couple more shirts and pairs of jeans, which I can pick up cheap at the Salvation Army, but I want *new* underwear, and the mercantile has the most reasonable prices in this overpriced tourist trap."

Scowling, Marcello avoided eye contact. Probably wasn't comfortable discussing women's underwear. He didn't say another word until he pulled to the curb in front of Foster's Mercantile, a big, old-fashioned general store that still carried the basics despite the latte bar in back and the three aisles devoted exclusively to souvenirs.

As Nevada was unfastening her seat belt, Marcello turned to her, still looking uncomfortable and a little embarrassed. "Do you need money?" he asked. "An advance against your wages?" She wouldn't receive her first week's pay for another two days, and Marcello knew that.

She smiled, caught off guard by the thoughtfulness and generosity of his offer. "Thanks, but I'll manage," she said and let herself out of the Jeep.

Forty-five minutes later, she walked into the historical society headquarters, the proud owner of some colorful new underwear, socks, three pairs of secondhand jeans, a pink sweater, and four nearly new T-shirts. Plus, she had over two dollars left.

Jonathan Calhoun, apparently engrossed in a book, didn't glance up until she was halfway across the room.

"Ms. White." The corners of his mouth trembled for a moment, as if they were trying to smile but couldn't quite remember how.

"Call me Nevada, Mr. Calhoun."

"Call me Mr. Calhoun, Nevada." He did smile then, a miserly little stretch of the lips, there and gone in a flash, but a smile nonetheless. "No, I'm joking. Call me Jonathan." He set his book aside and got up out of his armchair. "I didn't expect you this early."

"I took the afternoon off," she told him. "So what new information did you dig up about Blanche Smith?"

Jonathan studied her over the tops of his glasses. "I found a list of the items mailed to her next of kin after her death. It was stuck in between the pages of one of Miss Opal's account books."

"May I see?"

"Of course." He crossed to the desk on the opposite side of the room, found the list he was looking for, and handed it to her. "Careful," he warned. "The paper's old and fragile. If you have trouble deciphering the words, I can help. I've had a lot of experience reading nineteenth-century script."

Nevada handled the yellowed paper carefully, tilting it to get the best light. The handwriting was faded but easy enough read. She skimmed through the list. "One gold amulet," she read aloud. The last item on the list.

"Check out the scribbled notation at the bottom of the page," Jonathan suggested.

Nevada squinted, trying to make sense of the squiggles. Whoever had added the line at the end hadn't been quite the stickler at penmanship as the person who'd penned the original list. "Okay, I give up. What does it say?"

Jonathan's smile was just this side of smug. "It's a personal note from Silas Granger, telling the Smith family how sorry he is for their loss."

"Was that standard procedure," she asked, "for brothel owners to write notes of condolence?"

Jonathan shook his head. "No. Definitely not."

She frowned. "Then why?"

"Good question." Jonathan pursed his lips. "Perhaps he was truly sorry."

"Or maybe he was guilty as hell and trying to throw them off the scent." Nevada stared at the yellowed paper. "The Smiths," she said. "They were locals then?"

"Oh, no." Jonathan looked surprised that she would suggest such a thing. "They were Romanichal, British Gypsies."

"So they were English?"

"Originally, though at the time of Blanche's death, the family was living in San Francisco."

Her heart gave a little jolt. The address that had been attached to her file at the Appleton Institute was in San Francisco.

Trick studied the photograph of Blanche Smith on the wall in the dining room, struck afresh by the woman's startling resemblance to Nevada.

"Strange, is it not," Marcello said from the doorway, "that two women from two different centuries could look so much alike?"

Trick nodded. "Nevada thinks she may be related to my ghost."

Marcello crossed the room, stopping in front of the stable. "Nevada does not remember her past. Correct? She remembers nothing of the time before she was committed to the Appleton Institute."

"What are you getting at?" Trick asked.

"What if she is older than she looks?"

Trick frowned. "I don't see—"

"Much older," Marcello suggested. "As in a century and a half older."

"What are you suggesting, Marcello?"

"Perhaps the reason Nevada looks so much like Blanche Smith is because she *is* Blanche Smith."

Trick turned to Marcello, waiting for a punch line that never came. Marcello wasn't joking. His expression was dead serious. Trick mustered a halfhearted laugh. "That's crazy."

"Not if she is a vampire," Marcello said.

"Are you serious? If she were a vampire, wouldn't she have to avoid the sun?"

"Have you never heard of sunblock?"

"But what about blood? Don't vampires crave blood? Hell, Nevada won't even eat rare steak."

"Perhaps she is suppressing her cravings," Marcello suggested.

"How?"

"With medication. She has a plastic bag full of pills. She takes one tablet every morning. I have seen her."

"That proves nothing. I take pills every morning, too. They're called vitamins."

Marcello gave him a pitying look. "Then you would have no objection if I had one of her pills analyzed?"

"Knock yourself out," Trick said. "You're wrong about Nevada, and the sooner you figure that out, the better."

"And if I am not wrong, what then?"

"Look," Trick said, "even if I believed she was a vampire—which I don't—I still wouldn't buy your theory that she's Blanche Smith."

"Why not?" Frowning, Marcello tapped Blanche's photograph. "The resemblance is undeniable."

"Nevada can't be Blanche," Trick said, "because Blanche is a ghost, and by definition, a ghost is dead."

"I know you think you've heard the ghost."

"Wrong, Bellini. I *have* heard the ghost and seen her, too."

"According to Granger family legend," Marcello continued as if he hadn't even heard Trick's interruption, "the manifestation is a ghost, but what if it's not?"

"If it looks like a duck and quacks like a duck . . ." Trick said.

Marcello stared. "I do not understand the duck reference."

Trick suppressed a sigh of exasperation. "It's a saying. In other words, what else could my apparition be but a ghost?"

"I have been doing research," Marcello said. "Some experts estimate that over half of so-called hauntings are nothing but residual psychic energy leftover from emotionally traumatic events."

"Events like being stabbed to death?" Trick suggested, heavy on the sarcasm.

After dinner, Marcello stopped by Trick's room on the second floor to say he was going for a jog on the beach. Trick suspected his assistant was more interested in trying to catch the culprit responsible for dragging limbs onto Britt's beach than he was in exercise, but either way, Trick had no problem with the plan. The truth was, he could use some time to himself, time to think, time to poke a few holes in Marcello's ridiculous Nevada-is-a-vampire theory.

But he didn't get much thinking done. Trick had just settled back against the pillows, hands folded under his head, when he heard a shriek from the third floor.

The two fake cops, he thought. Somehow they'd slipped into the house and cornered Nevada. Galvanized by sheer terror, he took the dimly lit stairs faster than good sense dictated, then paused on the landing at the top, listening hard. No sound disturbed the stillness, at least nothing he could hear over the pounding of his heart. Light spilled out into the hallway from one of the bedrooms at the far end.

"No!" Nevada cried.

Visions of mayhem flashed through Trick's mind. He lunged down the hall and burst into the room, fully prepared to use his cane as a weapon, only to find Nevada standing alone under the ceiling fixture, studying something cradled in her palm.

"My God, you scared me to death," he said. "I thought you were being torn limb from limb."

Her puzzled gaze met his. "Why?" Then, slowly, re-alization dawned. "I must have shrieked, huh? Sorry."

"What was it? What set you off? A spider?"

"No." She smiled. "Though I have faced my share of cobwebs up here. I was cleaning out this old highboy." She patted the chest of drawers. "And guess what I discovered? A secret compartment. Look what I found inside." She extended her hand, palm up.

"Pebbles?" he said.

She laughed. "Not exactly." She passed him a hand-ful of stones. "Have a closer look. Unless I'm mistaken, those are—"

"Gold nuggets," he finished. "Nice. Worth quite a bit right now, too, with the price of gold through the roof. Was there anything else in the secret compartment?"

"I don't know. I was so fascinated with the nuggets that I didn't check any further. Look." She pulled out one of the top drawers. "Notice how deep it is?"

He nodded. "A foot, more or less."

"Okay, then. Compare this one." She pulled out the next drawer. "See? It's a good three inches shorter." She pulled out a third drawer that was the same length as the first. "The compartment is hidden behind the second drawer." She hooked the edge of the false back with her fingernail and nudged at it. "It slides side-ways."

He peered into the dark slot. "Hard to see all the way back in there. Hard to tell if there's anything else inside."

"I couldn't feel anything. Nothing loose. Just the nuggets."

"There's a flashlight in the drawer of the bedside table in my room. I think I'll go get it. I'd like to take a closer look at the secret compartment."

"I'll get the flashlight," she offered, and without waiting for a response, bolted out the door and down the stairs.

Trick studied the nuggets in his hand. Dull gold in color, rough ovals, smooth to the touch but with a few random pockmarks. Most of them were half an inch long or less, but three were over an inch in length. They would have represented a small fortune back in the 1850s. Who, he wondered, had hidden them? And why?

"Found it." Nevada dashed back into the room, flourishing his penlight. She directed its narrow beam into the secret compartment.

"Empty," he said, trying not to feel disappointed. He'd hoped for some clue to the nuggets' original owner.

"No," Nevada said. "I don't think it is." She leaned closer, holding the light steady with one hand while probing the narrow space with the fingers of the other. "There's something jammed up against the back of the compartment. See?" She shone the light on it. "That's not wood. It looks like fabric. Or maybe leather."

"You're right."

"Got it!" she crowed. Seconds later, she drew a small leather-bound book from the hidden compartment.

"Who would go to all that trouble to hide a book?"

Nevada leafed through the yellowed pages. "Not

a book," she said. "A diary." She met his gaze with a stunned expression, her cheeks pale.

"What?" he said.

"Look." She opened the diary, pointing to the name inscribed on the inside cover.

"Blanche Margaret Smith," he read aloud, then whistled softly.

SEVEN

Blurry-eyed from too little sleep and too much time spent deciphering Blanche's tiny, crabbed handwriting, Nevada took her morning pill like a good little girl, then trudged down the path to the beach.

The sky was still dark at a little after six, but the first hint of dawn backlit the mountains to the east with a ruddy glow. Fog hugged the lower slopes, trailing wispy white fingers through the pines. She shivered nonstop, not dressed warmly enough for the early morning chill in jeans and a sweatshirt. Ski pants and a parka would have been more appropriate. Still, there were advantages to being out here in the great outdoors—solitude for one thing. And the complete absence of dusty, musty, old-house smells. She breathed deeply. Room fresheners and dryer sheets might claim to be pine-scented, but nothing, she thought, could accurately duplicate the real thing.

On the other hand, room fresheners and dryer sheets didn't slap the unwary hiker in the face with their aromatic but dew-drenched branches. Nevada wiped moisture from her cheeks with the sleeve of her sweatshirt as she trudged downhill. She was just mopping away the last of the dampness when the lake came into view. The lake and Britt Petersen.

"Oh," Britt said, the way people did when they were caught doing something they weren't supposed to be doing. She dropped the pine bough she was dragging, trying hard to be casual about it but only succeeding in looking shiftier. "I promise this isn't what it looks like," she said.

"Okay." Nevada fought a smile. "What is it then?"

"I was . . . I was . . . returning this rubbish that floated over onto my beach."

Nevada glanced pointedly at the drag marks in the sand. Britt had clearly been hauling the big limb away from Marcello's trash pile and toward her own pristine strip of beach.

"Why go to so much trouble?" Nevada asked. "Are you that determined to tick him off?"

Embarrassment and then defiance flitted across Britt's beautiful face. "Okay, here's the truth, lame as it is. Marcello's the first man I've been attracted to in years. Unfortunately, the big, dumb Italian seems impervious to my charm. In fact, he totally ignores me. The only way I've been able to get his attention is to pick a fight."

"So when there's nothing to fight over," Nevada guessed, "you manufacture a problem . . . like the branches that keep mysteriously washing up on your beach."

"It sounds silly, I know," Britt said, "but I think it's working. Several times when he didn't think I was paying attention, I've caught him looking at me . . . I don't know . . . with a sort of hungry expression. Hungry and maybe a little speculative."

"Like he's wondering if you're as feisty in bed as out," Nevada said.

"Exactly." Britt nodded. "You're not going to tell him about my little subterfuge, are you?"

Nevada did smile then. "And divert the path of true love? No way."

Nevada burst into the kitchen, all rosy-cheeked, the wisps of hair that had escaped her ponytail curling around her face in tendrils. "Where's Marcello?"

"Good morning to you, too," Trick said. "Would you like to split an omelet?"

"As long as it doesn't have any eggs in it. Where's Marcello?"

Trick raised an eyebrow and planted one fist on his hip. "What do you mean 'as long as it doesn't have any eggs in it'? Haven't you heard? You can't make an omelet without breaking eggs."

"Exactly," she said. "That was my way of saying no, thank you. Where's Marcello?"

Trick cracked another egg on the edge of the counter, then dumped it into the bowl that already held two. He was hungry this morning. Apparently that was what happened when a ghost didn't keep you up all night. He selected a whisk from the kitchen implements bunched like flowers in an old blue enamel coffeepot.

"Marcello took the rowboat out early. Said he planned to do a little fishing."

"Oh, good. So he's not around to overhear. Wait." Nevada's eyes widened. "Did you say fishing? As in out on the lake?"

"Yes, on the lake. Where else?"

"Good point," she said. "Boats and lakes. A match made in heaven." A secretive smile tilted the corners of her mouth.

"What?" He dumped the egg mixture into the melted butter already sizzling in the omelet pan.

"Nothing."

He let it pass, even though it was perfectly obvious from the smirk on her face that something was up. "Did you get through Blanche's diary last night?"

She opened the refrigerator and pulled out a half gallon of milk. "Almost. I fell asleep about ten pages from the end."

"Really?" He raised an eyebrow. "I figured X-rated stuff like that was a guaranteed page-turner."

"X-rated? Oh, you mean you thought because of Blanche's profession, she'd dwell on all the erotic details. Well, sorry to disappoint you, but no. What she wrote was mostly day-to-day trivia—the weather, what she ate for breakfast, which of the girls were feuding, who was jealous of whom. She did include a little about her family and her hopes and dreams for the future, though. You'd never guess what Blanche's long-term goal was."

"To join a traveling carnival as a fortune teller," he tried.

"Not even close. Blanche planned to open a milliner's shop when she went back to San Francisco."

"And a milliner's shop is . . . ?" Trick flipped his omelet, then added chopped onions and grated cheese.

Nevada grinned. "I wasn't sure, either. Had to look it up. It's a place where they make and sell women's hats." She ducked into the pantry, returning a few seconds later with a box of cereal.

"Hats?"

"Those big fancy ones they wore back then, all feathers and froufrou."

"No wonder you fell asleep before you finished reading. I'd have been out like a light in five minutes flat if I'd had to wade through yawn-worthy stuff like that." He scooped his omelet onto a plate. "Sure you don't want any of this?"

"Thanks, but no thanks. I hate eggs." She poured herself a bowl of Rice Krispies, sprinkled on some sugar, drowned it all in milk, then leaned over the bowl, cupping her ear. "Yup. They're snap, crackle, and popping up a storm. You've got to love a cereal that comes with its own sound effects."

"You're a strange girl," he said.

"Thank you."

Trick was just finishing up the dishes when Marcello came in the back door. "Catch anything?" Trick asked.

"Anyone," Marcello said, tossing his jacket on a chair.

Trick frowned. "Either you're being obscure or I'm being obtuse."

Marcello buried his face in his hands. "Britt Petersen," he mumbled, as if that explained everything.

Okay, first Nevada came in acting weird, and now here was Marcello acting even weirder. Was it something in the air? "Britt Petersen," he repeated slowly. "Blond woman. Owns the lodge next door."

Marcello, his expression halfway between worried and upset, met Trick's gaze. "You know how angry it makes her when branches from my trash piles wash up on her beach? How she stomps over here and yells at me, demands that I clean up the mess?"

Trick nodded.

"As it happens, it is not my mess."

"I don't follow," Trick said. "Are you saying someone's deliberately scattering branches on her beach?"

"Yes," Marcello said.

"Who?"

"Britt."

"That doesn't make sense. Are you sure?"

"I saw her with my own eyes."

"From the boat," Trick guessed.

"Yes."

"But she didn't see you."

"No."

"How far away were you? Are you sure it was Britt? Maybe it was another blonde."

"It was Britt. I am positive. But if you do not believe me, ask Nevada. She also saw Britt. In fact, they spoke for some time."

Which might explain Nevada's odd reaction when

he'd mentioned that Marcello had taken the boat out. "Okay, so you think Britt's been dragging branches from your trash piles to her beach. That's pretty peculiar behavior. Why would she do something like that?"

Marcello shot him an impatient look, as if he thought Trick were being deliberately dense. "Because she enjoys provoking me. Because she wants me, and because on some level, she knows I want her, too."

Trick grinned. "And this is a problem because . . . ?"

Marcello looked grim. "You know why."

Nevada surveyed the row of drawers she'd lined up side by side on the hardwood floor of one of the second-floor bedrooms. *Everyone has secrets. For me, X marks the spot.* The cryptic entry from Blanche's diary had been driving Nevada crazy all day. What did it mean? Nevada didn't know. Presumably, there was an *X* somewhere in the house, an *X* that hid a secret. So far, though, she'd had no luck locating this mysterious *X* Blanche had written about. It certainly wasn't anywhere on these drawers or any of the other three dozen or so she'd checked, which meant she was rapidly running out of places to look.

"What are you doing?" Trick asked from the threshold.

She smiled. "Well, I started out cleaning this room, but then I got sidetracked by the chest of drawers. Does that second drawer look shorter than the others to you?"

"No," he said.

She heaved a sigh. "I didn't think so."

"You're looking for more hidden compartments," he guessed.

"Looking but not finding."

"Seems to me," he said, "that Blanche would restrict her hiding places to her own room. That's predicating that she had hiding places plural, not just hiding place singular."

Nevada frowned at the depressingly identical drawers. Trick was right, of course. "I cleaned her room from top to bottom, back to front, side to side. There's nowhere else to look."

"What is it you expect to find?" he asked mildly.

"I don't know." She shrugged helplessly. "A little more background information maybe? I mean, consider the situation from my perspective. I discover that a woman who lived here back in the mid-nineteenth century, a woman whose ghost is rumored to haunt the house still, looked very much like me. I keep thinking if I could just discover my connection to Blanche, then maybe I'd be able to figure out who I really am."

"Find your family, you mean."

That word. She'd tried very hard not to bring it up. Connections, relationships, and links were discussable, but family? She blinked away the tears that sprang to her eyes, tilting her head down in the vain hope that Trick wouldn't notice.

But that bright blue eye didn't miss much. He cupped her chin in one hand and forced her to meet his gaze. "You know, I can't even imagine being in your situation, not knowing who you are, where you come from, who your people are."

"Don't," she said.

"Don't what?" His expression held nothing but kindness and confusion.

"Don't be so nice and kind and comforting," she said fiercely.

He shot her a strange look. "Why not?"

"Because it makes me want to cry."

He pressed a quick kiss to her forehead. "Go ahead," he said softly and pulled her against his chest.

His gentle understanding nearly proved her undoing.

But crying didn't help. The Institute had taught her that. In fact, crying, betraying weakness of any sort, was to be avoided at all costs. If she'd learned one thing in the last five years, it was that people could and would use your frailties against you. "I'm fine," she lied, backing out of reach. Ignoring Trick, she busied herself reassembling the chest of drawers.

When she finally glanced over her shoulder, he was gone. She'd probably ticked him off, pulling away as she had. He probably thought she hadn't liked him putting his hands on her, that she thought he was trying to take advantage.

And damn it, she knew he hadn't been, but . . . Once again her vision blurred as her eyes filled with unshed tears.

By the time Nevada had finished putting the room to rights, she'd regained her composure. Feeling she owed Trick an apology, she made her way downstairs. No one was in the house, but she eventually located Marcello outside in the rose garden, hacking away with some lethal-looking pruning shears.

"Have you seen Trick?" she asked.

Marcello grunted. "What am I? Head of the missing persons' bureau?"

Her surprise at his surliness must have shown on her face because his expression instantly changed from irritated to contrite.

"I apologize for my rudeness," he said quickly. "My filthy mood has nothing to do with you. Trick drove to Reno with Britt Petersen. They will not be back until quite late this evening."

Britt? Nevada felt a little twinge under her breastbone.

Marcello attacked another hapless rosebush.

"Are you all right?" she asked. "Is there anything I can do to help?"

"There is nothing anyone can do to help," he said, as he sliced and diced the poor bush down to size.

"That bad, huh?"

"Worse." He hesitated for so long that she thought he was done talking, but then he spoke again, slowly, as if measuring each word. "The next time you run into Britt . . ."

"Yes?" she said, a little worried about what was coming. He sounded so depressed, so angry. This wasn't about Britt and Trick going off to Reno together, was it?

"Try to discourage her."

"Discourage her?" she asked, thinking she'd misunderstood.

"I saw her on the beach this morning. I know what

she was doing and why." He paused. "I saw you there, too, so please, do not pretend not to understand what I am saying. Britt is attracted to me." He paused again, as if waiting for confirmation.

But she couldn't say anything one way or the other. She'd promised Britt.

"And I . . . I am attracted to her, as well."

"Then what's the problem?"

"There are complications. Insurmountable complications."

"Such as?" she said.

His face went rigid as stone, but she sensed a fierce battle raging just beneath the surface stoicism. "I am married," he said.

Britt had called Trick a little after ten and said she needed his help. Would he be able to drive down to Reno with her? She was thinking about buying a new SUV but knew if she went into a car dealership by herself, the salesman would try to screw her over.

So he'd said sure, thinking it would be good to get out of Midas Lake for a while, away from the mansion, away from Nevada . . . and temptation.

Then, a mere ten miles out of town, Britt had uttered those terrifying words, the ones every man feared: "We need to talk." Followed by silence.

Trick gave it a minute or two, then asked, "Talk about what?" even though he had a sinking feeling that he really didn't want to know.

"Oh, nothing." Britt's attempt at breeziness fell short of the mark.

He gave it another minute or so, then tried again. "Well, if you change your mind, I'm here." Which was pretty stupid on his part, reminding her that she had a captive audience, because what if she wanted to talk about some embarrassing female thing?

Britt glanced sideways at him. Hard to tell what she was thinking behind those oversize sunglasses. "You're a good guy, Trick."

Which didn't sound like the prelude to a monologue on hormone-induced mood swings, but then again, you never knew. "I try," he said.

"I have to ask you something," she said, "and I want you to promise me that you'll tell the truth."

"Okay," he said, though what he was thinking was more along the lines of *oh, shit.*

"Am I ugly?"

Which was not exactly what he'd expected to hear. "What? No, of course, not!"

"Am I repulsive in some other way? My personality, for example?"

"No. God, no. You're beautiful, generous, intelligent, and sexy as hell."

She heaved a sigh. "There must be something wrong with me."

"Why do you say that?"

"Because Marcello seems to find me infinitely re-sistible."

"Not because there's anything wrong with you," Trick said hastily.

"Meaning what? There's something wrong with him?"

"Not wrong exactly, but . . ."

"Don't tell me he's gay."

"I wouldn't," Trick said.

"Because I don't believe it. I've seen the way he looks at me when he doesn't think I'm paying attention."

"I wouldn't know about that."

"So what's the problem?" she demanded.

"There's a problem?"

"With Marcello," she said. "You indicated that he has a problem. What is it? Is he . . . diseased?"

"God, no! I mean, I don't think so."

"Or maybe it's a different sort of physical problem. Erectile dysfunction or something like that."

"No, it's . . ."

"It's what, Trick?"

He's married, damn it, and way too Catholic to contemplate divorce. Only what he said out loud was, "Marcello's the one you should be having this conversation with."

Nevada spent the afternoon cleaning the rest of the third-floor bedrooms. She didn't find any more gold nuggets or hidden compartments, but she did discover a box of scrimshaw carvings tucked in a drawer in one room and a rather gorgeous Persian rug rolled up, tied with twine, and shoved in the corner of another.

"You know," she said to Marcello over dinner, a really excellent veal parmigiana, "Trick ought to have a reputable antiques dealer come out and value the furniture before he sells the mansion. I'm no expert, but I suspect he has some real treasures here."

Marcello raised an eyebrow. "Compared to the price-less Donatelli tapestries he already parted with?"

"Probably not," she admitted, "but even these lesser New World treasures are worth something."

"Humph." Marcello scowled out the window.

Nevada gave him a few minutes. Then, "Marcello?" she asked.

He turned his scowl on her. "Yes?"

"Do you mind if I ask you a question?"

He shrugged. "That would depend on the question."

"Okay, fair enough." She buttered a roll. "If Trick was this big-shot race-car driver, I'm guessing he earned a decent income."

Marcello nodded.

"Plus, I assume there was family money."

Another nod.

"So where did it all go? His medical bills couldn't have been that steep."

He stared at her in silence for a moment. "You are right," he said at length. "The bills were astronomical, yes, but it was not the doctors who stole his fortune. Trick was betrayed by a man he believed to be his friend."

"Betrayed how exactly?"

"While Trick lay in a coma, his trusted financial adviser, Philip Ellison, liquidated the bulk of Trick's assets and fled to Rio."

"Wow."

Marcello snorted. "A man is ruined by someone he trusts, and all you can say is 'wow'?"

"Okay, enough already. *What* is your problem? Is it me you hate, or are you just in a snit?"

He frowned. "What is this snit?"

"A bad mood."

His frown deepened. "Then yes, I am in the snit."

"You're not a female—"

"Obviously."

"So I can rule out its being that time of the month," she said, ignoring the interruption. "So why the snittiness? Have you had some bad news from home? Is it your . . . wife?"

Marcello's glare would have felled a lesser woman, but Nevada was used to the nasty, malicious glowering of Morgan the Orderly. "My snit and its causes are none of your business," he said. "Nor is my wife."

"I wouldn't have brought her up if you hadn't mentioned being married. I take it she's in Italy."

"Switzerland," he said, then scowled again, as if irritated with himself for letting more information slip.

"Why Switzerland?"

"Why not?"

Like talking to a brick wall, she thought. And yet, she just kept trying. "Any idea when Trick and Britt are supposed to be back?" She couldn't wait to show Trick the scrimshaw.

"They did not confide their plans to me."

Nevada was pretty sure she hadn't imagined the touch of asperity in Marcello's voice. "And that bothers you, doesn't it?" Though it shouldn't. Surely he didn't think there was any sort of chemistry between Trick and Britt.

"I am going out this evening," Marcello said, pointedly ignoring her question. "Will you be all right on your own?"

"Going out where?" she asked in surprise as he pushed himself away from the table.

"If you do not want to do the dishes, leave them and I will take care of them tomorrow."

"But where are you going?" Marcello never went anywhere at night. He was always there, always at Trick's beck and call, always available to pick up the pieces and smooth out the wrinkles. Steady, reliable, the perfect, unflappable personal assistant.

"Does it matter?"

"I suppose not, but what if Trick gets back before you do? What am I supposed to tell him?"

He crossed to the door. "Tell him I am taking a page from his book."

"Meaning?"

"I plan to drink myself into a stupor."

Trick really ought to paint the entire interior if he wanted to get top dollar for the mansion, Nevada thought as she studied the dingy walls of Blanche's room on the third floor. She'd scrubbed her way through two gallons of heavy duty liquid detergent and three pairs of rubber gloves, so she knew the walls were clean, though you couldn't tell by looking at them.

But if she could get Trick to spring for a few gallons

of paint—okay, *quite* a few gallons of paint—she could have the whole house looking as fresh as new. She'd have to broach the subject the next time she saw him.

And speaking of Trick—or more accurately, *thinking* of Trick—where was he? It was almost eleven. How long did it take to drive to Reno and back?

She scowled at the parquet flooring—also clean now but in serious need of a waxing. Once polished, it would . . . Was that piece of parquetry in the corner loose? It seemed to be tilted up on one end, a fraction of an inch out of alignment.

She stilled. Was that a motor she heard? Was Trick back?

She opened the heavy shutters and peered out into the darkness. No car. No Trick. And apparently no distracting her brain with mundane concerns like uneven floors. She sighed. Where was he?

With Britt, she told herself firmly, Britt who was thoroughly hooked on Marcello. Of course, it wasn't Marcello Britt had asked to accompany her to Reno.

Nevada frowned into the darkness. At the time, she hadn't thought a thing of it, but what if Britt had finally tired of Marcello's hard-to-get act? What if she'd decided to get her flirt on with Trick? Worse, what if Trick had taken Nevada's earlier withdrawal to heart? What if Trick and Britt were . . . ?

Damn it, think of something else.

She studied the board in the corner. It wasn't her imagination. The wood really was tilted out of line. Maybe if she applied a little pressure, she could shove it back into place.

She crossed the room, telling herself that Trick and Britt were both consenting adults and what they did with and/or to each other was none of her business, but that didn't stop the images that flashed through her brain—Trick and Britt kissing, touching . . .

Damn it.

And them.

And her for a silly fool who'd fallen for a man she barely knew. And what was even more foolish, a man who didn't know her at all.

"I'm just the hired help," she said aloud, which, come to think of it, wasn't exactly grounds for a pity party, particularly when compared with her previous stint as Subject 111.

Nevada peered down at the misaligned parquetry at her feet. She tried tapping it into place with her heel, but it didn't budge. Odd, she thought, as she knelt down to have a closer look. She pressed with her finger. Again it didn't move. It wasn't loose as she'd assumed.

She stood up, staring absently down at the offending board as she ran through various possibilities in her head. She could (a) try to fix it herself, (b) ask Marcello or Trick to hammer it back in line, or (c) just shove a piece of furniture over into the corner to camouflage the imperfection.

And yet . . . Something teased at her memory. She brought her gaze into focus and stared hard at the tilted board. It, along with three other pieces of parquetry formed a crisscross design, a design repeated all over the room. Like crosses or . . . *X*'s.

X marks the spot. That's what Blanche had written in her diary, and here Nevada was, in Blanche's old room where Blanche's old floor was littered with *X*'s. One in particular stood out, though. The flawed one.

"*X* marks the spot," she said aloud, then dropped to her knees once again.

Daniel glanced up from the proposed education reform bill he was reading as Consuela, looking wary and a little perturbed, edged into his office. "There are two"—she hesitated, as if searching for the right word—"gentlemen outside who insist on speaking to you. A Señor Collier and a Señor Branson. I told them you were busy, Señor Snowden, but—"

He cut her off with a wave of his hand. "Show them in."

Billy Branson shot a triumphant smirk at the housekeeper as she reluctantly ushered them into Daniel's office. "Bitch," he muttered as she closed the door.

"Mind your manners," Daniel snapped. "You're not riding with a renegade biker gang anymore."

Billy's smirk turned sullen.

"I assume you're here to tell me you found the girl."

Billy looked sideways at Sarge. Sarge stared at the floor. Neither said a thing.

"I'm waiting."

Sarge straightened, making eye contact. "No sign of her in San Francisco."

"Did you try the outlying areas? Oakland? Alameda? San Leandro?"

"Checked 'em all and came up empty," Billy said.

"You asked at all the cheap motels? The vagrant camps?"

"We looked everywhere, boss," Sarge said. "She's not there. She's not in San Francisco."

Daniel's acid reflux kicked into high gear. "What do you mean she's not in San Francisco? Earlier, you said you were sure she was headed that way."

"Oh, we found the girl, all right," Sarge said and Daniel's heartbeat picked up. "The girl who worked those couple days at the fast-food place here in Sacramento. Only she wasn't your sister."

"Half sister," Daniel corrected him.

"She wasn't your half sister," Sarge repeated.

"You're sure?"

"Positive," Billy said. "This chick was only about seventeen."

"Whitney might look younger than she is."

"But I'm betting she don't have half the pinky on her left hand missing," Billy said, "and a big old tramp stamp in the small of her back."

"What's a tramp stamp?" Daniel asked.

"Tattoo," Sarge translated. "In this case a butterfly."

"So the whole trip was a wild goose chase," Daniel said.

"Pretty much." Sarge nodded. "I'm thinking the trip here to Sacramento was a waste of time, too. I don't think your half sister ever came within fifty miles of the city."

"But you told me she'd hitched a ride here to Sacramento."

"Because that's what we were told," Sarge said, "and,

at the time, we had no reason to question the source. Only what if the two guys in the Jeep were lying through their teeth?"

"Why would they do that?" Billy demanded. "They thought we were cops."

"Maybe they wanted the girl for their own purposes." Sarge licked his lips. "Pretty little thing like that . . . I can think of half a dozen reasons to keep her hidden."

"They didn't seem—" Billy started, but Sarge cut him off.

"Freaks don't always look like freaks." He spread his hands. "Case in point."

"But—"

"No buts," Daniel said. "They're the only lead we have. You know where they live, so what's the problem? Go have another talk with them."

Sarge stood a little straighter. "And by talk you mean?"

"Beat the truth out of them if you have to, but find my half sister."

EIGHT

From his vantage point in one of the rustic Adirondack chairs scattered across the broad front porch of the Lakeshore Lodge, Marcello watched from beneath lowered lids—the wine had made him sleepy—as Britt zoomed past in a brand-new Ford Expedition, then slowed sharply for the turn into Trick's drive. She would take him home first, of course, before returning to the lodge.

He wondered how her run-in with the police had turned out, whether she would end up paying a fine or just get a slap on the wrist. Stupid woman. She had bloodied that poor tourist's lip and for no good reason. The redhead had done nothing to deserve a punch in the mouth. Quite a pleasant woman really, not to mention easy on the eyes.

Though maybe that was the root of the problem. The redhead—Tara? Tina? Tanya?—was beautiful, and therefore, Britt had perceived her as a threat. Britt reacted out of jealousy.

Marcello smiled a particularly self-satisfied smile.

And yes, he probably should be ashamed of himself for gloating, but it was quite flattering to know Britt felt that way about him. Of course, it was also depressing and more than a little worrisome.

His smile faded. He frowned into the darkness. Britt Petersen was strong, beautiful, and intelligent, everything a man could ask for in a woman. Everything *he* could ask for in a woman, something he had noticed the first time they had met, something that had become increasingly clear as time went on. He cared for Britt Petersen. A lot. Given half a chance, he could love her. But that would be wrong. He had no right to fall in love. He was, after all, a married man.

Five years ago he had pledged himself to another strong, beautiful, intelligent woman. It was not Antonia's fault that everything had changed.

Nor his.

But marriage vows made before God and blessed by a priest were forever. No exceptions. Britt was not for him, and the sooner he made that clear to her, the sooner she could get on with her life.

The Expedition pulled out of Trick's drive, but instead of turning into the lodge parking area, it sped off toward Midas Lake. For some reason, Britt was not coming home.

And maybe that was a good thing. He needed more time to unmuddle his wine-soaked brain, to find the words that would crush any hopes that the two of them might have a future together. Sometimes it was necessary to be cruel in order to be kind.

Marcello settled back in the chair to wait.

• • •

Trick let himself in the back door, wondering what the hell Nevada was thinking, leaving the door unlocked like that. Anyone could have walked in—a burglar, a vagrant, one of her pursuers. "Nevada?" he called, switching on the overhead light in the kitchen. "Are you still up?" A good bet since the third floor was lit up like the candles on an octogenarian's birthday cake.

"Coming." Her voice echoed hollowly down the back stairs.

He leaned his cane against the wall next to the door. The doctor had said as long as he wore his brace, he could start weaning himself off the cane. He'd only taken it along today in case he and Britt had ended up doing a lot of walking, which they had.

He flexed his knee carefully. A little stiff, but no pain.

He limped across to the counter, settling onto a barstool just as Nevada came clattering down the back stairs. "Did you have a good time in Reno?" she asked, then grinned in response to his sour expression. "No, I guess not."

"Why do women have such a hard time making up their minds?"

"*Women* meaning Britt?"

"I don't know how many car dealerships we visited. I lost count after the first half dozen or so."

"So your afternoon sucked, huh?" For some reason, she sounded pretty pleased about that.

"The afternoon was tedious," he corrected her. "It

was my evening that sucked. We got back almost two hours ago."

"Two hours ago?" She frowned.

"As we were on the final leg, driving through downtown Midas Lake, Britt spotted the Jeep parked in front of the Gold Rush Saloon."

"Marcello moped around all afternoon," she said, "before deciding to go cry into his beer."

"Wine," Trick said. "He was drinking wine and, when we walked in, getting hit on by a redhead who seemed pretty anxious to have him give her new boob job a test drive. Britt tossed the wine in Marcello's face, then decked the redhead."

"What!"

"One punch and Red went down. Of course, the bartender called the cops, and they hauled Britt off to jail, tried to charge her with drunk and disorderly, though she hadn't been drinking, so the drunk part didn't stick. Still took almost two hours to get her released."

"What about Marcello?"

Trick shrugged. "Still drinking, I guess. How was your night?"

"Fantastic. I was working up on the third floor—"

"Working and fantastic don't seem to go together."

"And I found buried treasure," she finished.

"Wait a minute. Buried treasure on the third floor? Doesn't *buried* imply digging, as in shoveling dirt? I know the mansion's filthy, but . . ."

"Come see for yourself," she said, leading the way up the back stairs at a near run.

Trick followed more slowly, favoring his injured knee.

"This way!" Nevada called when he finally reached the third-floor landing.

He made his way to the room at the far end of the hall. "This is Blanche's room, the room where you found the nugget," he said, glancing around. No holes in the walls or floor, which was somewhat reassuring.

"The nugget and Blanche's diary," she said, "which included one cryptic entry: *X* marks the spot."

"Which," he said, "any good pirate can tell you means that's where the treasure's hidden. Only this isn't exactly a desert island."

"No," she agreed, "but look at the floor. *X*'s everywhere you look."

"The design in the parquetry, you mean?"

She nodded. "See this board? It's tilted a little off horizontal. Watch." She pressed on the slightly depressed end, and it tilted up to disclose a space underneath.

"Empty," he said, feeling obscurely disappointed.

"Empty now," she told him. "But look what I found inside!" She extended her hand, palm up, to show him an ornate gold band.

"Pretty," he said, "but I doubt it's worth much. I wouldn't exactly call it a treasure."

"Depends on your point of view, I guess. This is Blanche's secret cache, and it looks a lot like a wedding ring to me."

Trick examined her find more closely. "Or an engagement ring."

"If Blanche was married, or even just engaged, she was probably planning to leave the brothel."

"Okay," Trick agreed. "That makes sense, but it's hardly a motive for murder."

"Marcello?"

Stiff, cold, and wretchedly uncomfortable, Marcello dragged himself from the depths of sleep, forcing his eyelids open with a superhuman effort only to find Britt staring down at him, her expression a curious mixture of exasperation, anger, relief, and tenderness.

"I've been looking everywhere for you, you stupid man. The Jeep was still parked in front of the Gold Rush, but you weren't there. No one was. They'd closed down for the night."

"I walked home," he said, his tongue feeling thick and clumsy. "I had had too much to drink. Driving would not have been safe."

"Less than a mile on deserted streets?"

"Not even that far. The risk is too great. Ask Antonia." He frowned.

Britt just looked confused. "Who's Antonia?" Her eyes narrowed. "The redhead?"

He heaved a sigh. "No, that was Tina." He frowned. "Or maybe Tara?"

"Then who's Antonia?" Britt demanded.

"My wife."

"Your *what*?"

"My wife," he repeated, trying not to see the pain in her face.

"You're married? But . . . I don't understand."

"Antonia is in Zurich."

"She lives there?"

"If you can call it living," he said. "She does not speak. Cannot speak. Brain damage."

"I don't understand," she said again.

"Neither do I." The words tasted bitter on his tongue. "She was very like you—young, beautiful, athletic, an avid skier. We were on our honeymoon in the Alps when she was run down by a drunk driver. He did not even stop." Marcello met her gaze. "So no; I do not drive when I have been drinking. I owe Antonia that much."

"There's something written inside this ring," Trick said. "Here, look." He passed it back to Nevada.

"Doesn't look like words to me," she said. "My guess is, it's the jeweler's mark."

"Very likely," he agreed. "I think I'll have someone look at it. Might be smart to make an enlargement of Blanche's photograph and get a professional's input on the amulet, too." He glanced up then and caught the look of pure panic that flashed across Nevada's face. "What?" he asked.

"Nothing." She looked away quickly, but he caught her chin and tilted her face up to his.

"What's the problem? I thought you wanted to find out who you really are."

"I do, but . . ."

"But what?" he asked softly.

"What if I don't like the answer? What if I *am* as bad as those men claimed?"

"Nonsense," he said firmly.

"But what if?"

"Nonsense," he repeated. "You've been here for over a week now. Do you honestly think you could live in such close proximity to Marcello and me for that long and not reveal your true character? I might not know your real name, Nevada, but I know you, and you don't have an evil bone in your body. If you killed your father—and I don't for a second think that you did—but *if* you killed him, you must have had a good reason."

"Does insanity count as a good reason?" Her voice quavered as if she were on the verge of tears.

"You're not insane." He pulled her into his arms and held her close until gradually her rigid muscles relaxed. "You're not insane," he said again.

"You don't know that for certain," she said, her words muffled against his chest.

He moved slightly away from her, tilting her face up so he could make eye contact. "Yes, I do. Marcello did a Google search on your Dr. Poison Apple and his institute."

"He did?" Her eyes mirrored surprise and something else he couldn't quite pin down. Fear? Betrayal?

"We can't protect you if we don't know who all the bad guys are."

"The doctor's a bad guy?"

"Technically speaking, no," Trick admitted, "though his methods seem a little extreme."

"A little?" she echoed faintly. "I don't know what he did to me, but considering that I can't even remember my name, I think I'd label his methods as off-the-chart extreme."

"But not illegal," Trick said.

Nevada didn't say a word, just stared up at him, her face expressionless. Trick wasn't sure what she was thinking. All he knew for certain was that she'd stiffened up on him again, her muscles tense and rigid.

Concerned and trying not to show it, he continued. "The Appleton Institute outside Boston is a private facility, supposedly catering to the needs of the mentally disturbed."

"Supposedly?"

He forced a smile. "You caught that, did you?"

She didn't smile back.

"Marcello discovered that although Appleton has a degree in psychiatry, his primary interest has always been the field of psi phenomena. He's passionately interested in paranormal events and the study and observation of psychics."

"Lab rats," she said, and there was no mistaking the bitterness in her tone. "He treated us like lab rats, experimenting with various drug regimens, prodding and probing, trying to find the right buttons to push to make us perform on command."

"I'm sorry," Trick said, meaning it.

"Who committed me to that hell?" she asked, her voice raw with emotion. "Did Marcello's snooping discover that?"

"He wasn't snooping," Trick protested. "Information is power. We were trying to protect you."

"You said that already," she said coldly. "I didn't believe it the first time, either."

His hands tightened convulsively on her upper arms. "Nevada—"

"Don't!" She wrenched herself free. When he started to pull her back into his arms, she threw up her hands in a defensive posture. "Just don't."

"Okay." He took a step back.

"Who committed me?" She rapped out the words.

He shook his head. "We don't know. There's nothing like that online. No admittance records. No patient records of any kind."

"Wouldn't matter if there were," she said. "Yelena checked my file. There were no names. No background information at all aside from an address."

"An address?"

"In San Francisco," she told him.

"Why do I not feel better?" Marcello asked himself as he trudged down the drive toward the Granger mansion. After all, he had told Britt the truth, that he was married. And yes, perhaps he had lied as well, if only by omission, by not telling her how he felt about her, but it was better if she did not know, better to make a clean break, better that she hate him than pine for something that could never be.

But he still felt sick to his stomach.

And yes, part of that probably stemmed from all the wine he had drunk. He was going to have one truly wretched headache tomorrow. That much was certain.

But part of it—a big part of it—was due to the fact that Britt had reacted to his bombshell with such equanimity. True, she had seemed a little taken aback, but she had not yelled or looked hurt or even as if she cared very much one way or the other. Had he made a fool of himself by opening up his private life to her scrutiny? Had he misread all the signals? Had she never been interested in him in the first place?

Doubts haunted him, and some dark, indefinable emotion stirred.

Was it Trick she had wanted all along?

He had assumed Britt had invited Trick along on her car-shopping trip just to make Marcello jealous, which he had to admit had worked, but what if Trick had been the target of her affections from the beginning?

Pain and chagrin knotted his stomach, and when he glanced up to see Trick silhouetted against the kitchen blinds, anger added itself to the emotional stew.

Marcello covered the remaining distance at a near run, slamming dramatically through the back entry and into the kitchen. Trick, slumped over the counter staring at something cupped in his hand, did not even look up.

Which made Marcello's anger flare even hotter. "How was your trip?"

"Completely uneventful, at least until Britt spotted the Jeep parked in front of the Gold Rush. That led to some pretty major drama," Trick said. "How's the redhead? Or maybe I should ask, who's the redhead?"

"A tourist," Marcello told him. "No one of importance."

"That wasn't the way Britt read the situation."

"Are you accusing me of flirting?"

"Were you?" Trick asked.

"Were *you*?" Marcello countered.

Trick shot him a baffled look. "What?"

"Were you flirting?"

"With the redhead?"

"No, with Britt."

Trick was so startled that he dropped the object in his hand. A ring, Marcello realized. It went rolling across the room, coming to rest finally at the base of a cupboard. Trick bent to retrieve it, then shot Marcello a quick grin. "Britt's apparently not the only one with a jealous streak."

"I am not jealous," Marcello said with all the dignity he could muster. "Merely protective. Britt is a decent woman, deserving of respect." He paused. "I would hate to think you had taken advantage of her vulnerability."

"Vulnerable? Britt? Did you see what she did to that redhead?"

"Do not attempt to change the subject," Marcello said. "Just answer one question. Did you sleep with her?"

"What would it matter if I had?" Trick shrugged. "You're not going to."

"You bastard." Marcello took a clumsy swing at him, but Trick was able to step out of the way. "She deserves better than you."

"She deserves better than both of us put together," Trick said. "Unfortunately, she's determined to have you."

The shock of it stole Marcello's breath for a moment. Then, "Me?" he managed.

"You," Trick said with a smirk.

Marcello failed to see any humor in the situation. "No longer. I told her about Antonia."

The smirk disappeared. His words had taken Trick by surprise. "Told her everything?"

"Enough," he said. Enough to make her hate him. Enough to make her keep her distance.

"Pretty well pissed off, was she?"

Marcello nodded glumly. He knew what he had done was for the best, but . . .

"Welcome to the club," Trick said.

"Britt is angry with you, too?"

"Not Britt. Nevada. She wasn't happy when she found out I had you dig up information about Dr. Appleton and his institute."

"Women," Marcello said with feeling.

"Amen," Trick agreed.

NINE

Though it had been well past midnight before she'd gone to bed, Nevada woke a little after six. She figured she'd have the kitchen to herself, but Trick was up already. He'd used the last of the milk to make hot chocolate to go along with his omelet and English muffins. Used the last of the English muffins, too, which meant she had her choice of dry cereal or leftovers. She decided to go with the leftovers.

"*What* are you doing?" Trick asked.

"Wrapping this veal parmigiana in aluminum foil."

"Let me rephrase. Why are you doing what you're doing?"

She turned the oven control to 350°. "Because I don't want to eat my breakfast cold."

"Veal parmigiana for breakfast?" Trick made a face.

"I'd have had cereal," she said, "only *someone* used all the milk."

"But—" he started.

She talked right over the top of him. "Or I'd have had a muffin, but *someone* ate all of them, too."

"Sorry," he said, looking suitably chastened.

"No biggie. I like veal parmigiana. Maybe not for breakfast, but . . . How long do you think I should set the timer for? Twenty minutes?"

"I don't know." He shrugged. "I only do omelets and steaks."

"You really ought to spring for a microwave," she said.

"We aren't going to be here that long—just until we sell the place."

"You could take the microwave with you when you leave."

"Not where I'm going."

She eyed him closely, her head tilted to one side.

"You look like an inquisitive robin," he said.

"You look like a pirate."

"It's the eye patch," he told her. "Are you sure you wouldn't like some of my omelet?"

"I told you before. I hate eggs."

"So you do. I'd forgotten."

"Where are you going that you can't take a microwave?"

"I'm not exactly sure," he said. "Somewhere warm. Probably an island in the South Pacific. Possibly Tahiti. I speak passable French."

"The Caribbean's more pirate territory, isn't it?"

He slid his omelet onto his plate alongside his buttered muffins. "Hmm? Oh, well, I don't plan to go into the pirate business. I was thinking more of a charter boat. Cap'n Trick's got a nice ring to it, don't you think?"

"Honestly? It sounds like a cereal."

"What do you think of Cap'n Granger?"

"Better," she said. "How about Marcello? Will he be signing on as first mate?"

"That's up to him," Trick said. "Marcello, are you planning to sign on as first mate when my ship comes in?"

Nevada turned to see Marcello propped against the doorjamb, pressing his temples with his fingertips.

"Ungh," he said.

"Is that a yes or a no?" she asked.

"I think it's a where-the-hell's-the-aspirin?" Trick translated as he dug through the medicine in the cupboard next to the refrigerator. He passed the aspirin bottle to Marcello, who dry-swallowed three tablets before passing the bottle back to Trick.

"*Grazie*," Marcello muttered, then collapsed in a chair, once again clutching his head.

Apparently he hadn't been kidding when he'd told her he was taking a page out of Trick's book.

"The oven's hot," Trick told her. "The light just went out. You can stick your veal parmigiana in whenever you're ready."

Marcello raised his head and stared at her with bloodshot eyes. "Veal parmigiana?" he asked. "For breakfast?"

"I don't see why everyone has such a hard time with that."

Marcello's eyes widened so far the whites were visible all around his irises. He gagged, then slapping both hands over his mouth, lurched from his seat and dashed for the bathroom.

Nevada spent the day waxing floors. Trick had agreed that fresh paint was a good investment. He'd sent Marcello off to pick up some at the nearest Home Depot in Carson City. So she figured between finishing up the floors and painting the walls, there was enough work to keep her busy for another week. Maybe two or three. By the first of June at the very latest, she should be ready to continue her search for the truth about her past.

But somehow, the idea didn't excite her as much as it should have, and she wasn't sure how much of that lack of enthusiasm was due to the lurking fear that she really was a psycho nut job and how much was merely a natural reluctance to move on since Midas Lake in general and the mansion in particular had become her comfort zone.

After dinner—steaks, since it was Trick's turn to cook—she wandered down to the lake, where she found Britt Petersen skipping rocks across the water's surface with all the concentration of a true Olympic champion.

"Am I interrupting?" Nevada asked.

Britt shot her a grim look. "You're not bothering me, though I warn you, I'm not the best of company right now. Harry Wagner, my manager, all but physically tossed me out of the lodge, said I was scaring the guests." She lobbed another rock. It skipped four times before sinking below the water.

"I've been terrorized by the best. Or maybe I mean

the worst. Anyway, your sour mood doesn't bother me."

"Good," Britt said. She chose another flat rock from a pile at her feet, then straightened abruptly, turning to Nevada with an apologetic expression. "That came out wrong. I didn't mean good that you'd been terrorized. I meant—"

"I knew what you meant," Nevada said.

Britt smiled, a shaky and somewhat unconvincing smile, but a smile nonetheless. Then she skipped her rock. A three-hopper this time. "How's . . . everything at the mansion?"

And by everything, she meant Marcello. Or so Nevada suspected. "We're making progress," Nevada told her. "The wiring's officially up to code now. Every scrubbable or dustable surface has been scrubbed and dusted. The front lawn's been reseeded. The roses have been pruned and fed. The kitchen . . . well, I don't think Trick's going to do a major overhaul on the kitchen, though he's thinking about replacing the old linoleum with tile, and we may be able to talk him into a new sink and countertops.

"I spent my day waxing wood floors while Trick tinkered with the plumbing. It probably needs to be replaced, too."

Britt skipped a couple more rocks. "How about Marcello?"

Nevada smirked. "Spent most of the morning on the upchuck express. Then Trick sent him down to Carson to buy some interior latex. He's not back yet."

"Oh," Britt said, her voice so utterly neutral that it was a dead giveaway.

An awkward silence fraught with unvoiced questions enveloped them. Nevada tried skipping a rock herself, but it sank the second it touched the water. "Trickier than it looks," she muttered, then, "Did they take your mug shot?"

Britt whipped around to face her. "What?"

"Trick told me what happened at the Gold Rush Saloon last night."

Britt muttered an extremely rude word. "Why doesn't he just take out an ad in the paper?"

"No need. The story's bound to make the next edition of the *Nugget*. Maybe not the front page, but . . ."

Britt scowled. "You're enjoying this, aren't you?"

"No," Nevada said quickly, then, "Well, maybe a little."

Britt skipped three rocks in a row without saying a word, then she turned back to Nevada. "No," she said.

"No what?"

"No mug shot," Britt told her. "The redhead refused to press charges—God knows why, because if I'd been in her situation, I sure as hell would have. But since she didn't, the cops let me off with a warning. I think Jan Hooper, the officer who hauled me in, thought the whole thing was hysterically funny, but I wasn't laughing."

Nevada wasn't, either, though she wanted to. "Marcello's a mess."

Britt snorted. "At least you didn't say Marcello's a mess, *too*."

"He's upset," Nevada said.

"Tough," Britt snapped.

"And confused."

"And married," Britt said bitterly. "Don't forget married. Damn it, why didn't he just tell me that up front? Why wait until I'm . . ."

What? Nevada wondered but hesitated to ask.

Trick eyed the sixty gallons of paint that filled the front entry and smiled to himself. Twenty-one rooms to paint. A job of that magnitude ought to keep Nevada busy for a while.

And that was good, because he didn't want her to leave yet. He didn't want her to leave at all. He wanted . . . well, damn, that was the thing. He didn't know exactly what he wanted. Not when it came to Nevada.

Okay, that was a lie. He knew what he wanted. He wanted her—smart, funny, hard-working, egg-hating Nevada.

Trick's smile grew wider as he pictured the way her upper lip quirked when she was trying not to laugh, the way her jaw tilted when she was pissed. She fascinated him. He liked everything about her from the sweet, soft curves of her body to the thick, dark hair that floated around her shoulders in a billowing cloud. And best of all, he liked her lovely, almost classically beautiful face, especially those expressive dark green eyes that seemed to glow when she was happy, shoot sparks when she was angry, and cloud over whenever she was worried or frightened. She hid her thoughts whenever she felt threatened, hid herself, and that vulnerability spoke to him, too.

Nevada White appealed to him on many levels and

provoked strong reactions—a fierce need to protect her and an even fiercer need to possess her. It was that second one that concerned him, because, after all, they scarcely knew each other. She'd been in Midas Lake less than two weeks now.

Whereas he'd known Luisa Gallo all his life and had truly believed she'd cared for him, though, as it turned out, his money was all she'd really cared about. They'd been together on and off for almost three years, but after his accident, she hadn't even stuck around long enough to see if he would regain consciousness. He'd thought he loved her. He'd thought she loved him. He'd been wrong on both counts. Obviously, when it came to women, his judgment was sadly flawed. Equally obviously, he had no business now mooning over a woman he barely knew.

Hell, the truth was, Nevada didn't even know herself.

And wasn't that a nightmare scenario? He tried to imagine what that must be like, not to know your name or where you came from. The questions, the uncertainties must have nagged at her constantly.

Which reminded him, he needed to tell her what the jeweler had said about the ring. She would be wondering if that information would help her in her search.

So tell her he would, and if part of him knew he was just making up excuses to be with her, the rest of him ignored it.

He'd seen Nevada head down toward the beach earlier, but she hadn't returned to the house. If she'd come back up the trail, she'd gone straight to her apartment.

Trick let himself out the front door. The evening air was crisp but not cold. Summer, even here in the mountains, lurked just around the corner. Wouldn't be long before the rose garden Marcello had worked so hard to restore was full of blooms.

He circled around to the back of the house, then paused by the sundial to enjoy the sunset, a rich vermillion backdrop for the sharp peaks to the west. Higher up, ribbons of color faded to fuchsia, then rosy pink and lavender as they stretched across the evening sky.

Even though Marcello had invested a lot of time in thinning out the trees, you still couldn't see the beach from this vantage point. Trick eyed the trailhead dubiously. Probably not the smartest idea to try to hike down to the water on his gimpy leg, and it wouldn't help to go back for his cane, either. Covered in a thick layer of pine needles, the terrain was too uneven, the path too slippery for a man with a bum leg.

He could manage the steps up to Nevada's apartment, though. Might as well check there first anyway.

He was standing on the landing, poised to knock, when he heard her call from down below. "Need something?"

He turned. "Just to talk to you for a minute. I had Marcello run an errand for me this afternoon."

She crossed the rose garden quickly, moving with athletic grace. "Besides buying all the antique white latex interior paint in Carson City?"

Trick laughed. "He did get kind of carried away, didn't he?"

She took the stairs two at a time. "Why don't you come inside?" she said, leading the way. "Have a seat." She waved him toward the lumpy couch, but he ignored her. Once burned, twice shy. Last time he'd risked that sofa, he'd damned near emasculated himself on a loose spring. He chose the wooden chair instead, figuring the worst that could happen to him there was to collect a few splinters in his backside.

Nevada leaned against one arm of the sofa, arms crossed, legs extended casually. He was no expert at body language, but even he could read the mixed messages there. "So," she said. "What's up?"

He shot a quick glance her way. Her expression assured him the double entendre had been unintentional, and he felt like a jerk for suspecting otherwise. "I sent the ring and an enlarged photo of Blanche's amulet down to Carson with Marcello. He showed them to a jeweler there who specializes in antiques. According to him, the ring likely dates back to the early-to-mid-nineteenth century—"

"Which we knew already," she said.

"Which we suspected," he corrected her. "He was even able to identify the goldsmith who made it, Thaddeus McKelvey of San Francisco."

"And the amulet?"

"The jeweler couldn't say for sure just from studying a photograph, but he suspected the amulet was even older."

"But the ring definitely came from San Francisco?"

Trick nodded. "The markings we saw on the inside of the band? That was the goldsmith's 'signature.' Of course, Thaddeus McKelvey's long dead, but McKelvey Fine Jewelry is still in business."

"So there should be records."

Trick hated to be a wet blanket, but . . . "Unless they were destroyed in the earthquake of 1906."

"But it's still a solid lead," she insisted. "Finding McKelvey Fine Jewelry is bound to be easier than tracking down relatives of a girl named Smith who's been dead over a century and a half."

"Just don't get your hopes up," he warned.

Nevada's gaze slid away from his. She frowned at the threadbare carpet for a moment or two, then suddenly shoved herself upright. "I'm a terrible hostess. Sorry. May I get you something to drink?" She nodded toward the minifridge that did double duty as an end table.

"No, thanks," he said. "I don't mean to discourage you. It's just—"

"You're a pessimist by nature," she said.

"No," he corrected her. "Not a pessimist. A realist. And not by nature, either. It was a lesson I learned the hard way." He stood up. "I really should be going."

"And now you're offended."

"I'm not offended." Though he was.

"Then why are you in such a hurry to leave?" Her mouth did that twitchy almost-smile thing. "Hot date with ESPN?"

"Lukewarm," he said. "Why? You got a better idea?"

"Britt told me it's karaoke night at the lodge."

Oh, God. Well, he *had* asked. "You sing?"

"Not really," she said. "But I've never been to a karaoke night. How about you?"

"Sad to say, I've not been as fortunate as you have in avoiding them. Marcello's dragged me into karaoke bars on three continents."

She shot him a startled look. "Seriously? I thought karaoke was strictly an American phenomenon."

"No, I'm pretty sure it started in Japan."

"That's not really what I was asking, though," she said. "What I meant was, can you sing?"

"Lord, no." He gave a snort of laughter. "Can't carry a tune in a bucket."

"Britt is an amazing woman," Nevada said as she and Trick headed back toward the Granger mansion on foot. "Not only a former Olympic champion skier but a fantastic singer as well."

"Plus as gorgeous as a movie star and built like a goddess," Trick added.

"True." Nevada shot him a quick sideways glance. Was he more interested in his neighbor than she'd realized? Here she'd thought Marcello was the one who . . .

"But not really my type," Trick said. "I prefer brunettes to blondes, green eyes to blue."

Nevada stopped in her tracks, halfway across the parking lot. Was he coming on to her?

Trick stopped, too. "Something wrong?"

"I don't know. Are you flirting with me?"

Trick laughed softly. "All night long. Hell, don't tell me this is the first time you noticed." He shook his head sadly. "I really must be losing my touch."

"Trick, I . . ."

"I know." He gave her a quick hug. "No pressure."

No pressure. Easy for him to say. He obviously didn't have a full-fledged war raging inside his body—hormones versus good sense. His touch—even a casual touch like that arm he had wrapped around her shoulders—was enough to weaken her knees and set her heart racing. Damn it, she was such a fool.

Nevada started walking again, dislodging his arm in the process.

"Hey!" Trick protested. "Slow down. My knee's still not limber enough for a four-minute mile."

"It's not a mile back to the mansion."

"Okay, a two-minute half mile then," he called after her.

She slowed, then stopped to wait for him to catch up.

"Jackrabbit," he said.

She shot him a quizzical smile. "Okay, that was random."

"Not really." A wicked grin curved his lips. "As fast as you move, you should have called yourself Jackrabbit instead of Nevada."

"I know how to run," she admitted. "It's what I'm good at." She didn't smile, though, because it wasn't a joke.

"I didn't mean it that way," he said, his voice gentle, his face serious.

She didn't respond. What could she say? Instead, she started walking again.

"When we get back, you're not going to invite me in, are you?"

She took a deep breath, held it a second or two, then

exhaled slowly. "No," she said. Though God knew she wanted to so badly she was trembling with the effort not to voice her need.

"Just as well," he said. "Because if you did ask me in, I wouldn't say no, even though I know I should. You're not ready. I'm not ready. We're not ready. But . . ."

Yeah, but . . .

They completed the rest of the walk in silence. Trick didn't climb the stairs to her apartment with her or try to kiss her before she started up, but when she glanced back over her shoulder just before slipping inside, he was still standing there at the bottom of the staircase, still watching her. When he realized she'd seen him, he smiled and blew her a kiss. Very Romeo and Juliet. Then he turned and walked toward the mansion.

"Idiot," she muttered under her breath as she let herself into her apartment, though, to be perfectly honest, she wasn't sure if she was talking about Trick or herself.

She turned on the floor lamp, then collapsed on the sofa with a sigh.

Only gradually did all the disturbing little anomalies impinge upon her consciousness. She hadn't left two beer bottles on the coffee table. She didn't have any beer, didn't like it, never drank it.

She was pretty sure she hadn't bunched all the throw pillows up at one end of the sofa, either.

And she was absolutely positive she hadn't tossed hamburger wrappers and leftover fries on the floor at the end of the couch.

Somebody had been here while she was gone.

Correction, she thought as she heard the toilet flush, somebody was here now.

She bolted out of her seat and across the apartment to the door. One of the men who'd been following her, the big African American with the shaved head, emerged from the bathroom just as she jerked the outside door open. For once, he wasn't wearing his sunglasses, and his eyes seemed to glow red in the instant he spotted her.

"Don't run away," he said, his voice a deep, rumbly bass that sent chills down her spine. "Party's just about to get started."

"Not much of a party girl," she said. She ducked out the door and raced down the steps.

He lunged after her, but she didn't look back. Instead, she focused all her energy on getting away.

"Stop her!" Rumbly voice shouted from behind her.

"I'm planning to." The second man loomed up out of the darkness, blocking her escape. A self-satisfied smirk twisted his lips. "Looks like we've got you sandwiched in, sweetheart."

Nevada didn't think. She just reacted, running scared, hyped on adrenaline. Screaming at the top of her lungs, she flung herself over the railing, a six-foot drop into a hedge of rose bushes that scratched at her skin and snagged at her clothes.

Trick let himself in the back door, expecting to find Marcello either playing solitaire on his laptop or watching an old B movie on TV. Instead the house was dark. Dark and silent. Dark and silent and cold.

As if there were a window open somewhere. Only why would Marcello leave a window open when the temperature outside was in the forties?

Trick stood there with his hand poised above the light switch, listening hard, but the only sounds were the predictable ones, a dripping faucet, the hum of the refrigerator, the ticking of the grandfather clock at the end of the hall.

He turned on the light, half-prepared for chaos, but the kitchen looked the way it always did at this time of night, tidy and undisturbed, the dinner dishes drying in the dish drainer, the counters and stove wiped down, the table empty.

"Marcello?" he called.

No answer, which didn't mean anything. If Marcello had already gone to bed, he wouldn't have heard a thing from up on the third floor.

Trick moved into the hall, switching on lights as he went. It was colder here.

He checked the dining room next, then the room that had once been the brothel office, but again, like the kitchen, both rooms were in order.

He headed next for the big living room, the room that had once been the parlor. Much colder here, he noted, then quickly realized why. One of the front windows had been broken out. Glass littered the polished wood floor. Smaller fragments sparkled like glitter across the deep red and blue pattern of the Turkish rug. "Marcello?" he tried again, louder this time.

The broken window wasn't the only sign of damage, either, he realized as he took a good look around.

There'd been a fight here. Furniture was shoved out of place, one antique table crushed, as if something heavy had landed on it, a lamp overturned, a glass-fronted knickknack cupboard lying on its side, the collection of china teapots scattered across the room, many of them ruined. And *holy shit,* was that blood smeared across the floor and spattered on the wall beside the fireplace?

Frightened now at what else he might find, Trick turned a slow three-sixty. "Marcello? Where the hell are you?"

This time he was rewarded with a groan that seemed to come from behind the sofa. Trick crossed the room in three long steps. Marcello lay there, his hands bound behind his back, his bare chest covered with what looked like a dozen or more cigarette burns. The worst of his injuries, though, appeared to be a gaping gash in his forehead. He looked as if someone had painted half his face red, but it wasn't paint. It was blood. With a grunt, he managed to shove himself to a sitting position. "What happened?"

"I was just going to ask you the same thing." Trick knelt next to Marcello, cutting him free with a pocket-knife. "Looks to me as if someone tortured the hell out of you."

"Tortured?" Marcello frowned, his face a mask of confusion. Then his eyes narrowed, and he swore a blue streak, a creative blend of Italian and English. "Two men," he said. "The same two men who were looking for Nevada before."

"They were here?"

Nevada!

Trick tossed Marcello his cell phone, then headed out the back at a dead run. "Call 911," he shouted.

He raced toward Nevada's apartment as fast as his stiff knee would take him, grabbing up a shovel Marcello had left leaning against the house. As weapons went, it wasn't much but better than nothing.

Nevada screamed then, and he realized she wasn't upstairs in her apartment as he'd assumed. She was in the rose garden. He changed direction, spotting her the second he passed the sundial. One of the men had pinned her to the grass with the weight of his body. At first, Trick assumed he'd interrupted a rape. Then he realized what was really happening. The intruder reared back and the moonlight gleamed off his fangs in the second before he lunged forward and sank them into Nevada's throat.

Too angry for fear, too angry for caution, Trick charged. The second man appeared out of nowhere, though the truth was, Trick didn't see him until after the bastard had kicked his legs out from under him. He hit the ground with a jolt, losing his grip on the shovel. The ebony-skinned giant aimed a second kick at Trick's head, but Trick saw the blow coming and rolled out of the way. He grabbed the shovel by the handle and staggered to his feet.

"We've got company, Sarge," the giant warned.

"You sure do," someone shouted from the pines that bordered the far side of the rose garden.

The giant turned toward the voice, but it was already too late for him. A bolt from a crossbow buried itself in his chest. He made a sound, a grunt of surprise, and the next instant he exploded in a shower of dust. There one second, gone the next. Trick would have been flabbergasted if he'd given himself time to think about it, but he didn't have time.

The monster called Sarge still had his fangs buried in Nevada's throat. She was fighting, thrashing in a vain effort to throw him off.

Trick lurched forward, planning to slam the shovel into the back of the bastard's head, but the hidden crossbow shooter's blood-chilling whoop of triumph broke Sarge's concentration. He glanced up to see what all the noise was about.

Realizing he was about to be brained, he rolled sideways to avoid the blow. In desperation, Trick tossed the shovel like an ungainly javelin. It caught Sarge edgeways across the side of his head. He let out a howl, but before Trick could follow up with his fists, Sarge scrambled to his feet and raced toward the trees.

Screaming invective-laced threats, Trick grabbed the shovel again and lobbed it at the cowardly bastard.

This time the handle caught the vampire across the back of his knees. He stumbled but recovered quickly. A second crossbow bolt missed him by inches, thumping into the stable wall. But Sarge didn't hesitate. He kept running, and within seconds, he had disappeared.

TEN

Nevada! Nevada!" Someone was shaking her and shouting her name.

She pried her eyelids open with an effort. Why did she feel so weak? "Where am I?" she asked. "What happened?" But no sooner had she gotten the questions out than her memory returned, providing more information than she could process.

Her gaze locked on Trick's worried face. "The men who're chasing me," she said. "They came back." She fumbled for her neck, trying to find out how badly she was hurt.

Trick grabbed her hand. "Don't touch the wounds," he said. "You'll start them bleeding again. Marcello called 911. The paramedics are on the way."

A second face moved into her line of sight. "Faraday?" she said. "I thought you'd left Midas Lake."

"I did. I'm only back because the vampires are back."

"You could have given us a heads-up," Trick said

bitterly. "It's a damned miracle Nevada wasn't killed. Marcello, too."

Nevada's stomach clenched. "Marcello's hurt?"

"They tortured him, burned him with cigarettes among other things."

"To get him to tell them where to find me." Guilt sickened her. A man had been tortured because of her.

"It's not your fault," Trick told her.

"Then whose fault is it?" she demanded.

"Sarge's would be my guess." Faraday set his crossbow down. "Cigarette burns are kind of his signature."

"At least he's the only one left to worry about. You nailed the other guy," Trick said.

"Dusted," Faraday corrected him.

Nevada wasn't sure what he meant by that, but she felt way too rotten to worry about it.

"We need to get our stories straight," Faraday said. "You start spouting off about vampires, and you'll end up at the funny farm."

Panic gripped Nevada. She shot a look of wordless entreaty toward Trick, who squeezed her hand tightly, then shook his head, as if to say, "Relax. Faraday's choice of words was sheer coincidence. He doesn't suspect a thing." But she wasn't as convinced of that as Trick seemed to be.

"Wild animal attack?" Trick suggested.

"Dog, I think." Faraday crossed to the rear wall of the stable, leaned across the low hedge of roses, and yanked the bolt from the wooden siding. "Pit bull or German shepherd. Make it plausible. You don't want anyone asking too many questions or examining those bite marks too closely."

The wail of a siren announced the imminent arrival of the EMTs. Nevada tried to sit up, but Trick pushed her back down again. "Stay put," he said. "We don't know how much blood you've lost."

"I'm out of here." Faraday flipped a business card in Trick's direction. "If you spot Sarge again, give me a call. Anytime. Day or night." He took off at a lope, headed for the trees. By the time the ambulance pulled in, he was only a memory.

Trick studied Nevada's reflection in the rearview mirror. She didn't meet his gaze with a reassuring smile. She didn't even seem to realize he was watching her.

"She will be all right," Marcello said softly, not that it mattered whether or not he was overheard since he was speaking Italian. "The doctor said her injuries are superficial. As are mine."

"A splinter is superficial. A scratch is superficial. That psycho bastard burned holes in your chest and sank his teeth in her throat, and neither of those injuries qualifies as superficial in my book."

"Non-life-threatening then," Marcello said. He'd tried to get Nevada to ride in the passenger's seat, but she'd insisted on taking the back.

Downtown Midas Lake was quiet at this hour, both vehicular and pedestrian traffic light. A couple of bars were still open, but even their customers were starting to thin out. Trick stopped at the red light across from the train depot.

"Where did they park?" Nevada asked.

"Who?" he asked. "The train passengers? I think there's a parking lot on the other side of the depot."

"No," she said. "The vampires. They didn't pull into the driveway."

"Perhaps they left their car parked along the highway," Marcello suggested.

"I didn't hear an engine start up," she said. "When Sarge left, I mean."

"Maybe he escaped on foot," Trick said, though damned if he could see why it mattered.

"Possibly," Nevada agreed, then after a lengthy pause, "Probably."

The light turned green. Maybe it was the reflection that made her look so sickly. And maybe not. "You're staying in the house tonight," he said, prepared for an argument, but she didn't acknowledge his statement. He wasn't sure she'd even heard it. Nevada seemed to be in a world of her own, a nightmare world, judging by her haunted expression. "How does your neck feel?"

She put one hand to her throat, as if checking to see if it was still there. "Okay. Sore."

"She seems to be handling it well," Marcello said, again speaking Italian.

"Too well," Trick said in the same language.

Trick had made up a bed for Nevada in Blanche's room. "If you need anything in the night—even if it's only to talk—just yell. Marcello's room is at the other end of the hall. He can come get me."

"I'm fine," she told him, which was an out-and-out lie, but she didn't want him to worry, not any more than he was already worrying. She never should have stayed here, never should have taken him up on the job offer. Her pursuers—no, make that her pursuer—knew where she was now, and it was only a matter of time before he tried again. This room felt safe, but safety was an illusion. The monster named Sarge would just keep coming again and again until he finally succeeded in killing her.

And yes, that prospect terrified her, but what terrified her even more was the possibility that Trick or Marcello might get hurt—even killed—in the process. She couldn't—wouldn't—risk such an outcome.

"Nevada?" Trick frowned at her from the doorway. What did he see in her face to put that worried expression on his? "Are you sure you're all right?"

"I just need some rest," she said, even though sleep was the farthest thing from her mind. Tamping down the fear and guilt that threatened to overwhelm her, Nevada schooled her features into a pretense of calm. She could do this. After all, the Institute had provided her with years of practice at hiding her true emotions.

Trick hesitated for a second or two longer, as if maybe her mask wasn't fixed as securely in place as she'd thought, as if maybe he were picking up on some of that negative energy she was struggling so hard to hide. But in the end, he left, closing the door quietly behind him.

Nevada gave it an hour—long enough for Trick and Marcello to fall asleep—before she stirred. Moving quietly, she dressed, packed a few essentials in the second-hand backpack she'd found at the Salvation Army, made sure she had her money and her pills, then, carrying her shoes, tiptoed in her stocking feet across the room.

The door whined a protest when she opened it. She stood there frozen, waiting, her heart pounding. Ten seconds passed. Twenty. Thirty. A lifetime.

Gradually, she relaxed. Apparently the creaking door hadn't been loud enough to disturb Marcello. She could hear the faint sound of his snores from a room at the opposite end of the hall.

Slowly, she pulled the door shut. Again, it protested but not enough to cause a change in the rhythm of Marcello's snores. One hurdle crossed.

Silent as a whisper, Nevada made her way down one flight of stairs. She paused on the landing, listening hard. Nothing. If Trick was asleep, he wasn't snoring.

She fought the sudden foolish impulse to kiss him good-bye, proceeding instead down the last flight of stairs, then across the entryway to the front door. Quietly, she let herself out, then closed and locked the door behind her.

Nevada paused on the front porch just long enough to slip into her shoes, tying and double-knotting the laces. Then she glanced back up at the house, the closest thing to a home she'd had in as long as she could remember. She didn't want to go, but want and need were two separate animals. She needed to get away for her own good as well as for . . .

Damn it, she'd meant to leave a note of explanation.

What if Trick woke up and found her gone? What if he assumed she'd been kidnapped?

No. Ridiculous. One glance at the closed windows and securely locked doors and he'd know better.

Still, leaving this way felt wrong.

Another alternative occurred to her. She walked around to the Jeep, dug a pen from her backpack, and used it to scribble a quick note on an unused napkin she found lying on the floor in the backseat. She placed the napkin on the center of the dash where Trick couldn't miss it, then, before she could change her mind, set off for the main road at a fast walk.

Trick, who'd assigned himself to guard duty, woke with a start. The last thing he remembered he'd been reading the latest Elvis Cole mystery, but apparently he'd fallen asleep sitting up in his chair before even finishing the first chapter, which was no reflection on the book but spoke instead to his own exhaustion. It seemed a million years since he'd watched Nevada eating veal parmigiana at the breakfast table.

He stifled a jaw-cracking yawn, then stretched and shoved himself upright. Might as well make a quick patrol since he was up, check the doors and windows, make sure Marcello and Nevada were okay. He took a single step, stumbled, and nearly fell.

Glancing down to see what had tripped him up, he spotted his book. It stared accusingly back at him. "Abandon me in the middle of chapter one, will you?" it seemed to say.

He picked it up, placed it carefully on a table out of harm's way, and then set off on his rounds.

Once he'd reassured himself that all the doors and windows were locked up tight, the shutters latched across the broken window, reinforced now with a sheet of plywood, he made his way to the third floor. He paused outside Marcello's door.

His assistant was snoring softly. No need to disturb him.

Trick walked to the other end of the hall, pausing outside Nevada's door. No snoring. No sounds at all. He knocked softly but got no response. Carefully, he eased open the door so the light from the hall fell across the threshold, illuminating the bed.

The empty bed. If the covers had simply been tossed aside, he'd have assumed Nevada had just slipped down the hall to the bathroom, but the bed had been stripped, the sheets and blankets neatly folded.

So where was Nevada? Could she have returned to the apartment over the stables? Surely not. Not with the psycho vampire still on the loose.

Don't panic, he told himself. *There's probably a perfectly logical explanation.*

Right. Like she'd been sucked through a rift in the space-time continuum and ended up lost somewhere two centuries in the future.

Only in that case, would she have had time to fold up her bedding? Obviously not. So wherever she'd gone, she'd gone there of her own free will. She hadn't been coerced or kidnapped or even time-warped.

The question was, where would she have gone in the middle of the night?

And the answer was, away, somewhere far away, somewhere, hopefully, where there weren't any psycho vampires waiting to suck her dry.

She didn't trust him to protect her. She'd seen his pitiful showing in the battle earlier. Hell, a shovel. What had he been thinking?

But she must know she'd be safer with him and Marcello than wandering around on her own. What if she tried to hitch a ride and got picked up by another pervert like the logging truck driver? Or worse, what if the first car that stopped was Sarge's? Had she thought of that? No, she'd gone running blindly off into the night.

He paused in the midst of his mental rant, brought up short by an alternative scenario that had just occurred to him. What if she hadn't gone *running* off at all? What if she'd taken the Wrangler?

He crossed to a window overlooking the driveway. Moonlight glimmered off the Jeep's rear bumper.

So she *was* on foot.

No, calm down, think clearly, and quit jumping to unfounded conclusions. He didn't even know for sure that she'd left the premises and wouldn't until he'd done a thorough search.

Fifteen minutes later, having looked everywhere except the beach—the path was too slippery to risk—he was 99 percent certain she'd run. The only other possibility that occurred to him, admittedly a long shot, was that she'd appealed to Britt for help, thinking she'd be safer at the lodge, locked away in an anonymous hotel room.

He dialed Britt's private number.

"Yes?" She answered on the second ring, sounding groggy.

"This is Trick. Nevada's gone, and I'm worried. Have you seen her?" *Please tell me that you've seen her.*

"Not since yesterday morning. Why? What happened? I heard you had the EMTs out there earlier."

"Nevada and Marcello were attacked."

Britt drew in a startled breath. "Is he . . . are they . . . all right?"

"We thought Marcello had a concussion at first. He took a pretty nasty blow to the head. But the ER doctor said not. Apparently he has a harder head than I thought. As for Nevada, physically, the damage was minimal, but mentally, I think she was pretty traumatized. I tried to get her to talk about it, but she said she was tired and wanted to get some sleep. When I went up to check on her a while ago, she was gone."

"But where would she go?" Britt asked.

"I was hoping you'd tell me she'd shown up on your doorstep."

"No," Britt said. "I haven't seen her."

"Then she's on the run," he said. "Scared out of her mind and on the run. I've got to find her. But . . . may I ask a big favor of you?"

"Of course," she said without hesitation.

"The man who attacked Nevada and Marcello? He's dangerous. Dangerous and persistent. I have to find Nevada before she gets hurt, but I don't think it's safe for Marcello to stay here by himself. If his attacker comes back . . ." He let it trail off, hoping she would take the hint.

"You want Marcello to stay here at the lodge."

"Yes, I do, but not as a registered guest. There can't be any record. In fact, it would be best if no one knew he was there, not even the staff."

"But how? Oh," Britt said. "You want him to stay in my suite."

"Please, Britt. I wouldn't ask if I didn't think it was important."

"I know. It's just . . ." She paused for so long that he thought she was going to say no. "Okay," she said finally. "I know I'm going to regret this, but okay, he can stay here. Have him call when he's ready to come across, and I'll go downstairs to let him in the back door."

"Thanks, Britt. I owe you."

"Big-time," she said sourly.

He hung up without even saying good-bye. Ten rather traumatic minutes later, having convinced an extremely reluctant Marcello that staying with Britt was the only intelligent option, he grabbed the keys to the Wrangler and headed out the door.

Seemed like she'd been walking for hours. In all that time, Nevada had seen no more than a dozen cars, and none of them had stopped. Although this secondary road provided the most direct route to San Francisco, heading this way had probably been a mistake. Traffic was light at this hour, even lighter than she'd expected.

And that didn't bode well for her chances of catching a ride any time soon.

If she had a lick of sense, she'd hike back into Midas Lake and hitch a ride at the Stop 'N Go. But returning to Midas Lake would mean backtracking, and she didn't want to do that if she could avoid it. Too much chance of running into someone she knew, someone who might later report her whereabouts to Trick. She knew if he had any idea where she'd gone, he'd try to follow her. And *damn it*, she'd already put him in enough danger.

Time to stand on her own two feet. Literally.

She shivered in the cold night air. Her hoodie wasn't warm enough for the nighttime temperatures here in the mountains. Below freezing, judging by the way her breath made those little white clouds. She pulled up her hood, stuffed her chilly hands deep in the pockets of her sweatshirt, and walked a little faster.

Something moved with a furtive rustle among the trees on the opposite side of the highway. Startled, Nevada froze. The forest was full of animals, she told herself, most of them harmless.

But not all. Not bears. Not mountain lions.

More rustling noises broke the stillness. Then she heard the sharp crack of a branch breaking. Nevada held her breath, not sure if she should stand her ground or run and hide.

Then a doe came into view, carefully picking its way down the mountainside, and Nevada released her breath in a sigh of relief.

No sooner had the doe reached the graveled shoulder of the highway than a second doe appeared, following in the footsteps of the first. By the time the first doe had crossed the blacktop, a third had come inching its way down the hill, moving more slowly than the first two.

The first one had crossed the road at a trot, then disappeared into the trees on Nevada's side of the highway. After a moment's hesitation, the second had followed. Neither animal had spared Nevada a glance. But the third doe made it only to the center line before pausing midstep and fixing her with suspicious look.

Nevada didn't move a muscle. She didn't even blink.

Apparently reassured, the doe broke eye contact, clicked across the second half of the highway, then vanished into the trees.

Cheered by the encounter, Nevada resumed her hike, trudging another half mile or so without seeing a single living soul. She'd almost talked herself into turning around and heading back to Midas Lake when she heard a vehicle coming, the sounds faint at first but quickly growing louder. Something with a powerful engine, moving fast.

It roared up the incline behind her, the noise echoing off the steep mountainsides.

This one probably won't stop, either, she told herself but, standing well off the paved surface, her back pressed against the guardrail, she held out her thumb anyway.

Headlights appeared suddenly as the vehicle crested

the rise, two blinding beams bearing down on her at an alarming speed.

Surely the driver could see her. Her dark clothing provided a stark contrast to the white ribbon of guardrail behind her. But the car, something big and dark, flashed by without even slowing.

It missed her by a good five or six feet but created enough of a draft to pull down her hood and whip her hair into her face. *Jerk.* She was already cold enough without his help.

Perhaps the driver hadn't seen her until he was right on her, or perhaps he'd had a sudden change of heart. Whatever the reason, he suddenly slammed on his brakes, squealing to a stop fifty yards beyond the spot where she stood. Then he put it in reverse and began backing up.

The car was a Crown Victoria, she realized with a nasty jolt, the same model her pursuers had driven. Could it be the same car? What were the odds?

Run! her brain ordered. But before she could even decide which direction to bolt, the car pulled to a stop next to her. She searched the empty highway. No help. No help in either direction.

She glanced over her shoulder, trying to see how far she'd roll if she threw herself over the guardrail. Too far, she decided, since she couldn't see the bottom of the steep slope. Too far, too rocky, too dangerous.

The driver's window rolled down. "Need a ride?"

Not Sarge. Relief washed over her.

She couldn't see the driver very clearly; she could

tell, however, that he was both younger and slighter than the vampire.

The passenger leaned across the driver, another male, late teens or early twenties. "Yeah, babe, want a ride." She could smell the alcohol fumes from where she stood.

Babe?

"Where are you headed?" the passenger asked.

Maybe she could pretend they were going in the wrong direction. But no, that wouldn't fly. She'd stuck her thumb out, and why would she have done that if the car had been going in the wrong direction?

"We're on our way back to Auburn," the driver said.

"Hey, don't be so hasty, Travis," the passenger chided. "We're flexible. We'll take you anywhere you want, babe."

"Flexible? Hell, yeah, we're a bunch of damned rubber bands," she heard from the back seat.

So there were three of them then. Maybe four.

"I appreciate the offer," she lied. "Unfortunately, I have this rule about riding with drunk drivers, and it's pretty clear that you guys have been partying tonight."

"*We* have, yeah, but not Travis," the front seat passenger said. "He's our designated driver."

"Not to mention a stick-in-the-mud." A hand reached up to cuff the back of the driver's head.

"Knock it off," Travis said.

"What're you doing out here in the middle of nowhere anyhow?" someone yelled from the far side of the backseat.

"My boyfriend and I had a fight." She shrugged. "I took off."

"Looks like your boyfriend's stupidity is our good luck," the front seat passenger said.

"Amen!" The rear door swung open. "Get in. We'll move over." The burly young man sitting there gestured with his beer can for her to come closer.

"Better yet," the guy sitting on the other side said, "she can squeeze in between us. Emphasis on the *squeeze*." He laughed uproariously at his own lame joke.

"Thanks," she said, "but no thanks."

"Now, don't be like that." The blocky young man with the beer can stumbled out of the car, so drunk that he nearly took a header on the pavement. After regaining his balance, he staggered over to the shoulder of the road, a silly grin on his face. "Want a drink?" He shoved the beer can in her face.

She shook her head.

So he swigged the last of the beer, then pitched the empty over the guardrail.

With a sinking heart, Nevada listened to it clattering its way down the slope. Definitely not the escape route for her. "Look, I—" she started.

The drunk grabbed her.

"Let go of me!" She twisted and squirmed.

He grinned. "A hottie *and* a spitfire. Damned if this isn't my lucky night!"

His leering face moved closer and closer. The stale brewery stench of his breath filled her nostrils. Then his mouth closed over hers.

Fueled by revulsion and sheer panic, Nevada twisted loose, aimed a quick kick at his shin, then took off running.

"Smooth move, Liam," she heard one of the others say, the comment followed by a lot of raucous laughter.

No help there. The passengers were just drunk enough to be dangerous, and apparently the driver, Travis, didn't have either the balls or the decency to stand up to them. She heard a car door slam behind her. The engine started up with a growl.

Damn it, she couldn't outrun a car, but if she could just make it to the end of the guardrail, she might be able to slither down the slope at a point where it wasn't so steep.

She didn't have to look behind her to know the car was gaining on her. Not that the driver was moving fast. Quite the contrary. He seemed to be pacing her, prolonging the chase. They probably expected her to run out of steam. If so, they underestimated the strength of an adrenaline rush.

She was pretty sure she had a shot if she could just make it to the end of the guardrail. Five yards away now. Four. Three. But two yards shy of her goal, disaster struck. She got tangled up in a long strip of shredded truck tire, lost her balance, and landed with a jarring thud on her hands and knees.

Before she could get her feet back under her, three of them were on her. They jerked off her backpack and flipped her over. She hit the ground with a whump that drove all the air from her lungs.

"Come on, babe, don't be shy. How 'bout a kiss?" one of them said.

"Stop!" she shouted. "Help! Travis! Somebody!"

"Hold her still, damn it!" the blocky one shouted.

Nevada's struggles reached the frenzied level. She kicked and hit and bit at anything that came within range.

One of her attackers let out a howl as her foot connected with something tender.

"Son of a bitch!" someone else screeched as she got a good handful of hair.

"Hold her still, for crying out loud!"

"Car coming!" Travis yelled.

Then suddenly, a second set of headlights lit up the scene.

Nevada blinked in the glare. "Help!" she screamed, her cry echoing off the mountainside.

"Oh, shit," someone said. "We've got to get out of here."

Shoes pounded the pavement, doors slammed, an engine revved, tires squealed. And then they were gone.

Shaky now that her adrenaline was wearing thin, Nevada levered herself to a sitting position. She'd just finished jerking her sweatshirt down and was reaching for her backpack—her damaged backpack, she noted, one of the shoulder straps ripped completely loose—when the crunch of footsteps on gravel alerted her that someone was coming. Presumably the driver of the second car. Hastily, she shoved herself to her feet.

"Nevada?" Trick sounded as shocked as she felt. Or at least as shocked as she would have felt if she could have felt anything at all. "Nevada?" he said again, his voice raspy, a little uneven.

And then she was folded close to his chest, wrapped

in his arms. He felt so good, so safe. She started to shake as reaction set in.

"You're freezing," he said.

Was she? She hadn't noticed.

"Come on. You need to get into the Wrangler. I'll turn the heater on high, so you can thaw out."

"Not yet," she whispered. "Just hold me for a little while longer. Please."

So he held her tight right there on the side of the road, and she wasn't sure, not absolutely, but she thought maybe his lips brushed the top of her head.

ELEVEN

Trick kept shooting concerned glances in Nevada's direction, as if worried she was about to freak out. The truth was, she was miles beyond the freak-out threshold and fast approaching the zombie zone. But at least she wasn't shuddering nonstop anymore. Hands buried in the pockets of her sweatshirt as much to hide their trembling as for warmth, she huddled in the passenger seat and stared at the road ahead, mesmerized into a fragile facsimile of calm by the comforting repetition of the dashed center line.

What if Trick hadn't come along when he did?

The trembling in her hands immediately spread throughout her body.

No, she told herself. *Don't think about the what ifs. Think about the what nexts.* The problem was, she wasn't sure at this point what she should do next, though she knew at least one thing she shouldn't do—return to Midas Lake. Now that Sarge was aware she'd been staying there all this time, he'd be back. Trick and

Faraday might have frightened him off for a little while, but no way would he stay away. The first chance he got, he'd return, probably with reinforcements.

"Are you insane?" Trick asked suddenly.

She turned sideways to frown at him. "I don't think so, but I was institutionalized and I do sometimes see things other people don't, so who knows? Why do you ask?"

"You're safe now," he said.

"Yes, but—"

"No thanks to your own rash actions."

"You think I encouraged those drunken punks?"

"Just being there that way—alone—was all the encouragement they needed. Why did you run away in the first place? What were you thinking?"

"I explained that in my note."

He stared at her. "What note?"

"I left a note . . . on the . . ." She faltered to a halt, having spotted the napkin lying near her left foot. When Trick had opened the door to get inside, the napkin must have fluttered off onto the floor. So much for good intentions. "Never mind," she said.

"But I *do* mind," Trick said. "What if Sarge had been the one to stop for you?"

"When I first saw the Crown Victoria, I thought it *was* Sarge."

"So did I." He reached across to grasp her hand. "I was scared, Nevada."

"Me, too," she said. And then, damn it, she just dissolved, shaking and crying, incoherent and out of control.

Trick eased the Jeep to the side of the road, shifted into park, unfastened his shoulder harness, and pulled her as close as he could with the gearshift in the way. "Don't," he said.

As if she had a choice. As if . . .

His touch—both soothing and arousing—calmed and disturbed her at the same time. Tears slid faster and faster down her cheeks. She was shaking all over now, an 8.7 on the Richter scale.

"It's okay," he said. "You're safe now."

"Th-those boys . . . They wouldn't have killed me. They might not even have raped me, but . . ."

"After Sarge's attack earlier—"

"It was too much, too similar. I . . . don't know what I would have done if you hadn't shown up when you did."

"Don't think about it," he said.

As if she could empty her mind that easily. "He's not going to give up," she said. "Sarge, I mean. He'll get to me eventually, no matter who's standing in his way. That's why I can't go back to Midas Lake."

"But—" he started to argue.

"No," she said. "Staying there now would put both you and Marcello in danger."

He framed her face in his hands, forcing her to look at him. "You can't go off on your own. It's not safe."

"Safe?" She gave a sharp, semihysterical bark of laughter. "Safe? Don't you get it? Nowhere's safe for me, not as long as he's out there. He's not going to stop. He's going to keep coming and coming until . . ." She pulled herself free of him, staring resolutely out the windshield into the darkness. "I want you to take me to the nearest town and put me on a bus."

"No bus stops before Midas Lake," he said.

And she couldn't go back to Midas Lake. Too risky. "Then turn around and take me all the way to Sacramento if you have to, but find me a bus stop."

"Sarge isn't the one you have to worry about," Trick said.

"No?" She turned to him in surprise.

"No." He frowned. "It's whoever hired those two monsters to come after you. He, the mystery man, is the one you need to worry about."

"But I don't know who he is." Once again she trembled on the verge of hysteria.

"Then we need to find out," he said firmly.

"We?" Her voice broke midsyllable. She couldn't help it. "The last person who tried to help me ended up dead."

"Yelena, you mean? Your surrogate mother?"

"Yes."

"Don't worry. I won't be as easy to kill. I know what to expect and how to defend myself."

Sudden anger supplanted her fear. "How? With a crossbow?" she demanded, her words heavy with sarcasm.

"If need be, though I'm sure a stake would work as well. Or fire. Or even just sunlight."

"You're the one who's insane," she said.

"Right," he agreed. "Insanely worried about you. We need to find out who you are and why someone thought it necessary to steal your memories of the past."

Her identity, her *life*.

"That's the person you should fear," Trick was saying. "That's the person with the most to lose. Obviously, you know something—"

"*Knew* something," she said.

"Knew something," he repeated. "Something dangerous."

When Trick pulled to a stop in the parking lot of a Best Western, Nevada woke with a start. She'd fallen asleep about forty miles back, her head mashed against the door, and had the creases in her right cheek to prove it. "Why are we stopping?"

Trick gave her a weary smile. "Because I need some rest. I can't afford to fall asleep at the wheel."

"I could take a turn driving."

"Could you?" he asked. "Do you drive?"

Nevada frowned. "I'm not sure."

"We both need sleep, and I, for one, could use a shower." He could use a change of clothing, too, but he wouldn't get one, not until the stores opened in the morning.

"But if we stop," she said, "we're giving Sarge a chance to catch up."

"He doesn't know we're together," he objected.

"Marcello knows. You called him, right?"

He had, and he was sure his face confirmed it.

"So what's to stop Sarge from returning to the mansion long enough to torture the truth out of Marcello?" Nevada spoke urgently, her eyes wide and dark with concern.

Trick covered one of her hands with his and realized she was trembling again. "Marcello's not in the mansion. He's staying at the lodge for the time being."

"That's still too close." Nevada's lower lip trembled. "Sarge is bound to find him."

"No," Trick said. "He's not even registered. He's staying in Britt's suite."

"With Britt?" Her eyes widened.

He smiled. "Presumably. Now, let's check in before I pass out."

Nevada's shouts woke Trick from a sound sleep. He fumbled for the switch on the lamp that sat on the table between the two queen beds. On the third try, he finally managed to connect. He wouldn't have been surprised to have found Nevada in a fight for her life with her vampire stalker. Instead, she was still asleep, apparently locked in a nightmare as she battled to free herself from her tangled sheet.

He threw back his own covers, slid out of bed, then sat on the edge of her mattress. "Hey! Wake up." He shook her gently. "Wake up. It's just a dream."

Something penetrated, either his touch or his voice. As abruptly as if someone had turned off a switch, her thrashing ended. She opened her eyes, blinking once or twice. "Where are we?"

"In a motel in Sacramento."

"Sarge," she said. "The car full of drunken teenagers."

"You remember."

"All too well. They were holding me down. In my dream, they were holding me down. I couldn't get away. I couldn't move." Her voice rose.

"They're gone," he said. "You're safe. You just got yourself twisted up in the bedding, that's all."

She rose up on one elbow, surveying the tangled sheet. "What happened to my blanket?"

"I think at some point during the struggle, you must have used some fancy karate move to flip it off the end of the bed. Apparently broke its spirit in the process, too. It's just lying there limp as a rag."

Unfortunately, being in close proximity to Nevada was having quite the opposite effect on a certain portion of his anatomy, an effect that was going to be really hard to camouflage once he stood up.

Nevada frowned, then grabbed his arm and cinched down hard. "The Jeep. What if he—they—trace us by tracing the Jeep?"

He laid his hand over hers. "Why would they? They don't even know we're together."

"But it's a logical assumption," she argued.

"You're right. It is." He gave her hand a comforting squeeze, then gently detached it from his arm. "We'll switch cars, but not until tomorrow. For now, you need to rest."

She frowned again. "I'm not sleepy."

"Well, *I* am," he lied.

She brushed her fingertips across his chest. "Hold me," she whispered. "Please."

He pushed her hand aside almost roughly, and

when he spoke, his voice sounded raspy. "If I hold you, I can't guarantee I'll stop at just holding."

Nevada's gaze never faltered. "I was hoping you'd say that."

She didn't understand what she was suggesting. Hell, she was still half asleep. "Nevada, I—"

"Shh." She pressed a fingertip to his lips.

Or maybe he was the one who was asleep. Maybe this was all a dream. A titillating, X–rated—

"Hold me." Nevada draped her arms around his neck. "Kiss me. Love me."

She felt real enough, warm and soft, a living, breathing temptation. Cherries and oranges. The faint scents teased his nostrils. Probably just her shampoo. Or maybe her lip balm. But *damn* . . . "You smell delicious."

She nibbled at his lower lip. "And you taste delicious."

He pulled back, frowning. "This is crazy."

"Probably." Her smile was both sweet and seductive.

God help him, he wanted her. Fiercely. Desperately.

Nevada drew one of his hands to her lips and pressed a kiss to his palm. "I need this right now," she whispered. "I need you."

God, who could resist? Not him, for damned sure.

She smoothed out her top sheet, then tossed it back and moved over to make room on the bed. Nevada might have the face of an angel, but there was nothing innocent about the lush curves that rose above the top edge of her bra or the tight nipples straining against the silky white fabric.

Wordlessly, he slid in beside her, then let his hands

drift over her curves, squeezing here, rubbing there, learning the texture of her skin.

Her eyes widened and her cheeks flushed. He wondered for a second if she'd changed her mind, but then she said, "Aren't you going to get the light?" her voice a little shaky, and he realized she was just embarrassed.

He trailed the pad of his thumb down her neck.

Her pulse raced. Her breathing quickened. "I—"

"You're beautiful," he told her, leaning forward to nuzzle the unbandaged portion of her throat. "Too beautiful to hide in the dark."

"Beautiful? You think so?" She pulled back, and he saw that a fresh wave of color had tinted her cheeks a delicious pink. "But my hair's all messy and my—"

He pressed a finger to her lips. "Beautiful," he repeated. Then he used that same finger to trace the soft skin along the top edge of her bra. "And sexy." He leaned over her, pressing a kiss to her abdomen halfway between her navel and the narrow elastic band on her panties. "And very, very desirable."

She was shivering again, but not, he suspected, with cold this time. "Oh, God."

"If I start to go too fast, say something, and I'll slow it down," he told her. "It's been a long, dry period for me."

"Me, too." Her voice emerged shaky and breathless. "In fact, I literally don't remember the last time it rained."

"But you *have* had sex before?"

"I must have." She gasped as he slid one hand between her thighs. "According to my medical records, I'm not a virgin."

"Only you don't remember having sex with anyone, do you?" he persisted as he stroked her. Back and forth. Back and forth.

She gave a muffled groan. "No."

"So it'll be like I'm the first."

"Yes." Though she was breathing hard, obviously aroused, a smile once again played at the corners of her mouth. "But no pressure."

Trick's eyebrows rose. His mouth curved in a devilish smile. "No pressure?" he repeated softly.

Nevada's nipples hardened in response.

Trick noticed. She knew he did. As his narrowed gaze raked her body, she experienced an actual physical sensation, a tingling shiver of anticipation.

He made a sound, half growl, half groan. Then he shifted lower, suckling one nipple right through her bra while the hand between her thighs teased her unmercifully.

Her tension escalated into the unbearable zone. She squirmed and shuddered, not sure whether she wanted him to stop the torture or to continue it forever. She burned. She ached. She needed. She . . .

A sudden burst of ecstasy took her by surprise. She gasped, then surrendering herself to sensation, rode the seemingly endless crest of pleasure. On and on. Peak after undulating peak. Every time she thought it was over, Trick would use his clever mouth and talented fingers to tease her right back to the summit.

She collapsed against the pillows when he finally released her. "Oh," was all she managed to say, which didn't make a whole lot of sense, but damn it, her thoughts were totally scattered and completely incoherent. Hard to know what she thought—if she thought—but easy to identify what she felt. Bliss. Utter bliss.

"Nevada?"

She forced her eyes open with an effort.

Trick, propped on one elbow, stared down at her, smiling faintly as if he liked what he saw.

"Mmm?"

"You want to try that again?" He leaned down to brush her lips with his.

She uttered an inarticulate moan. "Again?"

"The real deal this time."

"Mmm," she said. If the man could spark multiple orgasms, using nothing but his mouth and a couple of fingers, what undreamed-of level of ecstasy could he trigger if he put himself into it body and soul?

She glanced back at Trick, who was frowning un-certainly, apparently unsure how to interpret her muted response. "What do you say, Nevada?"

"Yes," she told him. "Yes, please."

His eyebrows shot up, and fire seemed to flicker for an instant in the depths of his eye. "She begs." His mouth twisted in a sardonic smile, and he looked—*oh God*—he looked every inch the pirate.

"I didn't beg," she protested. "I just asked politely."

His smile grew into a wicked grin. "Nothing polite about what I have planned for you, lady. Take off the underwear."

"Yours or mine?"

"Already lost mine," he said.

She glanced down and realized he had. Trick was naked. Extremely naked. Insistently naked.

She stroked him, surprised at how warm and velvety soft the tautly stretched skin felt against her fingertips.

His groan of pleasure seemed to restore her energy. One minute, she was lying down, sated and a little drowsy. The next, she'd stripped off the constricting underwear and shoved Trick onto his back so she could climb astride him.

"Hey," he muttered in a halfhearted protest. "Who's seducing whom here?"

She lowered her mouth to within a whisper of his. "You talk too much, mister. Shut up and kiss me."

So he kissed her. It started as a soft little brush of the lips, slowly deepening into a wildly arousing tangle of tongues, hot and desperate.

He cupped. He caressed.

She teased. She touched.

He suckled. He spanked.

She squirmed. She squeezed.

But when she started to lower herself onto him, Trick stopped her. "Condom," he said, sounding strained. He crawled out of bed to rummage through his discarded clothing.

Nevada curled into a ball. What was wrong with her? Had she completely lost her mind? She'd almost had unprotected sex—would have had unprotected sex if Trick hadn't stopped her. A reckless move. Foolhardy. And yet, she could hardly bring herself to care. Her body's insistent clamoring drowned out the voice of reason. She wanted him.

God, what was taking him so long? Her breasts ached. Her mouth hungered. Her whole body felt tingly and needy. Unfinished.

Trick dug a condom from his wallet, ripped it open, and pulled it on. Then he all but flung himself onto the bed, and when she would have climbed on top, easily flipped her onto her back, pinning her arms down as he drove himself into her with one long, steady thrust. His hands and mouth were everywhere at once, touching her, stroking her, tasting her, teasing her.

"You feel so good," he said, his voice hoarse. He nuzzled her neck and squeezed her breasts as he filled her again and again in powerful, rhythmic thrusts. Desire licked at her like flames, burning, burning. She wanted. She needed. She needed. She wanted.

One more wild thrust and she'd ignite. Simply go up in flames.

Suddenly, Trick pulled out of her and she moaned a protest, which he stifled with one, long, soul-searing kiss. He rolled off her, then smiling in an unspoken promise, suckled her breasts and flicked at her sensitized clitoris until she was moaning and writhing uncontrollably. She stared wordlessly when he spread her trembling thighs. She gasped when he buried himself in her.

Then he started again. Thrust after thrust. Over and over. And once again her tension escalated, each jolt pushing her closer to the edge until at last she toppled headlong into an abyss of sensation. A burst of pleasure, intense and shockingly, frighteningly out of control, seemed to affect her on a molecular level, as if Trick's final thrust had splintered her into a million throbbing fragments of ecstasy. Incredible. Exquisite. Like nothing she'd ever imagined.

Neither of them spoke for a long, long time.

When Nevada's body finally quit tingling, when her brain finally quit spinning, when all her bits and pieces finally coalesced once more into a coherent whole, she nudged Trick's shoulder. "Is it always like that?"

He roused himself enough to twist his head so he could look her in the eye. "Like what?"

She thought about that for a second. How was she to describe that tsunami of incredible sensation? "Like . . . wow?" she said uncertainly.

Trick smiled. "Maybe we should try it again and see."

At intervals throughout the night, Trick had pleasured Nevada with exquisite care. Sometime after three, he'd finally turned out the light, and mindless, boneless, bodies snuggled close, limbs entwined, they'd both drifted into sleep on a wave of utter contentment.

But that was then, and this was now. Nevada was ready for more. No, desperate for more. How long had she been asleep?

No light leaked in between the slats of the blinds. Still night then. She lifted herself up so she could see the alarm clock's glowing green numbers. Seven after five. Not night. Morning. Very early morning.

She grazed Trick's shoulder with her teeth, sucked at his earlobe, nipped at his lower lip. "Wake up, sleepyhead."

Moving pretty quickly for someone who'd been

snoring softly only seconds ago, Trick grabbed her hand and wrapped it around his erection. "Am I going to have to use my last condom?"

She gave him a squeeze. "What do you think?"

"I think I need that condom."

He covered himself and then lay down, linking his hands behind his head. "I'm all yours."

Trick had tortured her with a slow seduction, but this time she was in control, and slow wasn't what she had in mind. Straddling him, she eased him inside, then rocked back and forth, squeezing hard.

He groaned. "Hey, take it easy."

"No way." Her excitement spiked with each squeeze. His, too, judging by the sounds he made. "You feel so good in me," she whispered.

He managed another inarticulate groan.

"Really, really good." She rocked faster, squeezed harder.

He caught the rhythm then, his thrusts coinciding with the clenching of her internal muscles. Faster and faster. Harder and harder.

She gasped in response to a particularly well-placed thrust. "Touch me. Please." Her breasts, she meant. Swollen and tender, they ached with need.

He made another sound, half growl, half agreement. Then he reached up, cupping her breasts in his hands.

"More," she begged, leaning down toward him. So close. She was so close.

He rolled one nipple between his thumb and fore-finger, then sucked the tip of the other into his mouth, licking and sucking until she was crazy with need.

An orgasm took her, endless waves of bliss. On and on and on it went until she thought she'd die if it lasted another second, knew she'd die if it didn't.

Trick stilled for a second, his muscles clenched tight, then he groaned his release, and a pleasure so intense that it verged on pain, rocked Nevada in an explosive finale.

Gradually, her pulse slowed. She snuggled close to Trick. Neither of them said a word for a long time. Then Trick shifted his position, removed the used condom, and dropped it in the waste basket. "Just so you know, that was the last of my protection."

She wriggled closer, laying her head on his chest, comforted by the steady sound of his heartbeat under her ear. "Just so you know," she said, "I'm all out of energy. But . . ." She hesitated. "You were planning to buy more condoms once it's light, right?"

"Right." Trick wrapped his arms around her.

Nevada had never felt safer.

A telephone call had awakened Daniel Snowden from a sound sleep, but that in itself didn't explain his anger. He sat on the edge of his bed, grinding his teeth together in an effort to control his fury, an effort that was not altogether successful. "Would you mind repeating that?" he said into the phone, his voice quiet but edged with a deadly menace his political opponents would have recognized. And feared. But Sarge Collier wasn't an opponent. He was part of Daniel's team.

The big vampire and former Army Ranger cleared his throat. "Billy Branson got himself dusted."

"That's what I thought you said. What the fuck happened this time?"

"Faraday, that demon hunter who used to be a deputy up north, shot Billy through the heart with a crossbow."

"And how did Faraday know where to find Billy?"

"Lucky guess?" Sarge said.

"Try again," Daniel snapped. "You two have been feeding on humans again, haven't you? Leaving a trail of blood a blind man could follow."

"No," Sarge protested.

Daniel jumped to his feet and strode naked back and forth across his bedroom. "No?"

"Okay, maybe one. A homeless kid, teenage girl we found turning tricks on a street corner in Oakland."

"And that's it? Just the hooker?"

"Well," Sarge said. "I guess maybe there was one more, though she hardly counts. Old lady we spotted sitting all alone in an all-night Laundromat."

"Damn it, Sarge. Where was that?"

"Vacaville, I think."

"You *think*?"

Sarge grunted. "Could have been Fairfield, I guess. Or maybe Davis. No." He paused. "Davis was where . . ."

"Where what? Do I have to drag this out of you one word at a time? Or are you going to tell me the whole thing?"

"There was this smart-ass college kid, see? And he was giving Billy a raft of shit. You know Billy. That is, you knew Billy. He didn't take shit from anybody."

"Killed the kid, did he?"

"Beat him to a pulp, then drained him. We dragged

the body out into the country, dumped it in an irrigation canal. Guess some farmer must have found it."

"It's a damned good thing Billy's dead," Daniel said, "because if that stupid bastard was alive, I'd dust him myself. And Sarge?"

"Yeah?"

"If you don't straighten up, I'll dust *your* ass. Got it?"

"Got it," Sarge said.

"Where's Faraday now?" Daniel asked.

Silence on the other end. "I don't know," Sarge finally admitted.

"Is there any chance he could have followed you?"

"No, I don't think so, but—"

"Good. Confine your blood-sucking to wild animals and strays. That's stray animals, not stray people. Got it?"

"Got it."

"Stay under the radar, and you'll be able to avoid demon hunters." He paused for a second or two, somehow sure he hadn't heard the worst of it yet. "What else aren't you telling me?" he asked at length. "Where are you now?"

"Midas Lake," Sarge answered, his tone a fraction away from sullen. "We did what you told us to, came back here to beat the truth out of the two guys with the Jeep. Only one guy in the house when we got here, though. After a little persuasion, he admitted the girl had been there all along, living in the caretaker's apartment. He claimed he didn't know where she was. I figured he was lying. Unfortunately, Billy got carried away, hit him a little too hard and he lost consciousness, so we just left him tied up, then headed over to the apartment to wait for the girl to get back from wherever the hell she was."

Daniel's heart beat a little faster in anticipation of some good news at last. He licked his lips. "You eliminated her?"

"I had her down, was getting ready to finish the job, but then all hell broke loose. Some guy came after me with a shovel and Faraday dusted Billy. I was damned lucky to escape without being dusted myself."

Daniel slammed one clenched fist down on the window sill. "So she eluded you again."

Sarge didn't say anything.

"You really are a worthless piece of scum, Collier."

"I'll get her. I promise. Just give me a little more time."

"You know where she is then?"

"No, I . . . the bastard hit me a hell of a blow with that shovel, addled my brains for a minute or two—"

"A minute or two?" Daniel murmured.

"And Faraday was right on my tail. I finally managed to elude him, pretended I was headed toward Reno, then circled back this way after I lost him."

"But when you got back to Midas Lake, the bird had flown."

"I . . . yes. The Jeep was gone, the house locked up."

"I presume you searched it anyway."

"I did. The place was empty, looked like they'd left in a hurry, too. I thought . . . the reason I called you was, I thought maybe you knew somebody who could trace the license plate, maybe report the Jeep stolen and put out an APB."

"Sarge, you surprise me," Daniel said. "I hadn't thought you capable of such a rational approach."

"Thanks," Sarge said, sounding a little dubious about it, as well he should.

"But if I use my connections, my influence, to draw official attention to the Jeep and those in it, what do you suppose might happen when at least one of its occupants turns up dead. Where might the authorities look to find the culprit?"

"I hadn't thought of that," Sarge said.

"And why," asked Daniel, "am I not surprised?"

Someone thumped the door two or three times.

Nevada woke with a start. Sarge, she thought, her heart racing, but then realized almost immediately how ridiculous that was. Bad guys didn't knock.

Another couple of thumps on the door were followed by a woman with a thick Spanish accent saying, "Housekeeping."

"Come back later," Nevada called.

Apparently, the maid didn't hear her because the lock clicked as a keycard was inserted.

The door was fully open and the cart shoved halfway into the room before the maid realized her mistake. She gasped. "*Lo siento.* I come back later." Then she backed out about twice as fast as she'd entered.

Nevada didn't blame her. Must have been quite a shock to see a man's bare backside in a room she'd presumed to be empty. Trick lay facedown on the bed, a pillow over his head, the rest of him as naked as the day he was born. Next to him lay Nevada, equally naked but at least partially covered by the sheet. "Should have thought to hang up the Do Not Disturb sign," she muttered to herself.

"Hmm?" Trick said.

"A woman from housekeeping was just here."

"What time is it?" He tossed the pillow aside and twisted onto his side to squint at the clock. "One thirty-six. Holy shit. I knew I was tired, but hell, we've got to get moving."

"Moving where?" Nevada asked. "We can't go back to Midas Lake. It isn't safe."

"Can't go anywhere," Trick said, "until we get some new wheels. You were right about the Wrangler being too easy to trace."

"When the maid knocked, I thought at first it was Sarge," Nevada confessed. "Silly, I know, but . . ."

Trick draped a comforting arm around her shoulders and planted a kiss on her cheek. "Not silly. Wary. And under the circumstances, wary makes a lot of sense. Wary's what's going to keep you alive."

"Alive is good," she agreed. "But the thing is, your chances for longevity would increase dramatically if you'd just go your own way. I am not your responsibility, Trick."

"No," he said. "You're my weakness."

Nevada felt as if he'd stabbed her right through the heart. "Look, I have feelings for you, too. I admit it, but if things were switched around, I wouldn't insist on accompanying you."

"Yes, you would," he said.

"No," she insisted. "Chivalry's part of a male's genetic

makeup, the same way nurturing's part of a female's."

"Maybe so, but—"

"I don't want to argue with you, Trick."

"Then don't."

"Face it, I'm a danger magnet. I don't pretend to know why, but facts are facts. Look what happened to Marcello. All my fault." She held his face between her hands, forcing him to make eye contact. "I don't want the same thing to happen to you. This is my problem, and it's up to me to find the solution."

"Or fail in the attempt," he said, his expression grim.

Releasing him, she nodded. "Or fail in the attempt."

This time he was the one to initiate eye contact. He tilted her chin so she was forced to meet his gaze. "Let's go to Mexico," he said. "Just you and me. We could blend in with the tourists in Acapulco or Puerta Vallarta. You'd be safe. The bad guys would never find you there."

She nodded. "Probably not. But I'd still be Subject 111. I still wouldn't know who I was or where I came from. And I need to know. Can you understand that?"

"Even if the search puts your life in danger?"

"Even then," she said.

His jaw set stubbornly. "Okay, but you're not going to launch this search on your own. I'm going with you."

"But—"

His kiss effectively silenced her. Blew a few circuits in her brain, too.

"We're in this together."

"Together," she repeated, hardly aware of what she was saying.

He kissed her again, and her mental capacity degraded even further. All she wanted in that moment was for him to keep doing what he was doing with his lips and tongue and yes, with the thumb that was brushing back and forth across her nipple in the most maddening way possible.

His mouth left hers to feather kisses across her cheekbone. "What's our next move?" he whispered in her ear.

"Insert tab A in slot B?"

He laughed softly. "No more tab slotting," he said. "Not until I buy more condoms. That wasn't the kind of move I was talking about anyway. What I meant was, where do we go from here? How do we go about finding out who you are?"

"I have an address in San Francisco," she told him. "It was the only thing approaching personal information that was included in my file at the Institute."

Trick sat up. "The jeweler who made Blanche's ring was from San Francisco, too."

"So was Blanche herself."

"Looks like San Francisco, here we come," Trick said. "But first I need to shower and shave."

"We could shower together," she suggested. "Save a little hot water."

He grinned. "Not until I buy those condoms."

TWELVE

Marcello glanced up from his laptop as Britt let herself into the suite. Her face was flushed from her afternoon run, her eyes bright, her long blond hair tousled. She had never looked more desirable. He tore his gaze away from her, focusing once again on the laptop's screen. "Did you have an enjoyable run in Pioneer Park?" he asked politely.

"It was okay, a little windy. I had to dodge a few kids flying kites."

"Your cheeks are pink," he observed before he could censor himself. Then to make matters even worse, he added. "You look very . . . healthy." What madness had prompted him to make personal observations, observations that might be construed as compliments, albeit clumsy compliments?

Britt's color deepened, but she made no reply. "Do you need anything? A snack or whatever?"

"I am fine," he said.

"Well, uh, okay then. I'm going to take a shower."

And did that not present a tantalizing visual? Marcello was suddenly thankful that he was sitting down.

"Oh, wait. I almost forgot." Britt paused with one hand on the knob of her bedroom door. "Guess who I ran into at the park?"

A twinge of jealousy pinched at his chest. "Ethan Faraday?"

"Who?" she said, looking puzzled.

"Faraday. He stayed here a while back."

"Oh, right," Britt said. "I remember. Big guy with cowboy boots and permanent beard stubble, looks kind of like Matthew McConaughey."

"Matthew . . . ?"

"Movie star," Britt said. "And no, it wasn't Faraday. It was Jonathan Calhoun from the Midas Lake Historical Society."

"I am not familiar—"

"He's the one who's been helping Nevada research Trick's ghost."

"I see."

"Seems he found a tell-all letter written by Silas Granger and addressed to Blanche. It was wedged into one of the brothel ledgers."

"Fascinating, I am sure."

"It will be to Nevada. Jonathan said he planned to call her with the news, but I told him she was out of town. Did Trick say anything when you talked to him about when he planned to check in next?"

"This evening sometime."

"Any idea where they are?"

"No." Marcello frowned. "And I prefer it that way. I cannot reveal what I do not know."

Fear flickered across Britt's face. "You think he'll come back, don't you? The man who . . ."

"Tortured me? It is all right to say it. And yes, I think he will return. I also think that if he can find me, he will torture more secrets from me." He paused, frowning unseeingly at his laptop's screen. "I never questioned my own integrity, never dreamed I would betray another to protect myself, but all it took to persuade me to talk was a few cigarette burns. The worst part is, I know in my heart I would do it again. That is why I do not want to know where Trick and Nevada have gone or what they are doing." He took a calming breath. "When Trick does contact me, I will pass on the information about the letter. Nevada can contact Mr. Calhoun."

Britt's expression softened. "You're too hard on yourself, Marcello. You think you're a coward, but you're not. Anyone would have caved in that situation."

He did not respond. What was the point in arguing? Britt could make all the excuses she wanted, but he knew the truth. A truly brave man would not have talked. No matter what.

They'd checked out of the motel almost three hours late, which meant Trick had had to pay for an extra night. Nevada had felt a little guilty about that expense on top of the truly sumptuous lunch Trick had treated her to, so when he pulled into a mall, she was moved to protest. "Why are we stopping here?"

"If we expect to stay with my great-aunt Leticia for the next few days, we'll need proper luggage."

"We're staying with your great-aunt Leticia?"

"I figure it'll be easier to keep a low profile if we stay at a private residence instead of registering at a hotel."

"Okay, but what is your great-aunt going to think when we just show up on her doorstep with no warning?"

"She's had warning. I called her earlier while you were in the shower."

"And she didn't mind the unexpected company?"

"Mind? She was ecstatic. The woman adores entertaining, and I'm her favorite great-nephew."

"Meaning what?" Nevada asked, skepticism edging her voice. "You're her only great-nephew?"

"Yes." Trick grinned. "But that's beside the point." He got out of the Jeep, then came around to open Nevada's door. "Time to shop."

She let him help her out and herd her toward the mall entrance. "Shop for what?"

"I told you already. We'll need proper luggage and all the clothing and toiletries necessary to fill it."

"And we're going to pay for this how? If you think I'm going to squander my little hoard of hard-earned cash just to impress your great-aunt—"

"It's not Great-aunt Leticia who worries me. It's Rivers, her butler. The man's a dreadful snob, not to mention a terrible gossip."

"But—"

"Low profile," he reminded her. "We want to fly

under the radar. Hell, just think of it as camouflage."

"But—"

"Money's not a problem." He dug a stack of hundreds from his wallet and handed it to her.

"But I thought . . ."

"What?"

"I thought you were virtually broke. Marcello said . . ."

"Marcello said what?"

"That your former financial adviser had run off with all your money."

"Not *all* my money," he said. "Just most of it. I still have assets in excess of a million dollars. Of course in Granger terms, that makes me a pauper."

"I see." She frowned. "There's poor, and then there's Granger poor."

He grinned. "Otherwise known as middle class."

Daniel surveyed the crowd gathered at the Papillon Mall for the Mother's Day Weekend Blow-Out Sale. Carlos Santiago-Ortiz, his campaign manager, had arranged for Daniel, front runner in the race to be named the Democratic candidate for governor, to say a few words prior to the kickoff of the afternoon's special event, a donkey basketball game in the center courtyard. After all, what said Mother's Day like donkey basketball?

"I bet you could count the registered voters on the fingers of one hand," Daniel whispered to his stepmother, Regina. Still beautiful at fifty, Regina just smiled and waved to the crowd, as if she, not he, were the one running for office.

"You're up," Carlos said, passing Daniel the microphone.

He launched into his prepared speech, full of humorous anecdotes and a saccharine reference to Regina, then finished with a joke at the current governor's expense, earning laughter, applause, and a few cheers.

With a smile glued to his face, he endured half an hour of baby kissing and handshaking before his security people started moving him toward the exit and the waiting limo.

A few feet from the exit, Regina suddenly leaned forward and squeezed his arm. "Look! Over there by the bookstore. I could have sworn . . . but no. That's absurd."

"What's absurd?" he asked, distracted by a glimpse of a seven-foot-tall basketball player riding past on a four-foot-tall donkey.

"I saw a woman, and for a second, I thought it was Whitney."

Daniel stopped dead in his tracks. "Whitney? Are you sure?"

Regina gave her trademark tinkle of laughter. "No, silly. Of course, it wasn't Whitney. I just thought so for an instant. Something about her profile."

"Where?" Daniel demanded, his gaze darting about the mall's enormous central court.

"She was over by the bookstore, but she's long gone now." Regina, more accustomed to sycophantic cajolery than abrupt demands, spoke haughtily.

Damn it. Was it possible? Could he be this lucky?

"Carlos!" he raised his voice just enough to catch his campaign manager's attention.

"Yes, Representative Snowden?" Carlos turned to face him. "Is there a problem?"

"I want you to do me a favor." He dug a picture from his wallet and handed it to the other man.

Carlos glanced at the photograph, then back up at Daniel, confusion written across his face. "Yes, sir?"

"Have some of the security team members stay behind and search for the young woman in this picture." He turned to his stepmother. "What was she wearing, Regina?"

"I don't remember. Nothing special. Certainly not a designer label."

"Slacks? A dress?"

"No, jeans and a sweater, I think. Possibly a sweatshirt."

"What color?"

"Black. No, navy. No, black, or maybe a very dark green." His impatience must have shown, because her nostrils flared. "Don't give me that pissy look, Daniel. I told you I didn't remember."

Wincing mentally, hoping no one of consequence had overheard that "pissy," Daniel glued an amiable expression on his face.

"I don't see why you're making such a fuss anyway. Let's just go," Regina said. "The limo's waiting."

"You go. I'll be there in a minute. I need a word in private with Carlos."

She shot him a narrow-eyed look, then flounced toward the exit.

He waited until she'd disappeared from sight before turning once again to his campaign manager.

At first, Nevada had thought she was being completely paranoid. How ridiculous, she'd lectured herself, to feel so exposed, so vulnerable in a cheerfully crowded public venue like a shopping mall. But she hadn't been able to quell her jitters.

Twice now, she'd caught people staring at her as if she were some sort of three-headed monster. She'd shrugged it off the first time, telling herself that the woman she'd thought was gaping at her had really been looking at someone behind her, most likely one of the bizarre donkey-mounted basketball players that had seemed to be everywhere.

But the second time, there hadn't been any donkey-mounted basketball players around. In fact, there hadn't been anyone much around when she'd noticed the young man in a suit staring fixedly at her. So naturally, when she'd seen him speak into a walkie-talkie, she'd panicked and raced to the nearest women's restroom.

Which was a great solution in the short term, since it seemed fairly unlikely that Mr. Walkie-Talkie would come barging into the restroom after her. As a long-term solution, however, her restroom hideout left something to be desired, because really all Mr. Walkie-Talkie had to do was wait for her to make a break for it. And what was worse, he was probably using the damned walkie-talkie to call up reinforcements. Possibly even female reinforcements.

Okay, she told herself, *get a grip.* Just because the guy was wearing a suit didn't mean he was in cahoots with the monsters who'd chased her across the country. Lots of people wore suits. Lawyers and salesmen and funeral home directors. Professors and ministers and stockbrokers. But why take chances, especially when the risks were so high? Best case scenario, she could end up back in the Appleton Institute. Worst case scenario, she could end up an exsanguinated corpse.

She stared at the dusky pink walls of the stall where she'd been hiding for the last ten minutes and racked her brains for a workable escape plan. Okay, plan one: She could walk out into the hall and scream her head off if Mr. Walkie-Talkie so much as glanced in her direction. The possible drawback here was that such behavior was just as likely to get her tossed in the loony bin as it was to get him tossed in jail. So, she needed to keep thinking.

Plan two: She could escape out the window. Or not. By standing upright on the toilet, she could see over the stalls to the far wall. No windows. Not even a vent.

Which brought her to plan three. She could take a page out of the Hollywood playbook and escape through the heating-slash-air-conditioning ducts. Only that would require her to stand on someone's shoulders in order to reach the ceiling panels, and she didn't see anyone volunteering for that job.

Or . . .

A small mob of teenagers had come in a few minutes ago to primp in front of the mirror. If she timed her departure to coincide with theirs . . . Yes, it just might work.

She flushed the empty toilet, then emerged from her cubicle and made her way to the row of sinks on the opposite wall. She rushed through the hand-washing ritual, tossing a handful of paper towels at the waste bin before crowding her way into the middle of the pack of teens as they moved toward the exit.

Mr. Walkie-Talkie was right where he'd been when she'd first spotted him. Only now, he had company, a second man in a suit equipped with his own walkie-talkie. Luckily, she spotted them before they had a chance to spot her. She managed to pass within five feet of the pair without being seen by keeping a chunky girl in a lacy olive-drab tunic and camo-patterned leggings between her and them.

When she saw Trick waiting for her under the big clock in the food court just as they'd arranged earlier, she was so relieved, she nearly burst into tears.

"Let's get out of here," she said, doing her best to hustle him along.

"Wouldn't you like something to drink?" he asked. "Shopping is thirsty work."

So she told him about Mr. Walkie-Talkie.

"You say both men had walkie-talkies?" He started in the direction of the escalators, but she dragged him toward the staircase instead.

"Right." Nevada all but ran down the steps, dodging awkwardly around other shoppers, trying not to take anyone out with her heavy, overstuffed shopping bags. She paused for a second at the bottom to let Trick catch up.

"Guys with walkie-talkies sound more like mall security to me than bad guys."

"You didn't see the way he stared at me, Trick."

"Could be there's a perfectly reasonable explanation for that."

"Such as?" she challenged, edging around the outside of the central court where the donkey basketball game was still in full swing.

"Maybe someone reported a shoplifter and you fit the description."

"Okay," she conceded as they slipped out the main doors into the parking lot. "You could be right, and I could be paranoid, but—"

"But nothing." Trick grabbed her arm and pulled her down into a crouching position behind a big Dodge Ram pickup.

"What is it?" she asked, trying to peer around the truck's rear bumper.

"Let's just say I'm wrong, and you're not paranoid. Men in suits are watching the Wrangler."

"The Wrangler? So friends of Sarge's then. Mall security wouldn't know what we were driving."

"Friends of Sarge maybe, but not vampires," Trick said.

"How can you be sure? Oh! Because they're standing around outside in the sunlight," she said, answering her own question. "A major vampire no-no." She shot Trick a sideways glance. "Any idea how we can get to the Wrangler, unlock the doors, slip inside, and drive out of the parking lot without being seen?"

He shot her an exasperated look. "Not unless you know a foolproof invisibility spell."

"Sorry," she said. "My crazy doesn't come in that flavor."

"I didn't think so."

"So what's our next move?" she asked. "This escape's on your shoulders. I used up a year's worth of ingenuity sneaking out of that restroom."

"Well," he said, "we could find an unlocked car and hot-wire it."

"Steal a car? Surely there's another way."

"I hope so," he said, "because I'm not sure I *could* hot-wire a car."

She shrugged. "I suppose we could walk out to the main street and hitchhike from there. Or not," she added when she saw his expression. "I told you I'd used up my quota of ingenuity. Your turn."

He chewed thoughtfully on his lower lip. "How about this? I call a taxi on my cell phone. The taxi takes us to the airport where we rent a car and then drive to my great-aunt's house in San Francisco."

Nevada squeezed his hand. "That just might work."

Itchy. That was how Marcello felt, as if he had been cooped up for months instead of a day. He needed to exercise his body, not just his self-control.

Britt was driving him insane. Not on purpose, but still, it was the end result that mattered. Being around her all day every day—seeing her first thing in the morning in a figure-hugging tank top and silky pajama bottoms, her eyes sleepy, her hair falling around her shoulders in sexy disarray, and last thing at night as she moved with sinuous grace through her ritual pilates routine, her skin flushed, her eyes bright—was enough to drive any man insane with lust, let alone a man who had been infatuated with her for months. If he did not use up some of this excess energy, he was going to explode. Or do something inexcusable.

There was a workout room downstairs and an indoor pool, as well. Either would have provided a release for his growing tension. Unfortunately, both were off limits. He had to stay out of the public eye in case Sarge came poking around again.

Which in the abstract made perfectly good sense. He had not enjoyed that first round of torture and definitely was willing to do whatever it took to avoid a second. On the other hand, if he did not find some way to siphon off all this extra energy, he was liable to do something both he and Britt would live to regret.

Downstairs, lodge guests, along with half the population of Midas Lake, had gathered for a talent show Britt called Lakeshore Lodge Idol. Every once in a while, a contestant's high note would penetrate to the second floor. A few of them were even on pitch.

He paced restlessly from one end of Britt's suite to the other, glancing every so often at the clock on the mantle. Almost eight thirty. Trick should be calling back any time now. He had promised to check in once he and Nevada had settled in for the night, though he had been careful not to tell Marcello where exactly that would be.

Marcello paused at the big bay window in the sitting room and peered down at the moonlit beach. *Che diamine!* No one was down there at this time of night. No boats on the water, either.

Deserted.

The perfect place for him to vent his frustrations in a vigorous run.

Only he really should linger here until Trick called.

He glared resentfully at the phone.

If he called.

Of course, now that Marcello thought about it, was that not why answering machines had been invented?

Five minutes later, having changed into sweats and cross-trainers, he slipped unnoticed down the back stairs, through the deserted kitchen, and out the service entrance.

The mountain air was chilly but not unpleasantly so. On the whole, though he would never have admitted as much to Trick, he approved of the Sierras. In many ways, they reminded him of his beloved Alps.

The air smelled of pine resin and, as he drew closer to the beach, the not unpleasant, faintly fishy odor he associated with rivers and freshwater lakes. The trees thinned, gradually giving way to the beach, a strip of sand that stretched along the water's edge. Beyond, like an enormous mirror, the lake lay still and glassy with scarcely a ripple to disturb its surface. A half-moon, milky white against the glittering backdrop of a star-studded sky, was reflected in the placid lake, as if the missing half had broken free and fallen to earth, where it lay trapped beneath the surface of the water.

Back and forth he ran from the rocky outcropping that marked the beginning of Trick's property to the reedy area beyond the boat dock that marked the end of Britt's. Back and forth, back and forth, reveling in the repetitive movement, in the almost joyous expenditure of energy. And while his body labored, his mind drifted free.

Antonia.

They'd been just fifteen the first time they'd met at the wedding of Antonia's older brother, Matteo, to Marcello's second cousin, Paola. Antonia's effervescent personality alone would have made her stand out in that veritable crowd of bridesmaids even if she hadn't been the only diminutive brunette in a line of statuesque blondes.

He had danced with her at the reception, danced with her, talked with her, laughed with her, but he had not realized until almost six years later, that he had also fallen in love with her that night. Once the truth had finally dawned on him, he had proposed. Three months later, they had been married.

They'd had exactly two days of wedded bliss. And then his sweet, funny, vivacious Antonia had been run down by a drunk driver and left for dead.

Severe trauma to the brain, the doctors had said. She would most likely never emerge from the coma. But Marcello had refused to accept their pessimistic diagnosis. Fifty times a day, he offered up the same prayer: *Please, God, let Antonia wake up.*

Miraculously, twenty-six days after the hit-and-run, his prayers had been answered. Antonia regained consciousness.

But in a cruel twist, she had not recognized him, had not recognized anyone, had not spoken a word or responded to one. Antonia, his Antonia, was gone. All that remained was a soulless body.

Faster and faster Marcello ran, ignoring the tears streaming down his face.

THIRTEEN

Trick parked the rental car, an anonymous silver Toyota Camry, in the short steep driveway of his great-aunt Leticia's three-story Pacific Heights Edwardian. The house, which had been in the family since it was built shortly after the 1906 quake, perched on a hill above San Francisco Bay. Day or night, the view was breathtaking, and the drive up to Pierce Street, dramatic. Though Nevada, sound asleep in the passenger seat, had missed it. He leaned across to nudge her shoulder. "We're here." Several hours later than he'd originally planned after their late start and all the backtracking he'd done to be sure they weren't being followed, but here.

She moaned a protest. "What time is it?"

"Almost ten."

"So early? Feels like midnight." Nevada stretched and yawned.

"Ten's not early for an octogenarian. I hope Great-aunt Leticia hasn't gone to bed already."

As if on cue, the exterior lights lit up. "Someone's awake," Nevada said.

Before he had a chance to ring the doorbell, the front door swung open, revealing his diminutive great-aunt, exotic tonight in a flamboyant red wig and black satin lounging pajamas. Though pushing ninety, she didn't look a day under a hundred.

Behind her and to the left—and right—stood Rivers. At six feet seven and nearly four hundred pounds, Arthur Kiyoshi Rivers, looked more like a sumo wrestler than a butler.

"Patrick darling, come in. And you, too, my dear. I'd like to say my nephew has told me all about you, but the truth is, he's been quite deliberately reticent, which means, frankly, I can't wait to start grilling you."

Nevada glanced sideways at Trick, a panicky expression on her face.

He gave her hand a squeeze, but judging by the way she clung to him, her anxiety level remained high.

"Goodness, where are my manners? Come in, come in," Great-aunt Leticia trilled.

Trick led Nevada forward into the marble-floored foyer so Rivers could wedge his bulk in behind them and shut the door. "Great-aunt Leticia, this is Nevada White, the young woman I told you about. Nevada, my great-aunt, Leticia Granger."

Great-aunt Leticia wagged a reproving finger at him. "I think what you mean, Patrick, is that Nevada's the young woman you *didn't* tell me about." She grinned and her wrinkled face rearranged itself into a whole new configuration of lines and creases.

"Not much I *can* tell," Trick said. "She's in danger. Some very bad men are trying to kill her. We had an unexpected encounter with some of them this afternoon in Sacramento. That's why we're late."

Great-aunt Leticia's grin faded, giving way to a look of compunction. She leaned forward and patted Nevada's hand. "Forgive me, my dear. I'm a garrulous old woman with more curiosity than good sense."

"Don't believe her," Trick told Nevada. "She's sharp as a tack, knows everyone in the city."

"I do have a few useful connections," Great-aunt Leticia admitted, a hint of smugness coloring her words.

"I'm very pleased to meet you," Nevada murmured, though truthfully, she looked more stunned than pleased.

"And this is Rivers," Great-aunt Leticia continued. "He comes across a bit intimidating, I know, but he has a heart of gold, don't you, Rivers?"

"Quite, madam," Rivers said, his British accent presenting a sharp contrast to his distinctly Asian appearance.

"Rivers will bring in your bags," Great-aunt Leticia said, "while we get cozy in my sitting room." Moving very spryly in her beaded satin ballerina slippers, she led the way upstairs to a large east-facing room Trick remembered from childhood visits.

"This is the dragon room," he said.

"What a memory!" Great-aunt Leticia exclaimed. "You can't have been more than four or five at the most the last time you were here. I collect dragons," she told Nevada. "I keep them in that cupboard in the corner, everything from priceless Chinese porcelains to cheap plastic carnival trinkets. Playing with them used to keep Patrick occupied for hours on end." She waved one beringed hand toward the sofa. "You two sit there." She settled herself in a wingback chair, one foot tucked beneath her. "Now then, what brings you children to the Bay Area? Besides a sudden urge for my company."

Nevada shot him a quick sideways look, as if to say, "She's *your* aunt. You do the talking."

"I'm trying to track down the origins of a ring we found hidden under the floorboards in the former Silas Granger brothel. You knew I was staying there, right?"

"I heard you were planning to sell."

"Planning to sell but not having much luck."

"It's a buyer's market," she said. "Wait a few years and things'll turn around."

Trick made a noncommittal sound, then drew Blanche's ring from his shirt pocket and passed it to his aunt.

"A lovely piece," she said. "Simple and elegant. You say you found it hidden under the floorboards? Why, I wonder."

"We think it belonged to a woman named Blanche Smith."

"Isn't that the prostitute who died under suspicious circumstances? The one whose ghost is rumored to haunt the brothel?"

"It's no rumor," Trick said grimly.

Great-aunt Leticia had penciled in thin arching eyebrows half an inch above her natural brow line. They rose now, nearly disappearing beneath the red wig.

"Really?" she said. "Maybe I should visit you sometime. I've always wanted to run face-to-face with a real ghost."

"Not this one, you wouldn't. She keeps me awake all night with her sobbing."

Great-aunt Leticia turned to Nevada. "And you, my dear? Did the ghost disturb your rest?"

Trick eyed his great-aunt closely, suspecting that her question had been designed to find out whether he and Nevada were sleeping together, not whether Nevada had had an encounter with Blanche's ghost.

"Since I stayed in the apartment over the stables," Nevada said smoothly, "the noise wasn't an issue for me. What *I'm* curious about is why I resemble Blanche so closely."

"You suspect you're related to the Granger ghost?" Again, Great-aunt Leticia's eyebrows disappeared beneath her bangs.

"We have no proof," Trick said, "though the circumstantial evidence is overwhelming. We found an old photograph of Blanche Smith. Here. I brought along an enlargement. Thought it might prove useful." He passed the photograph to his great-aunt. "Do you see the resemblance?"

"Indeed," Great-aunt Leticia said. "The two could be sisters." She glanced from Nevada to the photograph and back again. "How very strange!" She stared fixedly at Nevada for a moment, then shifted her attention to Trick. "I was sorry to hear about your accident, Patrick."

"Not my finest hour," Trick said.

"At least you didn't die." She frowned. "I'm not a superstitious woman, but it's hard not to believe in that curse." She leaned toward Nevada. "My father dropped dead of a heart attack at thirty-two. My grandfather drowned in a boating accident at twenty-nine. And Patrick's father died at what? Forty?"

"Thirty-seven," Trick said.

"Airplane crash." Great-aunt Leticia sighed. Then in another abrupt shift of topic, she suddenly sat up straight and looked at Nevada. "Would you care for a drink? I usually indulge myself with a glass of sherry about now."

"No, thank you," Nevada said.

"How about you, Patrick?" Great-aunt Leticia shot him a laser-sharp glance from beneath half-lowered lids.

"No, thanks."

She smiled her approval. "So the rumors are wrong."

"What rumors are those?" Trick asked, though he had a feeling he knew already. "Someone been telling you I'm a lush?"

"Penelope Saxon. We're both active members of the Society for the Preservation of Bay Area Wildflowers. At a fund-raiser last week in support of San Francisco owl's clover, *Triphysaria floribunda,* she told me her daughter had confided that her best friend's son's girlfriend was vacationing in Tahoe a month or so ago and ran into you at Harrah's."

"Possible," he said. "What's Penelope Saxon's daughter's best friend's son's girlfriend's name?"

"I don't believe she mentioned a name, just that

the girl had seen you drinking whiskey at nine in the morning."

"Again possible," Trick said. "I was going through a bad patch."

"Alcohol in excess is not a solution, Patrick," she said sternly. "It's a problem."

"I've heard that," he said.

Great-aunt Leticia snorted. "Don't get smart with me, boy."

Rivers suddenly appeared in the doorway behind her. He cleared his throat discreetly.

"Yes?" she said without turning around.

"I've put Mr. Patrick's and the young lady's luggage in their rooms. Will there be anything else, madam?"

"No, thank you, Rivers. That will be all." She waited until the sound of Rivers's footsteps had faded away, then turned to Trick. "Your knee seems to be doing better. How's the eye?"

"They were able to save it." He flipped up the patch to show her. "But the optic nerve damage is irreversible, and the eye tends to wander. Hence the patch."

"I like it," she said. "Gives you a swashbuckling look. All in all, I'd say you've been lucky."

"Lucky?" He raised an eyebrow. "Did you hear about Ellison?"

"That would be the crook who took off with the lion's share of your fortune."

"And my girlfriend."

Nevada's eyes widened for a moment, but she didn't say anything.

"Ah," Great-aunt Leticia crowed, "but that's where

the luck comes in. Ellison did you a favor, boy, taking that grasping, disloyal, stone-hearted, money-hungry gold digger off your hands the way he did."

The phone was ringing as Marcello let himself back into Britt's suite. She was still downstairs, presumably supervising Lakeshore Lodge Idol, which meant he had to wait for the answering machine to pick up. He dared not risk answering himself. He was safe only as long as no one realized he was here.

The answering machine beeped. "Damn it, pick up already." Trick. Worse, Trick in a temper. No mistaking the irritability sharpening his voice.

Marcello grabbed the receiver. "Where have you been? I expected to hear from you hours ago."

"We ran into some trouble. The delay put us behind schedule, but we arrived safely at our destination about forty minutes ago."

"Safe arrival is the important part."

"How are things at your end?"

Frustrating. Maddening. Irritating. "Fine," Marcello said. "No sign of Sarge as yet. How do things look on your end?"

"We haven't seen Sarge, either, though we did spot a few of his fellow soldiers."

"*More* vampires?"

"Probably not, though I can't swear to it. Same army, I think, but different unit. One of them cornered Nevada in a mall restroom this afternoon, but she managed to slip out right under his nose."

"Clever girl," Marcello said.

"Yes," Trick agreed, "she is."

A little added inflection in Trick's voice made Marcello wonder if there was something going on between Trick and Nevada. Admittedly, a week ago such a development would have concerned him, but then a week ago he had been half-convinced that Nevada was a vampire. Since then, the lab results had come back on her pills—allergy medicine, not some exotic drug designed to suppress bloodlust.

"Listen," Trick said. "I have a job for you. Write this down, okay?" He rattled off an address in San Francisco.

Were Trick and Nevada in San Francisco? No, Marcello told himself. He was not going to speculate about that. The less he knew—or even thought he knew—the less he could reveal if Sarge caught up with him again. He touched the worst of the wounds on his chest, still painful and raw.

"Got it?" Trick asked.

"Yes," Marcello assured him.

"Good. I want you to get on your computer and see if you can find out who owns that property. If it's a corporation, try to figure out who's the linchpin of the organization."

"*Lynch* pin?" Marcello asked, certain he must have misunderstood, because he was almost certain *to lynch* meant the same as *to hang*. So what on earth, he wondered, could a lynch *pin* possibly be? A most peculiar language, English.

"The head honcho," Trick translated, though translated to what language Marcello could not have said. "Head honcho? This is like a hat?"

"No," Trick said. "The principal stockholder or the CEO, the man in charge."

"Oh." Marcello still did not see the connection, but he let it slide. "I can do that, yes."

"Good. I'll call again some time tomorrow to—"

"Wait!" Marcello said. "Do not hang up. I have a message for Nevada from Jonathan Calhoun, that funny little man from the Midas Lake Historical Society."

"You spoke to him?" Trick said. "Do you think that's wise? The more people who know you're still in Midas Lake, the more likely it is that Sarge will find you."

"Relax," Marcello told him. "I didn't speak to Mr. Calhoun. Britt ran into him, and he told her he'd found an old letter from your ancestor, Silas. He seemed to think Nevada would be interested in it."

"I'll mention it to her," Trick promised.

After getting off the phone with Marcello, Trick showered and shaved for the second time that day, then dressed in jeans and a T-shirt. He wondered how long it would be before Great-aunt Leticia went to bed. He really needed to talk to Nevada.

Okay, he admitted to himself, talking wasn't all he had in mind. Hence the showering and shaving, which, as it happened, had taken a little longer than anticipated. Rivers, well-trained servant that he was, had unpacked Trick's luggage. The problem was, Trick now had no idea where anything was. It had taken him almost ten minutes just to find the box of condoms he'd bought in Sacramento.

He glanced at his watch. Almost eleven. Surely his great-aunt had gone to bed by now.

And yes, maybe it was silly to worry about Great-aunt Leticia figuring out that he intended to share Nevada's bed, but he hated to be responsible for besmirching Nevada's reputation. He felt sure that was how Great-aunt Leticia would word it—besmirching. Old school, his great-aunt, and proud of it. Not to mention judgmental as hell. How was it she'd referred to Luisa Gallo, a woman she'd never even met? As a grasping, disloyal, stone-hearted, money-hungry gold digger?

Yeah, judging by that minidiatribe, he'd guess Great-aunt Leticia harbored a little animosity toward his former girlfriend.

Surprisingly, he didn't. Yes, Luisa had a streak of materialism a mile wide. She loved money and all the things it could buy, but even more than money, she craved adulation. And face it, who would envy a woman who'd tied herself to someone as physically imperfect as Trick? Yes, her defection had stung his pride, but his heart? No. After the fact, he'd realized that he hadn't loved Luisa any more than she'd loved him.

Nevada, on the other hand . . .

Someone knocked softly on his door.

A spurt of excitement set his heart thumping. Nevada, he thought. Then the door opened a crack and he heard Rivers's hoarse whisper. "Sir, are you awake?"

"Yes, come in," he said, unreasonably disappointed.

Rivers pushed the door open to its fullest extent but

remained in the hall. "I don't wish to disturb you, sir."

"You're not disturbing me. It's only eleven."

"Indeed. I was wondering, sir, if you'd like me to pull your car into the garage. There's an empty bay large enough to accommodate it."

"Great," Trick said. "I'd appreciate that." He handed over the keys and Rivers turned on his heel and headed down the hall.

Trick shut the door behind the butler, wondering again if it was safe to slip along to Nevada's room. His great-aunt, apparently operating on the theory that distance promoted virtue, had put Nevada at the opposite end of the hall in the room next to the master suite. The only way Nevada could be sleeping any farther from Trick would have been if his great-aunt had arranged for Nevada to stay in the house next door.

Another soft knock interrupted his thoughts.

"That was quick," he said as he opened the door, expecting to find Rivers, Trick's car keys in hand. Instead, it was Nevada, and she looked as if she'd been crying. He ushered her inside and closed the door. "What's wrong?"

"We need to talk." His heightened expectations took a nosedive. There they were again, those same four terrifying words he'd last heard from Britt on the drive to Reno.

"Okay." Talking wasn't necessarily bad, especially talking with Nevada, but those reddened eyes gave him a moment's pause. "Have a seat. Tell me what's wrong."

Nevada glanced at the room's only chair, buried at

the moment under a pile of discarded clothing, and chose to sit on the end of the bed instead. A good move, in Trick's opinion, since it meant he could sit next to her. *The better to wrap my arm around you, my dear.*

Or not, he thought as she inched away from him.

"I'm listening," he said.

She took a deep breath, then lifted her chin and turned to face him squarely. "Why didn't you tell me you had a girlfriend?"

"Had had," he corrected her, but she only gave him a puzzled look. "No longer have. Had in the past."

"Until she ran off with Ellison."

"Right. Though frankly, I doubt it was Philip Luisa lusted after so much as all the money he stole from me."

"Marcello told me about the money, but he neglected to mention your girlfriend."

"Because she wasn't important. She *isn't* important. Ours was a relationship based on convenience and mutual lust."

Nevada didn't say anything for a long time. Then she raised her head to look directly at him. "Is that how you feel about me, Trick? Is that all that's between us? Convenience and mutual lust?"

"I never said that," he protested.

Nevada frowned. "No, but you never told me you were just coming off a long-term relationship, either. Seems to me you've been holding out."

He took her hands in his and met her gaze straight on. "No, I haven't told you every detail of my life before I met you, just those things that seemed relevant. But you have to believe me when I tell you I didn't deliberately withhold anything important. Luisa is not important. You are. Nevada, I . . . care for you."

A tremulous smile lit her face. "Good. Because I . . . care for you, too." She leaned a little closer. Favorable body language.

And when he pulled her into his arms, she cuddled up to him with a sigh. Even more favorable body language.

So he tilted her chin up and did what he'd been dying to do for hours, pressed his mouth to hers.

At which point Rivers rapped once on the door before barging in, car keys dangling from one doughy fist. "Your keys, sir."

Nevada jerked herself away from Trick as if she'd been hit with a Taser.

Trick glowered at the butler. "Thanks." *Right. Thanks for screwing up my perfect tender moment.*

Rivers seemed quite impervious to Trick's irritation. "Will there be anything else, sir?"

"No, Rivers. Definitely not."

"How about you, miss? Is there anything you require?"

She shook her head, then shoved herself to her feet. "I was just leaving." She bolted for the door, which Rivers held open. In the space of three heartbeats, they were both gone.

Trick stared at the door. "Well, shit," he said.

All during dinner with a pair of potential campaign contributors, Latina firecracker Teresa Montoya and her squat, balding, up-from-the-barrio husband, Gaspar, Daniel had waited for the call telling him his people had caught up with Whitney, but his phone had remained stubbornly silent. It wasn't until he was pulling through the electronic gates into the grounds of the riverside estate he shared with his stepmother that a call finally came through.

"Yes?" One preemptory syllable.

"Representative Snowden, Zuckerman here, sir. I'm sorry to have to tell you the young woman suspected of stealing your stepmother's credit cards got away from us."

"How could that happen? I thought you told me earlier she was trapped in a restroom on the second floor of the mall."

"I can't explain it, sir, other than to tell you, we messed up. No one saw her leave, but she's not in the restroom any longer. In fact, she's not in the mall."

"How can you be so sure?" Daniel demanded.

"Because the mall closed an hour ago. There's no one left inside."

"But the Jeep. You had someone watching the Jeep."

"The Wrangler is still in the parking lot, sir. No one has approached it. No one at all. We've had it under close surveillance since this afternoon."

"I'm disappointed in you, Zuckerman."

"I let you down. I'm sorry, sir."

Daniel's rage threatened to send him spinning out of control. Mindful of his reputation as a demanding but reasonable public servant, he broke the connection before he could inform assistant head of security Michael Zuckerman what a lame-assed fuckup he was.

Still fuming, he snapped his phone shut, put his politically correct Prius in gear, and drove the final curved section leading to the house a little faster than common sense dictated.

Regina was waiting for him in the entryway, dressed in a short black trench coat, rhinestone-studded stilettos, and nothing else. He knew this because the trench coat was virtually transparent. "I gave the servants the night off," Regina whispered in the husky voice that told him she'd been hitting the vodka.

"Why?"

"Because this crafty cougar"—she stabbed her ample chest with one scarlet-tipped finger—"thought it would be fun to have the whole house to ourselves for once. Think about it, Danny boy. We can do it on the living room rug or out by the pool or, hell, under the mirrored ceiling in the conservatory if we want. What do you say?"

Daniel considered various scenarios, none of which had anything to do with fucking his oversexed stepmother. Though if all went as planned, the bitch would end up fucked all right. "Poolside," he said. He was too angry to smile, but Regina had never been a Mensa candidate. Chances were, she'd interpret the fury coming to a boil now as a different sort of passion entirely.

Nevada wasn't sure why she was crying, but she couldn't seem to stop.

Okay, admittedly, she was apprehensive. She'd have been a fool not to be considering the danger she was in. It was easy to run but hard to hide, especially when you weren't really sure who you were hiding from. So apprehensive? Yes. Wary? Yes. Out-and-out terrified? Not at the moment.

Nor was she depressed. Compared to her life at the Institute, where long periods of stultifying boredom were randomly interrupted by torturous experimental treatments, her life now, even plagued as it was with danger and insecurity, was a million times better, certainly nothing to be depressed about.

She wasn't even angry or hurt, not anymore. Trick had looked her right in the eye and told her that the only reason he hadn't mentioned Luisa before was because Luisa wasn't important. And Nevada believed him. He'd also said he cared for her. She believed that, too. And maybe that made her the front runner for Miss Gullibility, but . . .

Trick cared for her, and he wanted her, too. She remembered the blistering glare he'd shot in Rivers's direction. If looks could kill, the butler would be six feet under.

Feeling a little less weepy, she wiped her eyes and blew her nose.

Uncertainty, she decided. That was why she'd given in to her emotions. Not knowing who she was, where she came from, why she'd been locked away—all those holes in her memory had been eating away at her for weeks now. No surprise really that the pressure had finally found an outlet.

Nevada suspected the scratching had been going on for a while before she noticed it. At first, she thought perhaps Leticia Granger's piece of prime Pacific Heights real estate was infested with mice. But when her door opened a crack, revealing one bright blue eye and a narrow wedge of wrinkled skin, she rapidly revised her hypothesis. Not a mouse. An aunt.

"Are you all right, my dear? I thought I heard someone weeping."

"I'm fine." Nevada plastered a big fake smile across her face, hoping Trick's elderly great-aunt's eyesight was less acute than her hearing, because if not, then Nevada's swollen red eyes were going to be a dead giveaway.

Leticia Granger pushed the door open wider, wide enough for Nevada to see that she'd removed the red wig, revealing spiky white hair that stood out around her face like dandelion fluff. She'd changed her clothes, too, and now wore a long flowing white nightgown that bared her scrawny arms and bony shoulders. On her feet were red ladybug slippers, complete with spots, shiny black eyes, and waving antennae. "Don't try to fool me, dear. You've been crying." Apparently, those old eyes didn't miss much.

"My life lately . . ." Nevada shrugged. "I guess tonight I finally reached critical mass."

"It's Patrick, isn't it?" Great-aunt Leticia shut the door, then crossed the room, nodding in sympathy. "Men are such bastards."

"It's not Trick," Nevada said. "It's . . . oh, just everything, I guess, the weirdness that is my life."

"Patrick and a heavy dose of hormones." Leticia patted her arm. "I remember how it was. You should try a shot of tequila. Stuff works wonders. Three or four margaritas will fix you right up. Of course, I avoid margaritas myself. They remind me of the time I flew down to Mazatlán. There was this man—so handsome, so romantic—like . . . you're probably too young to remember Ricardo Montalban, aren't you?" She furrowed her brow for a moment. Then her eyes lit up and she snapped her fingers. "Like Antonio Banderas. Only his name wasn't Antonio. It was Raoul." Her withered face assumed a wistful expression for a second. Then she frowned. "Turned out he was married with six kids. Like I said, men are bastards."

Someone knocked on the door, a definite knock this time, not a mouse scratch. "Are you up?" Trick asked as he shoved the door open. Then, "Oh!" he exclaimed when he caught sight of his great-aunt Leticia, perched now on the end of the bed.

"We're having a little girl talk, Patrick," Great-aunt Leticia scolded, as if it were her room he'd just barged into. "What do you need?"

For a second, his face went absolutely blank. Then, "Aspirin," he said. "I came to see if Nevada had any aspirin."

Nevada shrugged. "Sorry."

"Headache?" Great-aunt Leticia slid off the end of the bed.

"Um." Trick blinked. "Yeah, headache."

Great-aunt Leticia turned toward Nevada, careful not to let Trick see what she was doing, and mouthed the words, "Not just a bastard, a lying bastard."

Nevada stifled a spurt of laughter.

Trick shot her a questioning look that she pretended not to see.

"Follow me, Patrick," Great-aunt Leticia ordered. "I have a great big bottle of extra-strength aspirin in my medicine cabinet."

She marched out of the room in her ladybug slippers. Trick trailed behind, leaving Nevada to wonder why he'd really come knocking on her door.

FOURTEEN

When Marcello entered Britt's sitting room the next morning, he found her curled up in her favorite chair with a cinnamon roll in one hand and the telephone in the other. "Bye, Mom," he heard her say. "Happy Mother's Day, and tell Dad, good luck with the alligator." She punched the disconnect button, then got up to replace the cordless phone on its base unit. "Help yourself to a cinnamon roll," she told Marcello. "I sneaked them from the kitchen when Molly's back was turned. The big Mother's Day brunch starts at eleven, but I was too hungry to wait."

Marcello selected a roll from the box on the coffee table and took a bite. Still warm, it seemed to melt in his mouth. Molly Jones, Britt's pastry chef, was a genius. Her doughnuts, éclairs, pies, and tarts were an unexpected but much appreciated side benefit of his stay.

"I made coffee, too." Britt waved a hand toward the small kitchen that opened off one end of the room.

Marcello set his roll down on a napkin and stepped into the kitchen to get himself a mug of coffee. "Alligator?" he asked.

"My parents retired to Florida," she said, as if that explained everything.

Marcello carried his coffee back into the sitting room and made himself comfortable on one end of Britt's tan leather sofa. "I do not understand."

"Florida." Britt held one hand out, palm up. "Alligators." She extended the other palm, then shifted her hands up and down as if they were a set of scales. "Can't have one without the other."

"Still, I do not understand." He took another bite of his cinnamon roll.

"My parents have a pool," she explained, "and alligators are attracted to water. The pool is fenced, but if an alligator is sufficiently determined . . ."

"Ah," he said. "Your parents have an alligator in their pool."

"Yes, and my father's trying to convince it to leave. Ordinarily, he'd call the cops or Fish and Wildlife, but"— she shrugged—"it's Sunday. And Mother's Day besides."

"Perhaps if he left the gate open?"

"Tried that last time and ended up with two alligators." She waved her hand, dismissing the subject. "The man's a retired college professor. He'll figure it out."

They finished their cinnamon rolls in a companionable silence.

"What do you have planned for today?" Britt asked suddenly.

Marcello helped himself to a second roll. "Trick

asked me to research something for him. Other than that, nothing. Do you need my assistance?"

"*Need*'s a strong word." Britt frowned thoughtfully. "But I'd appreciate your company. I have something I have to do, something I do every Mother's Day."

"Here at the lodge?"

"No, up the mountain at Granite."

"I am not sure it would be wise to leave the—"

"If I distract Molly, you could slip out through the kitchen into the garage. No one would see you if you rode in the back of the SUV."

"Still, I—"

"You don't know anyone from Granite, do you?"

"No," he admitted.

"Not that I expect to run into anyone where we're going anyway," she added.

"That is reassuring, I think, but . . ." But what? Why was he arguing? It was extremely unlikely that he would encounter Sarge in the daylight hours. His kind usually didn't come out until dark. And quite truthfully, Marcello would relish the opportunity to get out of the suite. Comfortable as it was, he was starting to feel like a prisoner. "All right," he agreed.

"Good." She studied him thoughtfully, her head tilted to one side. "But just as a precaution, it might be smart to disguise yourself."

"Disguise myself how?"

"Oh, nothing too elaborate." Britt disappeared into her bedroom, emerging in a few minutes with a navy blue sock hat and a pair of dark glasses. "This ought to do it."

Sneaking out of the lodge reminded him of all the nights he had crawled out his bedroom window as a teenager to sample forbidden pleasures with his friends, though generally speaking the sneaking out part had been more of a thrill than the forbidden pleasures part.

Marcello, who had planned a couple of James Bond–esque moves, was almost disappointed not to encounter anyone between the suite and the garage. Feeling cheated, he climbed into the backseat of Britt's shiny new Expedition to wait for her.

"Did you have any trouble getting down here unobserved?" she asked when she finally showed up ten minutes later.

"None."

"Maybe I should have taken the same route. One of my single guests cornered me, trying to get me to agree to give him a private guided tour of the falls. Ha! Like that's going to happen."

"Who is this guest? Would you like me to teach him some manners?"

Britt laughed. "I can take care of myself, Marcello. Besides, you're the invisible man, remember?"

The road up the mountain to Granite was little more than a series of tight switchbacks that had Marcello, in the backseat, regretting his second cinnamon roll. When Britt finally stopped, he all but catapulted from the SUV, gulping the fresh mountain air in an attempt to settle his queasy stomach. He was so busy trying not to vomit that it took him a second or two to realize where they were.

They stood in a small glade surrounded on three

sides by towering pines. The fourth side sheered off in a tumble of rock, providing for a spectacular view of Midas Lake far below. Marcello would not swear to it, but he thought he could make out a corner of the lodge. "What a lovely spot."

"I've always thought so." Britt spun in a slow circle, her arms outstretched, as if to embrace the sky, the trees, the wildflowers, the simple stones that marked the graves scattered across the old cemetery.

" 'John Kinsey Reynolds,' " he read aloud from the nearest moss-covered headstone. " 'Born May 4, 1831. Died September 30, 1857. Killed by a claim jumper. May he rest in peace.' What is this claim jumper?"

"A thief," she said. "And a murderer, who killed poor John Kinsey Reynolds for his gold. I've always wondered what happened to the claim jumper, whether he got away with his crime or ended up dangling from a rope. I guess it was pretty lawless around here in those days. Could have gone either way."

"Not entirely risk-free these days," he said, thinking of the gash on his head, the burns on his chest.

"Still," she said, "I love it here. I grew up in this part of California. Did you know that? I went to college in Colorado Springs, lived in Vail for a while, but eventually moved back here. This area—Midas Lake, Granite—has been home to my family for generations."

"You have ancestors buried in this graveyard?" Marcello asked.

She nodded. "At least one that I know of, William L. Rittenhouse, a great-great-grandfather on my mother's side." She paused. "But he's not the one I come to visit."

Something in her voice sent a chill down his spine.

"I make the pilgrimage faithfully three times a year: Mother's Day, Christmas, and October 17." Britt was smiling, but her eyes were so sad that Marcello could feel her pain as a tightening in his chest.

"Why October 17?" he asked, though he was afraid he was not going to like the answer.

Britt took his hand and led him to the far side of the small glade, where one grave stood at a short distance from the others.

"Samantha Leigh Halston. October 17, 2004," he read aloud.

"My daughter," Britt said quietly. "Born and died the same day."

"Halston?"

"Samantha's father. My husband. Ex-husband. We divorced within a year of her death."

"I am sorry," he said.

"My fault," she admitted, "though at the time I blamed Jared for everything—Samantha's death, our marital difficulties. It's no wonder he couldn't handle the strain. I acted like a crazy woman, either screaming, sobbing, and throwing things, or locking myself in the bedroom for days at a time."

"Grief affects us all in different ways."

"Yes, but most people don't go to the extremes I did. I was both unreasonable and inconsolable. Even my parents got fed up. Eventually, Jared filed for divorce. And I blamed him for that, too."

"He should have been more understanding." Marcello yearned to put a comforting arm around her shoulders, but in her present frame of mind, he was not at all sure how she would react. "You were grief-stricken."

"That's what I told myself," Britt said flatly. "And it was true, but only a part of the larger truth." She met his gaze straight on, and the pain reflected in her eyes made him ache for her. "I was also drowning in guilt, guilt I wasn't honest enough to acknowledge. Publicly, I blamed Jared and the doctor, the nurses, the hospital. But deep down, so deep I didn't even realize the feelings were there until almost two years after Samantha's death, I blamed myself. If only I'd eaten more vegetables. If only I had exercised less. If only I'd listened to more classical music. If only I hadn't forgotten my prenatal vitamins the day she was born. If only, if only, if only . . ."

"You did nothing wrong," he said.

"I know that now." She took a deep breath. Tears glistened on her cheeks. "No one did anything wrong. She just . . . died. Congenital heart defect. No way to prevent it."

"Britt." He did wrap her in his arms then, holding her as she sobbed. He wished there was something he could say, something that would make her feel better, but he knew it did not work that way. There was no cure for grief. Time might dull the edges of the pain, but it never went away entirely.

After a while, Britt regained control. She stepped back out of his arms, forcing a smile. "Sorry." She gave his hand a squeeze. "I didn't mean to fall apart."

"You have every right to mourn your loss. It is hard,

I know," he said, the image of Antonia's pale, still face flashing through his mind, "to come to terms with the might-have-beens."

Tears welled up again in Britt's big blue eyes. "I would have been such a good mother."

"Miss Granger is waiting for you on the patio," Rivers informed Trick when he and Nevada returned from a frustrating visit to McKelvey Fine Jewelry on Monday morning. "Lunch will be ready shortly."

"This way." Trick led Nevada through the French doors in the formal dining room out onto the stone-paved patio at the rear of the house. Great-aunt Leticia sported a glossy black wig today and oversize sunglasses reminiscent of those worn by Hollywood starlets in the 1960s.

"Oh, good!" she cried when she caught sight of them. "You're back! What did you find out?"

."Nothing," Trick told her. "It was a total waste of time."

"Maybe not." Nevada took a chair across from Great-aunt Leticia at the umbrella-shaded table. "The manager promised to have his executive assistant sort through all the old records. They're in storage, not kept on the premises," she explained for Great-aunt Leticia's benefit.

"The thing is, the McKelvey family sold the shop back in the fifties," Trick said. "The new owner kept the name, but it's really a completely different business. The manager wasn't even sure the old records went back that far."

Great-aunt Leticia nodded. "The earthquake."

"Actually," Nevada said, "according to the manager, McKelvey's came through the disaster with only minor damage."

"That's predicating he knew what the hell he was talking about," Trick said sourly.

"Language, Patrick," Great-aunt Leticia scolded. "There are ladies present."

After lunch, Great-aunt Leticia left for a meeting of her book group, and Trick went off to call Marcello, leaving Nevada to her own devices. She wandered the elegant high-ceilinged rooms of the house, admiring a chandelier here, a tapestry there. Her favorite room, though, proved to be the third-floor nursery with its magnificent old rocking horse, a bookcase full of novels like *Tom Swift and His Giant Cannon* and *A Girl of the Limberlost*, and an entire wall of dolls, enough to stock a small toy store. Crude stuffed rag dolls with yarn hair bumped shoulders with fine-featured porcelain princesses dressed in satin and lace. There were realistic-looking baby dolls, jointed metal soldiers complete with swords, and her favorite, a carved wooden Indian with leather clothing and a miniature feathered war bonnet.

She was examining a Little Lord Fauntleroy doll, whose blond pageboy appeared to have been made with real human hair, when Trick stuck his head in the open doorway.

"Oh, there you are. Rivers said he thought you'd come up here."

"This must have been your great-aunt's playroom when she was little."

"I assume so, since she was the last child to live in the house."

"No brothers or sisters?"

He shook his head.

"You don't have any siblings, either, do you?"

"No. According to the family tree, Grangers have been notoriously poor breeders for the last hundred and fifty years. One or two children per couple at the most. Great-aunt Leticia's branch of the family dies with her."

"How sad," she said, "that she never had children. They'd have loved this room. *I* love this room. The dolls. The books. Talk about little girl heaven."

Trick smiled. "Personally, I always preferred the rocking horse. She used to make deals with me. 'Eat all your veggies, Patrick, and you can ride Pegasus.'"

Nevada pictured a five-year-old version of Trick manfully working his way through a small mountain of spinach in order to earn the promised ride. "I bet you were an adorable little boy."

"If by adorable you mean impatient, stubborn, and reckless to a fault, then yes, I was extremely adorable."

She laughed. "Judging by those criteria, you're still pretty adorable."

He grabbed her hand and pulled her into his arms. "Am I?"

"Impatient," Nevada said. "Definitely impatient." She twined her arms around his neck. "Kiss me."

"No, it's your move."

She smiled. "And stubborn, too." She stretched up on her tiptoes and pressed her lips to his. She only meant to give him a quick little peck, but his lips were so soft, so shockingly sensual that she prolonged the contact in spite of herself. And then—Nevada wasn't sure exactly how it happened—they were lying on the rug in front of the fireplace and Trick had his tongue in her mouth and his hands up her shirt.

Sobbing for breath, she broke the kiss. "And reckless," she said.

Trick's gaze smoldered across the cleavage exposed by his wandering hands, but then the corners of his mouth twitched. "Guess I am pretty adorable."

She stroked a thumb along his cheekbone. "And modest, too."

"Modesty may not be my strong suit, but I have my strengths."

His smile seemed to melt her bones, and even though she knew it was the height of impropriety, not to mention, stupid, all she wanted at the moment was to feel Trick inside her.

"Just ask Marcello. He'll vouch for me. He's known me forever."

Nevada knew he was talking, but the sense of his words didn't register. Her mind was too preoccupied with sensations and emotions to allow for rational thought. "Marcello?" she repeated, wondering idly what Marcello had to do with anything.

"Marcello," Trick repeated as his forefinger circled her left nipple in slow lazy strokes that seemed to sear her skin even through her bra.

And then the lazy circles stopped. No warning. One minute she was drowning in seductive sensation, and the next, she wasn't.

Trick sat up. "Marcello," he said. "Hell!"

And a good place for him, too, Nevada thought, as she stared at the star-studded ceiling. She tried very hard to hang on to her bliss, but all those lovely tingly feelings were ebbing away.

"Damn," Trick said. "I promised I'd call him back as soon as I talked to you, but then I got distracted." His finger did one more agonizingly slow circuit of her nipple.

She pushed his hand away, covering her breasts with her hands. "Don't start something you don't intend to finish." And okay, her voice held an edge of petulance, but damn it, he wasn't playing nice.

A cocky grin emphasized the harsh angles of his face. "Oh, I fully intend to finish, just not here and now."

"What's wrong with here and now?"

"Well, for starters, Rivers is apt to walk in at any moment. He seems to have a sixth sense about these things."

Nevada frowned. Trick had a point.

"And here's the biggie: all the condoms are in my room."

She shoved herself up on her elbows. "Then what are we waiting for? Let's go to your room."

"You're forgetting one important detail."

"Which is?"

"Marcello's still waiting for my call."

"So call him already."

"He wanted you to confirm the address I gave him."

"What address?"

"The San Francisco address from your file at the Institute. I had him look it up to see if he could find out who owns the property."

Nevada frowned. "I didn't ask you to do that."

"But wouldn't you like to know?"

"I was just planning to find the place, see if anything about it seemed familiar, maybe stake it out, watch the comings and goings to see if anyone looks familiar."

"But isn't it smarter to go in knowing as much as possible?"

"I guess so, but—"

"It was Broadway, right?"

Nevada nodded, repeating the address that had burned itself into her memory. "Why?"

"Because it's not a house, it's a mansion. Italian Renaissance neoclassical style valued upward of fifty million dollars. The current owner, Mitchell Harrington, is a restaurateur with a lucrative chain of upscale bistros that stretches up and down the West Coast from Seattle to San Diego. Marcello thought he must have gotten the address wrong."

"Because I'm not the sort of person whose family lives in a mansion," she said without rancor. She had a hard time believing that herself.

"No," Trick said, "because Mitchell Harrington is African American, and you're not." He stood. "I'm going to go call Marcello back, thank him for his hard work, and let him know it was the right address after all. And then—"

Nevada stood. "We have sex," she guessed.

"Yes," he agreed, "right after we check out the Harrington mansion."

Interesting, Trick thought, the way Nevada had deliberately kept steering the conversation back to sex. It was almost as if she were afraid to visit the mansion, as if she thought she might not like whatever she learned there.

He glanced sideways at her as he navigated the steep streets of Pacific Heights. She was doing a pretty good job of feigning nonchalance, but her hands gave her away, never still, one second pressing the dash, the next fiddling with the radio. "Anything look familiar?"

Frowning slightly, she studied the houses on both sides of the street. "No. Nothing. Well, that is if you don't count the fact that it looks a lot like the neighborhood where your great-aunt lives."

"True." He signaled for a left turn.

"How much farther?"

"Five or six blocks, I think." Yes, she was definitely tense. He could even hear it in her voice now.

The climb grew gradually steeper as they approached the crest of the hill. "No wonder it's so pricey," he said as the Harrington mansion came into view. "Bet you can see halfway to Hawaii from the top floor."

Nevada made no response. She just stared up at the graceful lines of the building, her face expressionless.

"Still not ringing any bells?"

She shook her head. "Nothing about it is familiar." She turned to him with a frown. "I'm not sure if that's good or bad."

Trick parked across the street. "Wonder if anyone's home."

"We can't just go waltzing up to the door and demand to be let inside."

"Why not?" He got out of the Camry, then walked around to open Nevada's door. "We'll say we're newlyweds. We were driving by, and you fell in love with the place."

"But there's no 'for sale' sign." She stepped out, and he locked the car.

"We're newlyweds," he said again. "I'll do anything to please you. If you're determined to have this house, then I'm going to do whatever it takes to get it for you. We'll make them an offer they can't refuse."

"That's ridiculous. No one's going to buy that story."

"Why not?" He took her hand in his, lacing their fingers together.

"Why not? Because who would do that?"

"How about Trick Granger, world-famous race-car driver?" He smiled at her surprised expression. "Just because you never heard of me . . ."

The temperature outside hovered at a pleasant seventy-four, but Nevada felt cold to the bone. The house didn't spark any memories. She hadn't lied to Trick about that. But it did evoke gut-level emotions—fear and dread.

"This isn't a good idea," she protested as Trick dragged her across the street. "They're bound to know we're lying. What if they call the police?"

"They won't," he said. "Quit worrying."

The climbed a flight of wide curved steps that led to an imposing entry. "But what if they do?" she persisted.

"They won't. Trust me." He rang the doorbell, and the muted sound of the sonorous bonging struck fear in her heart. She pressed her free hand to her breastbone, trying to slow the flutter of her heartbeat. Her fear was irrational. She knew that. Because if she'd lived in this mansion, standing here at the entrance would feel more like coming home and less like waiting for the judge to pronounce the death sentence.

"Nobody home," she said, turning away. "Let's go."

"Not so fast." Trick tugged her back around to face the door and rang the doorbell again.

As the bell faded away to silence once more, she studied the front of the building. Every window on this floor and the one above it was tightly shuttered. "I'm telling you, no one's home."

"You give up too easily," Trick said and rang the bell a third time.

"Ain't nobody gonna answer," a gruff voice said from behind them.

Nevada gave a start, but Trick turned smoothly to face the small, bandy-legged middle-aged man who stood there. With a leathery tan that contrasted sharply with a shock of gray hair and pale grape green eyes, he was dressed in khakis and work boots. He stood there frowning at them, a trowel in one hand, a galvanized bucket in the other.

"You're kidding," Trick said. "My fiancée wanted to show me around."

He'd demoted her to fiancée?

"She grew up in this house," Trick added.

The gardener just stared, not saying anything.

Trick gave the man a friendly smile. "That would have been before Mr. Harrington bought it."

Still the gardener said nothing. Nevada had just started to wonder if maybe he was deaf when he broke his silence. "Trick Granger? By the Lord, you're Trick Granger!"

"Why, yes. I am." Trick extended his hand.

The gardener set down his bucket and shook Trick's hand enthusiastically. "I am mighty pleased to meet you, Mr. Granger. Marvin Odell's my name, and I am your biggest fan." Grinning widely to display a set of square white teeth, he pumped Trick's hand a couple more times before letting it go. "I apologize, Mr. Granger, for not recognizing you at first. The eye patch kind of threw me for a loop."

"I was involved in an accident a few months back."

"Yes, sir, I know. Hell of a thing. All them sports commentators was saying at the time you'd probably never race again, but I figured they was exaggerating like they always do. I didn't realize how bad you was hurt."

"Yeah, not much demand for a one-eyed race-car driver." Trick had thought he'd gotten past the self-pity stage, but talking about his shattered dreams like this dredged up remnants of negative emotion.

As if she knew exactly what was going on in his head, Nevada leaned closer, wrapping one arm around his waist, then threading the fingers of her right hand through his.

Which reminded him that if he hadn't had the accident, he never would have met Nevada. His gaze locked on hers, and for a moment, the world seemed to stand still.

"For sure, the fans are gonna miss you," Marvin Odell said. And the spell was broken.

"Not as much as I'll miss competing," Trick told him. "Listen, Marvin, do you think it would be okay if my fiancée and I took a walk around the courtyard?"

"Oh, hell, why not? Mr. Harrington wouldn't mind. He's a big race fan hisself."

Trick angled away from the gardener and winked at Nevada.

"In fact, if you'd like to check out the inside"—Marvin hooked his thumb through the key ring that dangled from his belt loop—"that can sure enough be arranged."

Trick nudged Nevada.

"Oh," she said blankly, then, "Super."

"Super?" he mouthed.

"Thank you." She blessed Marvin with a dazzling smile while treading heavily on Trick's right foot. "I would love a little trip down memory lane. If you're sure the owners wouldn't mind?"

FIFTEEN

The interior of the Harrington mansion provided a stark contrast to the old-fashioned charm of Leticia Granger's three-story Edwardian. From the high-tech stainless steel appliances in the kitchen to the sleek lines of the massive living room where one entire wall was covered with museum-worthy examples of African art, the mansion had obviously been decorated to reflect the owner's excellent and rather sophisticated taste.

Despite what Nevada had told Marvin, she'd dreaded this tour, not certain until the second Trick had dragged her across the threshold that she would be able to force herself beyond the door, which was strange, since the mansion didn't seem familiar in the slightest. She had no rational explanation for her reluctance. Still, dread, unfocused but loaded with a powerful emotional charge, niggled at the edges of her consciousness.

"This here is my number one favorite spot in the whole dang mansion," Marvin was saying. Nevada, who'd been moving through the tour in a fog, gathered her scattered attention and focused on their surroundings. The gardener stood in the center of the master bath, a room larger by far than the average living room. "And this here's why." Marvin pointed to the enormous walk-in shower, tiled in peacock colors. "Eight separate shower heads," he gloated. "Eight. And," he added, "over here's a heckuva big ol' Jacuzzi tub. Multiple jets. Plus it's got its own online water heater."

"You're in the wrong line of work," Trick told him. "You should be a real estate agent."

Marvin gave a hoot of laughter. "Not on your life. I'd druther spend my time grubbing around in the dirt. Plants ain't as likely to tick you off as people."

"Good point," Trick said.

"Okay, then, next on our tour . . ." Marvin led them back through the master suite, an elegant cluster of rooms that hadn't made much impression on Nevada the first time through, despite being decorated in the same vivid peacock colors as the bathroom.

Their footsteps clattered along the terracotta-tiled hall. "Does it bring back memories, miss?" Marvin asked.

"Not really," she said quite truthfully. "Everything looks so different."

"No surprise there, I reckon. The Harringtons have done a bunch of remodeling and redecorating since they moved in three years ago."

The address appended to her file must have been a mistake. She didn't know this house. Nothing about it seemed familiar.

"Here's a spot you might recall from when you was little." Marvin drew them into what appeared to be a den. "This here study is the one room Mrs. Harrington hasn't tackled yet."

Shudders wracked Nevada's body in great shivering waves.

"Are you all right?" Trick asked.

"No," she meant to say. "No, I am not all right. I am very much not all right. Get me out of here. Get me out of here now." Only nothing came out of her mouth.

Her own reflection stared back at her from the large octagonal mirror that hung above the fireplace. Her mouth opened in a silent scream. Her eyes widened.

"Nevada?" Trick said, sounding scared. And then again, "Nevada?" Only this time, as her vision narrowed to a pinprick and her legs turned to jelly, his cry seemed to echo hollowly: "Nevada-Nevada-Nevada-Nevada."

And then nothing.

When Nevada returned to consciousness, she was no longer in the study. She lay on the cool tiles of the hall with Trick down on one knee beside her, supporting her head and upper body. Marvin Odell squatted nearby, leaning forward on the balls of his feet, arms braced on his thighs. Both men appeared shell-shocked. She suspected she didn't look much better herself.

"You all right, miss?" Marvin asked. "You took quite a turn back there."

She heard him, but the sense of his words didn't really register. Something slithered around at the back of her mind. A memory maybe. She could feel it, dark and threatening, but no matter how hard she tried, she couldn't bring it into focus. All she could make out was the vaguest of outlines as it clung tenaciously to the shadows.

"Nevada?" Trick said, this time without the echo-chamber effect.

"Dead," she blurted, which was pretty weird since what she'd meant to say was "yes."

"No, you're alive. You're going to be fine," Trick assured her. "You just bumped your head on the edge of the hearth when you fell."

"Not much more'n a scrape," Marvin said. "Bled some, but that's how it is with head wounds. Any itty-bitty little minor scratch and you can almost double deluxe guarantee you'll bleed like a stuck hog. Don't mean you're gonna die, though."

Trick didn't drive straight back to his great-aunt's house. Instead, he made a short detour to Lafayette Park. When he switched off the ignition, Nevada, who hadn't said a word since they'd left the Harrington mansion, turned to him with a puzzled expression. "What are we doing here?"

Trick got out of the car, then went around to open her door. "Enjoying some privacy."

She released her shoulder harness, hesitated a second, then placed her hand in his. "Why do we need privacy?" He was fairly certain he wasn't imagining the tension in her voice.

"So we can talk without worrying about being overheard." He led the way to a sunny patch of grass with a clear line of sight in all directions. Nobody would be slipping up on them unawares. In fact, the only people within ten yards were a couple of energetic preteens tossing a lime green Frisbee back and forth. "Make yourself comfortable," he said, indicating the grass with a wave of his hand.

Nevada sat, wrapping her arms around her knees.

He took up a position across from her, so he had a clear view of her face. Words were easy to manipulate; facial expressions and body language, on the other hand, seldom lied.

"What do you want to talk about?" Nevada eyed him warily.

"I think you know."

"My fainting spell." She shifted her gaze to a spot above his left shoulder. She could have been watching the kids with the Frisbee, but he didn't think so.

"Yes, your fainting spell. What did you see in the mirror?"

"I don't know. I can't remember."

"Was it the gardener? Does Marvin have a dirty little secret?"

"No."

"How can you be so sure? You said you didn't remember."

"It wasn't a flash. I know that much."

"Then what?"

She shook her head, then pressed her fingers to her temples as if she had a headache. "I don't know. A memory, I think, but I can't be sure. It's like I can almost see it, but then it's gone again."

"A memory." He jumped on that. "A memory from that house? You think you lived there once?"

"Lived there, visited there. I don't know. Maybe. I told you. I don't remember."

"But it's possible."

She glared at him. "Yes, damn it, it's possible. Even likely. Why else would I have been so nervous about going inside? Why else would I have fainted?"

"You said 'dead' when you woke up. That was the first word out of your mouth. I thought at the time you were worried about your injury, but that wasn't it, was it?"

"No," she said. "I didn't even realize I was hurt."

"So what were you talking about?"

She glared at him. "Quit badgering me!"

"Give me a straight answer, one I don't have to extract like an impacted molar, and I'll quit badgering."

"Okay," she said. "Here's the thing. I don't know why I said dead. I swear I meant to say yes. Only when I opened my mouth . . ." She uttered a shaky laugh. "I almost said, 'when I opened my mouth, dead came out.' Creepy image, huh?"

"I know what you said. The part I don't understand is why you said it."

She shrugged. "I don't understand, either. The word just popped out. It wasn't in my mind, I swear. And I don't have a clue what I meant by it. Only . . ." She paused, frowning.

"Only what?"

"It was something bad. A memory, I think. A really, really bad memory, so horrible I can't make myself remember. Or maybe my brain won't let me remember."

"Or," Trick said, "there's another possibility."

She glanced up in surprise. "There is?"

"Think about it, Nevada. Think about where you were between the time you lived in the Harrington mansion—"

"Hypothetically lived in the Harrington mansion."

"All right, hypothetically. Whatever. Between then and now, where were you?"

"At the Institute," she said, and then, "oh."

"Exactly. You can't remember because whatever happened is part of the artificial void their conditioning created. They erased your memory."

She heaved a tremulous sigh. "So maybe *dead* is short for dead end."

"Maybe not," he said. "I have an idea."

Nevada wasn't thrilled with Trick's idea, but since she hadn't been able to come up with anything better herself, she agreed to go along with it. To tell the truth, she'd been half convinced Great-aunt Leticia would refuse to cooperate, but no such luck.

No sooner had they retired to Great-aunt Leticia's sitting room after dinner than Trick and his great-aunt had begun moving furniture, lighting candles, and otherwise preparing the scene.

"Have you ever been hypnotized before, my dear?" Great-aunt Leticia asked.

"No." Nevada studied the old woman's lined face suspiciously. "Have you ever hypnotized someone before?"

"Oh, my, yes." Great-aunt Leticia batted her false

eyelashes, worn tonight to complement her silver sheath dress, diamond choker, and Marilyn Monroe wig. "I worked at the USO during the war—"

"World War II, she means." Trick moved the flame-stitch wingback to the center of the room.

"Yes," Great-aunt Leticia agreed. "People think the USO was all cookies and dancing, but my hypnosis gig was hugely popular, let me tell you. The boys thought it great fun to give their buddies posthypnotic suggestions. You know the sort of thing I mean. 'When you wake up, you'll think you're a frog.' Had that one backfire on me, actually. Fellow mistook the punch bowl for a pond . . ."

"No posthypnotic suggestions!" Nevada shook her finger for emphasis. "Repeat after me, both of you: No posthypnotic suggestions."

"No posthypnotic suggestions," the other two chorused.

"Spoilsport," Great-aunt Leticia muttered under her breath.

"I heard that," Nevada said.

"Okay," Trick said. "Sit in the chair, Nevada, and try to relax."

She could handle the first part. It was the second part that might prove problematic.

"We need a focal point for her to concentrate on." Great-aunt Leticia began rummaging in the drawers of her dainty little cherry wood escritoire.

"I have just the thing." Trick held up Blanche's ring.

"Perfect." Great-aunt Leticia took it from him and approached the chair where Nevada sat. She dangled the ring four inches in front of Nevada's nose. "Look at the ring."

"I'm trying," Nevada said, "but it's too close. My eyes keep blurring."

"Not a problem. Let them blur. Just keep focusing on the ring."

"Aren't you going to swing it back and forth? That's the way they do it on TV."

"Don't worry your head with preconceived notions," Great-aunt Leticia murmured. "Keep your eyes on the ring. Let your mind drift."

"Snowdrift," Nevada said, then frowned. "That's not right."

"Don't try so hard, my dear," Great-aunt Leticia advised. "Relax. Breathe in, breathe out."

Nevada breathed in and out. Her eyes went blurry. And then her mind went blurry.

The next thing she knew, Great-aunt Leticia was leaning over her, saying, "Wake up, my dear."

"Did it work?" Nevada asked Trick.

"If you mean, did she manage to hypnotize you? The answer's yes. If you mean, were you able to access those hidden memories, then the answer's no."

"Did I say anything? Anything at all?"

Trick shot a questioning look at Great-aunt Leticia, who inclined her head. "Nothing new," he said with a shrug.

Nevada studied his face closely. "I said *dead* again, didn't I?"

"You said dead, all right, but that was it. No context," Trick told her.

"I don't know what those horrible doctors did to you." Great-aunt Leticia looked distressed. "I've heard of brainwashing, but your brain isn't really cleansed. All the dirt's still in there, just locked away where you can't get at it, even in a hypnotic state. It's like there's a roadblock."

"Or a disconnect," Trick said. "Like maybe they didn't just shut down the pathway, they removed the pathway."

"And either way," Nevada said, "I still don't know who I am."

Britt was lying on the sofa, reading a novel by someone called Linda Howard. Marcello had never read a novel by Linda Howard, but he had noticed the book was making quite an impression on Britt. Every so often, she would snicker. Once, she sighed. And another time, she murmured a soft, "Oh my God." In between these verbal reactions, she would twist a lock of hair around her finger or wriggle her bare toes. Marcello knew this because he couldn't seem to take his eyes off her.

He had tried to divert himself with television, and when that had not worked, he had started a crossword puzzle. But he had found himself unable to concentrate. Not even computer solitaire had held his attention.

Whenever Britt murmured something under her breath, he zoomed in on her lips, soft and pink and kissable. Her sighs, on the other hand, drew attention to her chest, where her sweetly rounded breasts stretched the fabric of her T-shirt. And as for her toes . . .

He had never had a foot fetish or any other sort of fetish for that matter, but Britt's wriggly little toes with their pale pink nail polish were rapidly driving him insane. He kept fantasizing about sucking on them and then slowly licking and tasting his way up her body. He was not sure if that made him a pervert or just an oversexed bastard, but either way . . .

He turned a groan of frustration into a fairly believable cough.

Then Britt sighed again, low and breathy, the same exact sound she would make if he . . .

Cazzo! He had to get out of here before he did something they both would regret. He shut his laptop and shoved himself to his feet. "I am going for a jog. I need the exercise."

Britt frowned. "Do you think that's wise?"

Not only wise but necessary. Imperative. "No one is down on the beach this time of night."

"No, I suppose not." But she still looked uncertain. "I realize being cooped up like this probably has you bored stiff."

Bored and stiff. Two quite separate problems.

Britt yawned and stretched.

Marcello looked away, but not quickly enough to avoid another testosterone rush.

"You know," she said, "I'm about due for a break myself. Mind if I come along?"

Yes, he thought. *A million times yes.* But, "Suit yourself," he said.

"Great!" She sat up and the Linda Howard book went tumbling onto the carpet. "I'll go change."

Into something less comfortable, Marcello hoped. A ski suit would be nice. Or better yet, a ski suit, parka, and mukluks.

Of course, that did not happen, and ten minutes later, Marcello found himself alone in the moonlight on the deserted beach below the lodge with the woman of his dreams, a more terrifying predicament than one might suspect. Britt in a well-lit room had presented a temptation. Britt by moonlight was mortal sin made flesh.

"Thanks for suggesting this, Marcello," she said, a lilt in her voice. "It's lovely out here, isn't it?"

"Lovely," he agreed, though he was not referring to the beach.

She placed a hand on his forearm. An innocent contact but enough to set his imagination running wild. What if she let her other hand trail gently down his chest? No, what if she grabbed the front of his jacket, pulled his face down to hers, and kissed him until he begged for mercy? No, what if she shoved him backward onto the sand and—

"Race you to the dock," she said.

He was so caught up in his fantasies that she had a ten-yard head start on him before he realized he had just been issued a challenge.

"Slowpoke!" she tossed over her shoulder. A slur to which any healthy young Italian male would take exception.

Marcello managed to catch up halfway along the beach. "Who is the slowpoke now?"

Britt flashed him a mischievous grin. "You!" she shouted and lunged ahead.

Again, Marcello caught up with her. "Who?" he demanded.

"Me," she said, "though I do have one advantage over you."

· "What is that?" he asked, preparing to pull ahead.

"I have no ethics." Deliberately, she stuck out her foot and tripped him. He hit the sand, and she flew past.

"That is cheating!" he yelled as he dragged himself to his feet and sprinted after her.

But the race was hers. Britt touched the end of the dock a good six inches ahead of him, then jumped in circles. "I won! I won! I won!"

He grabbed her arm. "Get down."

"What?" She shot him a questioning look.

"I said, get down." He pulled her to the sand.

"What's going—"

"Shh. Listen."

She cocked her head, frowning slightly. "I don't hear anything. Oh, wait. A motor?"

He nodded. "Someone is coming up the lake, and I would rather not be seen."

The boat drew steadily nearer, passing within a meter or so of the far end of the dock, close enough for them to see there was only one person aboard. A man. A large man. But that was all Marcello could tell for certain.

A dozen meters farther along, the tenor of the motor changed.

"He's slowing down," Britt whispered. "Do you think he spotted us?"

"No," Marcello said. "I think he has spotted his destination. The beach below the Granger mansion."

"But why would anyone—" Britt fell silent as the logical answer occurred to her. "Do you think it's—"

"Sarge," Marcello said. "He has returned."

"You don't know that," Britt said. "It could be someone out for a moonlight ride."

"I might believe that if there had been more than one person in the boat. And if he was just out for a ride, why did he douse his lights and kill the motor just as he approached the Granger property?"

"I don't know, but there might be a perfectly innocent explanation."

Marcello raised his eyebrows. "Such as?"

"Maybe our mystery boater's a thief."

"You have an interesting definition of *innocent*," Marcello observed. "Look, we both know the odds are it is Sarge. In fact, it makes sense. If you recall, we never found where he and his partner parked last time. Perhaps that is because they came by boat, not by car."

"Okay, that does make sense, but—"

"We are wasting time," Marcello said. "Stay here. I am going to try to get a little closer to see if I can make a positive identification."

"No!" Britt grabbed his arm with both hands and held on tight. "Are you crazy? What if he spots you? The man's a psycho. Remember what he did the last time he caught up with you."

"Do not worry," he told her. "I have no intention of allowing him to torture me again. There were two of them last time, and they caught me unawares. This time I have the advantage." He pried her hands loose and pressed a kiss to her forehead. "I will be careful. I promise."

Marcello jogged back across the beach, trying to act casual about it in case anyone was watching. A large stone outcropping marked the end of Britt's beach and the beginning of Trick's. Unlike Britt's stretch of sand, which extended a good twelve meters from the water up to the lawn, Trick's beach was much narrower. Above the stone outcropping, the trees grew thickly. Below it, a narrow four-meter strip of beach extended across the property, a ribbon of sand separating the forest from the lake. Marcello melted into the shadows of the rugged rock formation, listening hard for sounds of movement.

Nothing.

He peered cautiously around the lower end of the rock formation. A speedboat, one of the rentals from the public marina across the lake, was tied up at one end of the dilapidated dock, but there was no sign of whoever had come across the lake in the boat. Marcello scanned the beach carefully. Nothing. No one.

But perhaps if he tried a better vantage point . . . He levered himself up the rock and peered down from above. Still no one in sight, though he could definitely see where someone had plowed through the sand toward the path that led up through the trees to the house. He sat back on his haunches to wait.

The house was locked up tight, not that Marcello thought for a moment that locks would stop Sarge—if, indeed it was Sarge—from getting inside. But this time, he would find no one to intimidate.

The burns on Marcello's chest were well on their way to healing, but he would never forget the pain nor the obvious pleasure Sarge had taken in inflicting it. The excitement glittering in his eyes, the quickening of his breath, and the sinister smile twisting his face had all betrayed his delight in the torture, his glee at forcing Marcello to talk.

And Marcello had talked. That shame that would follow him to the grave.

"If Sarge returns, don't confront him. Just keep an eye on him if you can. See which way he goes when he leaves." That was what Trick had said.

Had Trick guessed how difficult it would be for Marcello to follow those orders, how loudly would his instincts be shouting for revenge?

Fire. Even monsters like Sarge feared the flames. It would not take Marcello ten minutes to slip up to the house and tamper with the natural gas line. He imagined the resulting explosion. An old house like that would go up like kindling.

The only problem with the scenario—aside from destroying Trick's property—was that it was not a hundred percent guaranteed to destroy the vampire. If Sarge was not knocked senseless by the initial blast, he might very well escape the building before the fire had a chance to reach him, and then Marcello's desperate and violent act would have been all for nothing.

Worse, Sarge would realize someone nearby wanted

him dead. And Britt's lodge was the only place nearby. Marcello had a sudden ghastly vision of the vampire pressing the tip of a burning cigarette to Britt's tender flesh.

No. Marcello could not risk that. He would hide and watch as Trick had instructed.

Fifteen minutes later, Sarge strode into sight, the scowl on his face clearly illuminated by the moonlight.

Marcello did not linger. He took off for the lodge at a dead run, knowing if he expected to beat Sarge back to the marina, he would have to hurry. He met Britt near the back door.

"What happened?" she asked, looking worried.

"He is getting away, and I need to know which way he goes. May I borrow your SUV?"

"Of course," she said, handing him the keys. "But I'm coming with you."

Marcello did not waste time arguing. They cut through the lodge to the attached garage, where Britt was parked. She punched the automatic garage door opener while he started the engine.

"How do you chase down a man in a boat using an SUV?" she asked as she buckled herself into the passenger seat. "Where are we going?"

"The marina," he said. "I need to see which way he heads from there."

"And then what?" she asked. "We're not going to follow him, are we?"

"No." he gave her a reassuring smile. "As soon as I know which way he is headed, I will contact Faraday."

• • •

As Trick climbed out of the shower, he heard his cell phone ringing. Figuring no one but Marcello would be calling this late, he grabbed a towel, wrapped it around his waist, then dripped his way into the bedroom to grab the cell phone he'd left on the dresser along with his wallet and the rest of the contents of his pockets. "Yeah?"

"Trick?" Definitely Marcello and he sounded upset.

"What is it? What's wrong?"

"Sarge came back to Midas Lake."

"Did he hurt you? Britt? How's Britt?"

"We are both fine. We saw him. He did not see us."

"You're positive?"

"Absolutely. We saw him approach the mansion by water."

"Good thing you were at the lodge instead of holding down the fort by yourself."

"Fort?" Marcello said.

"Never mind. What else happened? You said he didn't spot you, but you sound upset."

"Britt and I drove to the marina, assuming he had left his vehicle there when he rented the boat. We were anxious to see which direction he went when he left."

"You sound strange, Marcello. What's wrong? What haven't you told me?"

"The boat . . ." Marcello faltered. "Sarge had not rented it." He swallowed audibly. "After he drove away, heading down toward Sacramento, by the way, not into Midas Lake—"

"Did you let Faraday know?" Trick asked quickly.

"I called him before I called you."

"The license plate. Did you think to get the license plate?"

"I tried. It was obscured with mud, purposely, I think."

"That's not the end of the story, though, is it?"

"No."

If Trick hadn't known better, he'd have thought his friend was on the verge of tears. "Marcello, what is it?"

"Mr. Spinelli, the man who runs the North Shore Marina . . . ?"

"Short, stocky old guy with a hula girl tattoo on his left biceps. Told me once he was a sailor in World War Two."

"He is dead," Marcello said. "After Britt and I watched Sarge drive off, we went into the office to see if Mr. Spinelli could give us any additional information." Marcello paused. "But he was not able to tell us anything. Sarge had seen to that. Mr. Spinelli was lying there on the floor with his throat ripped open, and the blood . . ." He paused again. "The blood—his blood—was everywhere. The place looked and smelled like a slaughterhouse. I thought Britt was going to faint. I thought *I* was going to faint."

"I assume you called the police."

"Britt did."

"So they'll be looking for him, too," Trick said.

"Only they do not realize they are looking for a monster."

SIXTEEN

"Such a pity," Great-aunt Leticia said, glancing up from the newspaper.

Trick helped himself to scrambled eggs from the buffet set out on the sideboard, then took a seat at the breakfast table across from his great-aunt. "What's a pity?"

Great-aunt Leticia frowned. "Regina Snowden's disappeared. A possible abduction, according to the police, though so far, there's been no ransom demand."

"Maybe she just ran away," Trick said.

"Who ran away?" Nevada asked from the doorway.

"Stepmother to one of our state representatives," Great-aunt Leticia said. "And I very much doubt she disappeared of her own accord. I can't say I know the woman well, but she's always been very supportive of her stepson's career, very active in his campaigns. I can't see her taking off just as he's about to throw his hat in the ring again."

"The stepson's running for something?" Trick asked.

"Governor," Great-aunt Leticia said. "He's heavily favored to win the Democratic primary even though he hasn't officially announced that he's running."

Trick noticed Nevada then, still standing in the doorway, an odd abstracted expression on her face. "Is something wrong?"

She blinked, then frowning, shook her head. "I don't think so. For a minute there, I . . . No, it's nothing."

"You're probably just hungry," Great-aunt Leticia said. "There's food on the sideboard. Help yourself. Only I'd skip the fried tomatoes if I were you."

"I heard that, madam," Rivers said, hardly surprising since he was standing next to the sideboard, adjusting one of the chafing dishes.

"Then take a hint already," Great-aunt Leticia told him. "No one but you likes the nasty things."

Trick caught Nevada's gaze and winked.

She smiled back, though she seemed a little preoccupied.

"Well, then." Great-aunt Leticia smiled first at Trick and then at Nevada. "What do you two children have planned?"

"For starters," Trick said, "I thought I might pick your brain."

"Don't pick too hard, Patrick dear. We seniors are fragile, you know." She finished off her scrambled eggs and popped a strawberry into her mouth.

"Do you know the Mitchell Harringtons, by any chance?"

"I've met them."

Which didn't exactly sound like a ringing endorsement.

"You don't care for them?" Nevada asked tentatively as she took a seat next to Trick. Apparently she, too, had noticed a lack of enthusiasm.

"He's quite an admirable man, rich as Croesus and earned every penny of it himself."

"But . . . ?" Trick prompted.

"Pamela's father is Tony Blaine," she said as if that explained everything.

"Who's Tony Blaine?" Trick asked.

Great-aunt Leticia widened her eyes. "Tony Blaine," she said. "*The* Tony Blaine."

"Never heard of him." Trick took a bite of his toast.

She shook her head sadly. "Patrick, Patrick, Patrick."

"Humor me, okay? I've lived out of the country for years."

"Tony Blaine's the premiere Beverly Hills exercise guru," she said. "He started as a stuntman back in the seventies, but he made a fortune later in life as a fitness expert. Half the stars in Hollywood owe their abs and booties to the Tony Blaine workout. Tried it once myself. Crippled me up for a solid week. Could barely move from my bed to the bathroom."

"So Mrs. Harrington's father's something of a celebrity," Nevada said, dragging the conversation back on track.

"Who spoiled his daughter rotten." Great-aunt Leticia gave a dismissive head toss that set her Shirley Temple ringlets bobbing.

"Define *rotten*," Trick said.

"Pamela Harrington would rather fly to L.A. to shop on Rodeo Drive than help to raise money for a worthy charity."

"She turned up her nose at your pet cause," Trick guessed.

"Acted like I was a batty old lady to care what happened to the Presidio clarkia." She frowned. "I may be old, but I'm not . . ." She turned to Trick. "Why did you bring up the Harringtons in the first place, Patrick?"

"Do you know their place on Broadway?"

"The old Smith mansion, you mean?"

Great-aunt Leticia's casual correction seemed to have an unnerving effect on Nevada. All the color left her cheeks. By contrast, her eyes looked like dark holes. Trick turned back to his great-aunt. "Smith is the name of the people who sold it to Harrington, I presume."

"Oh, no. The Smiths were the original owners, the family who built the place. Before the Harringtons, the mansion belonged for a brief time to a wealthy man from Colombia. Rumor had it he was a drug lord, but I never actually met the man, so I can't say."

"Meaning you could say if you'd met the man?" Trick teased.

"Anyone who's lived as long as I have, Patrick Donatelli Granger, is bound to be an astute judge of character."

"What sort of person am I?" Nevada asked in a strangled voice.

Great-aunt Leticia's penciled eyebrow arches disappeared beneath her curls. "Why do you ask, my dear?"

"Because I'd really like to know." Pain rippled across Nevada's face. "I don't remember who I am. I could be a thief or a liar or . . . a killer."

"Nonsense," Great-aunt Leticia said briskly. "You're nothing of the sort."

"Then what am I?" Nevada demanded.

"You're a fairy-tale princess. Right now you're lost in the enchanted forest, which is why you can't remember who you are, but sooner or later you'll find your happy ending."

"And my memory," Nevada said.

"And your prince," Rivers added.

The others turned to stare at him in surprise. Trick, for one, had forgotten Rivers was still in the room.

He shrugged. "One can't have a happy ending without a prince, can one?"

Great-aunt Leticia shot him a pointed look.

"And before the Colombian drug lord?" Trick asked in an attempt to divert her before she could comment on his role in Nevada's fairy tale.

Great-aunt Leticia screwed her forehead into a ferocious frown. "I believe"—she put her wrinkles through yet more contortions—"the Snowdens owned it prior to that. Oh, my!" she exclaimed. "Isn't that strange?"

"What?" Trick asked.

"What a coincidence! About the Snowdens, I mean. Mrs. Snowden sold the Smith mansion after her husband's death, and just this morning I read in the paper that she's disappeared."

Nevada looked as if she were about to faint.

"What is it?" he asked.

She shoved herself to her feet. "Excuse me," she said and all but ran from the room.

Nevada lay curled in a tight ball in the center of the bed, eyes shut, fists clenched. Her fear was like a giant python, coiled tightly around her chest, squeezing tighter and tighter with every breath she took. The past was still a blur, but red-tinged now and terrifying. She'd wanted to remember. For years, she'd wanted nothing more than to remember, but now, she wasn't so sure.

The veil was lifting. She knew it, and she was scared to death of what might be revealed. Dead, she'd said at the Smith mansion and then again under hypnosis. Dead.

Someone knocked softly on her bedroom door. "Nevada?"

She recognized Trick's voice, recognized, too, his concern for her. She must have seemed like a maniac, fleeing the breakfast room that way. "I'm not feeling well," she called.

Trick didn't take the hint. He let himself inside, then closed the door.

"I want to be alone," she told him.

"Yeah? Well, I want two good eyes and my racing career back. Guess we're both doomed to disappointment, huh?"

"Trick, go away."

"Not happening, lady." He sat on the edge of the bed and pulled her into his arms.

She stiffened at his touch.

"Nevada, relax. I'm not the enemy. I'm here to help. Look at me."

"No," she said, feeling as stupid and childish as she sounded.

"Look at me," he repeated softly as he brushed the hair gently away from her cheek. "Look me in the eye. What do you see?"

"The reflection of a crazy woman."

"Not crazy," he said. "Just distraught. Try again, and this time go deeper."

Once again she met his gaze.

"What do you see, Nevada?"

Love. She saw love, but how could that be? How could he love her when he didn't know who she was?

"What do you see?"

"Someone who . . . cares about me," she said.

He pressed a gentle kiss to her forehead. "That's right. I care about you, and I want to help you, but I can't do that if you won't tell me what's wrong?"

"I'm scared," she said.

"I got that."

"I used to be afraid because I couldn't remember, but now it's even worse. The fear, I mean. Because now I'm afraid that I *will* remember."

"Great-aunt Leticia's mention of the Smiths was the trigger, wasn't it?"

"No. Yes. I don't know. Maybe. The Smiths and then the Snowdens."

"I think the Snowdens are involved. I think they're part of what you're so terrified to remember. I need to call Marcello," he said.

The invisible snake gave another vicious squeeze. "Why?"

"I need him to do some research. Unfortunately, I left my cell phone lying on the dresser in my room. Will you be okay alone here for a while?" Even as he spoke, he extricated himself from her and stood up.

Nevada had never felt so alone in her life, but she managed to nod.

He crossed the room, then paused with one hand on the doorknob. "Promise me something?"

"What?"

"Promise you won't run away again."

The thought had barely skirted the edges of her mind. How had he known what she was thinking?

"Promise," he said, more forcefully this time.

"I promise," she said.

And then he was gone, leaving her alone with her fears.

Trick stared at his reflection in the mirror above the dresser, hardly daring to believe his hunch had panned out. "Could you repeat that?"

On the other end of the line, Marcello patiently re-read the newspaper account of James Snowden's death.

"A bullet through the temple, you say?"

"A bullet from his own gun, yes," Marcello agreed. "Because there was no sign of forced entry, it was eventually ruled a suicide even though he left no note."

"And it says his daughter found the body?"

"Yes," Marcello said. "You think Nevada's the daughter, do you not, this Whitney Snowden?"

"I think so, yes. You should have seen her face when she saw the room where Snowden committed suicide. She fainted, Marcello, just collapsed."

"James Snowden was a wealthy man, Trick."

"Your point being?"

"If Nevada is his daughter, then why was she virtually abandoned in a research facility thousands of miles from her home? If she were traumatized by her father's death, one would expect the family to have placed her under the care of a first-rate psychiatrist."

"The article doesn't say anything about what happened to Whitney after she found her father's body?"

"No. I read you the whole thing."

"Then you need to keep searching," Trick told him. "Dig up everything you can find on Whitney Snowden. On the rest of the Snowdens, too."

When Trick returned to Nevada's room half an hour after he'd left to call Marcello, he found her still lying curled tightly in a fetal position in the center of the bed. "Nevada?" he said softly, not wanting to wake her if she'd fallen asleep.

But she wasn't asleep. When she sat up, turning to face him, her eyes looked enormous, dark and haunted. "Did I kill him?"

"What? Who? Oh, you mean Snowden. No! Of course not. Why would you even think such a thing?"

"Are you sure?"

"Yes, I'm sure. According to the newspaper article Marcello located online, James Snowden wasn't murdered. He committed suicide."

Her face went completely blank, as if this were a possibility that hadn't even occurred to her. "Suicide?"

"That was the official finding."

"Suicide," she said again.

"He shot himself in the head."

She stared at him in confusion. "That doesn't sound right."

"I thought you couldn't remember, so how would you know if it sounded right or not?"

"I can't remember," she said slowly, "but I can almost remember. It's like when you recognize someone's face, but the name eludes you, so you start running through the alphabet. Nine times out of ten you can zero in on the right first letter even if you can't nail down the name."

"And suicide doesn't sound like the right first letter," he said.

"Something like that." She frowned. "What else did you learn?"

"His daughter was the one who found the body. In the study," he added.

"The same study where I fainted."

He nodded, watching her closely.

"And you think I'm the daughter?"

"Aren't you?"

"I don't know."

"Not for sure, but you know whether or not it sounds like the right letter."

"And if I am?" Her lower lip trembled. A look of fear rippled across her face. "Why would my family have institutionalized me? Because I murdered my own father. That's the only scenario that makes sense."

"Why would you murder your father?" Trick asked reasonably.

"Crazy people don't need rational reasons for violent acts."

"Okay, but there are two huge gaping holes in that theory. You're neither crazy nor violent."

"Maybe I lost my temper. Maybe I killed him, but it was an accident."

"And the family covered up the crime by making it look like a suicide, so you didn't have to spend time in prison."

"It's possible," she said.

He narrowed his gaze. "So why then, after saving you from prison did they incarcerate you in the Appleton Institute three thousand miles from home?"

"Because they were afraid of what I might do next?"

"That argument doesn't hold water. We've already established that you aren't violent."

"Not now," she said. "But maybe I was before. The treatments I had at the Institute could have altered my brain chemistry."

"Okay," he agreed. "You think about that. Run through the alphabet and see how it sounds."

Nevada didn't say anything for a full minute.

"It doesn't compute, does it?" he said.

She shook her head.

"Because you're not insane and you never were. The only thing that sets you apart from 'normal' is your psychic ability."

"Limited psychic ability," she corrected him. "I have no control over it. The flashes just happen."

"Okay, consider this," he said. "We have a young girl—you'd have been what five years ago? Eighteen? Nineteen?"

"Eighteen."

"We have an eighteen-year-old girl who goes waltzing into her father's study to talk to him about something and finds him dead, an apparent suicide. So naturally, she screams. Other people come running. And let's say the first one on the scene is the person who actually murdered the girl's father and set it up to look like a suicide. But the instant the girl sees the murderer's reflection in that mirror on the wall of the study, she realizes what really happened and she goes berserk. Maybe she's acting so wild and out of control that she has to be sedated. I mean, there had probably been previous incidents, psychic flashes that led to odd behavior. How difficult would it be to convince everyone that the trauma of finding her beloved father's dead body had pushed her over the edge?"

Nevada looked troubled. "Trick, I don't know."

"We should ask Great-aunt Leticia to hypnotize you again. The barrier is weakening, I think. This time she might—"

"No," Nevada said. "Not now. I need to think. And I need to be alone," she added pointedly.

"But—"

"Please."

He held her gaze for an endless moment.

"Please," she said again.

So he left her alone. It felt wrong, but he did it anyway.

Nevada spent the rest of the day in her room, not even emerging long enough for meals. Rivers, at Trick's insistence, had carried first lunch and then dinner to her room, but she'd ignored both the butler and the food.

Worried, Trick checked on her every half hour or so, and when night fell, instead of sleeping in his bed, he slept sitting up in a chair in the hall outside her bedroom door. Just in case.

Daniel woke with a start in the middle night, unsure what had disturbed his rest. He reared up on his elbows, staring into the darkness and listening hard. At first, nothing seemed out of the ordinary. Then he caught a sharp, medicinal scent and heard the whisper of the wind riffling through the leaves of the big eucalyptus tree outside his bedroom window, a window always shut and locked for security reasons, even on balmy spring nights like this one.

What the hell? He stared in disbelief as the heavy brocade draperies rippled and swayed.

But how? Who could have . . . ?

And then he smelled another scent. Smoke. More specifically, cigarette smoke.

He whipped around. A shadowy figure, black against charcoal, and male judging by its bulk, filled one of the club chairs flanking the hearth. The man drew on his cigarette, and the end glowed orange-red in the darkness.

Daniel groped for the Ruger he kept tucked between his mattress and box spring. Feeling more in control with the gun in his grip, he reached out with his left hand and turned on the light, hoping to startle his uninvited guest.

But he was the one who was startled. "Collier? What the hell are you doing? How did you get in here?"

"Crawled in through the window," Sarge said. "That alarm system of yours is shit worthless, by the way. Took me all of five minutes to disable it."

"I'll get my security people right on it first thing in the morning," Daniel said.

A slow smile curved Sarge's mouth. "Who says you're going to be around first thing in the morning?"

"What are you talking about?" Daniel forced a laugh. "I'm the one with the gun."

"And I'm the one with the bullets." Sarge extended one big hand palm up, and sure enough, there were Daniel's bullets. "Not that the bullets would kill me anyway, but I've got to admit, they hurt like hell. Kind of like a cigarette burn. You ever have a cigarette burn?"

Sarge's avid grin and menacing tone set Daniel's heart racing. Fear curdled his gut, and for a split second, he couldn't speak. Then he realized that showing weakness would only encourage the bastard. He needed to go on the offensive.

"What are you doing here, Collier? You're supposed to be hunting my half sister."

"Right. Hunting, not being hunted." Sarge took another pull on his cigarette.

"Someone hunting you?"

"The police, as if you didn't know."

Daniel scowled, aiming for righteous indignation,

though he wasn't sure how close he came to his target. Righteous indignation was hard enough to pull off when you were fully clothed. Being naked in bed added a whole new level of difficulty. "How *would* I know?"

"Because you're the one who set them on my tail."

"Why would I do that?" Daniel asked, genuinely surprised. "You work for me. Do you seriously think I'd take a chance on your spilling your guts to the cops?"

"If you didn't blow the whistle on me," Sarge said stubbornly, "then who did?"

"Oh, let me take a wild guess," Daniel said. "You left another mutilated corpse behind."

Sarge's expression lost some of its cockiness.

"That's what happened, isn't it? Only this time, someone must have seen you leaving and have given your description to the authorities. Or maybe"—Daniel paused for effect—"you didn't take quite enough blood, and the would-be corpse was the one who ratted you out."

"No way!" Sarge said. "That old guy was nothing but maggot food when I left."

"So I'm right. You have been feeding on humans again, even after I warned you."

"Old guy who owns the marina on Midas Lake caught me stealing a boat. Bastard threatened me with a shotgun. What was I going to do? Let him blow holes in me? Or worse, let him sic the cops on me?"

"Someone sicced the cops on you anyway. That's the kind of thing you've got to figure will happen if you leave a string of dead bodies everywhere you go."

"One old geezer is hardly a string," Sarge grumbled.

"Was it worth it?" Daniel snapped. "Did stealing the old man's boat get you any closer to finding my half sister?"

Sarge had the grace to look embarrassed. "She wasn't there. I took the boat across the lake to the Granger mansion, the place she'd been staying before, thought maybe I could squeeze a little more information out of the Italian that Billy and I had interrogated earlier. Only he wasn't there. No one was. Place was empty, locked up tight."

"You *did* go inside to be certain?"

"Yeah, I did." Sarge frowned. "House had an abandoned feel to it, like nobody'd been there in a while."

"And you know this how? Some special vampire sense?"

"Yeah," Sarge said. "My overdeveloped sense of smell."

Daniel raised his eyebrows in silent derision. "Right."

"Milk," Sarge said.

"I beg your pardon?"

"The milk in the refrigerator was sour, and there were no food odors in the air. When you cook, the smell lingers. No one had cooked in that kitchen for several days, maybe not since the last time I was there. Plus, there were a whole string of messages on the answering machine."

Daniel perked up. "I assume you had the good sense to pocket the tape."

Sarge shook his head. "No tape. It was one of those digital machines. Maybe there's an easy way to forward messages to a cell phone or something, but I'm not that techno savvy."

"Damn it, Sarge!"

He butted out his cigarette on the polished surface of Daniel's two-thousand-dollar end table, then smirked. "So I just copied them off by hand. Not that they're gonna help. Just a bunch of telemarketing shit."

SEVENTEEN

Nevada was sitting at the table in the breakfast room of the Pierce Street Edwardian, nibbling at a croissant and listening with half an ear as Trick's great-aunt, today in a sleek little Betty Boop wig, droned on and on about the endangered Presidio clarkia (*Clarkia franciscana*). Then, right in the middle of a rant about the shortsightedness of certain city officials when it came to choosing between protecting native species and promoting land development, she suddenly asked, "Why are you so angry with Patrick? You've scarcely spoken a word to him in the past two days."

"I'm not angry—"

"I realize he's been pushing hard to get you to remember the past, though any fool should realize that's the absolute wrong approach. He needs to back off and give you some breathing room."

"But he hasn't—"

"Nonsense. I heard him haranguing you earlier." Great-aunt Leticia paused, a spoonful of oatmeal suspended halfway to her mouth. "Oh my God! Perhaps I should follow my own advice. I've been bombarding city officials with my demands for the last six months, and where has it gotten me? Exactly nowhere. Maybe I need to back off and give them some breathing room. Or at least not pitch any more fits in public the way I did with that pompous ass George Westbridge at church last Sunday." She carried the spoon to her mouth, savoring the cinnamon-and-honey-flavored cereal with every appearance of enjoyment. Then, in another of her abrupt switches of topic, she asked, "Have you decided yet on your costume?"

"Costume?" Nevada echoed.

"For the ball tomorrow night," Great-aunt Leticia said.

"What ball?"

"The annual Bay Area Literacy League Ball. The BALL Ball. Get it?"

"Yes, and I'm sure it's an excellent charity, but—"

"Our goal is one hundred percent literacy in the city of San Francisco. To that end we donate books to both city and school libraries and fund a free tutoring program open to students of all ages."

"Yes, admirable work, I'm—"

"Crucial really, and none of it would be possible without the proceeds from the annual ball. Everyone who's anyone attends, including prominent figures from the entertainment industry, doctors, lawyers, politicians, sports heroes, artists, musicians."

"It's very kind of you to think of me, Miss Granger, but—"

Great-aunt Leticia raised both beringed hands like an ambidextrous traffic cop. "Stop! No buts allowed, my dear."

"I can't go to a ball. I have nothing to wear."

"That's the beauty of the BALL Ball. It's a costume affair, and I have closets full of costumes."

"But I don't have an invitation."

"Don't be silly, my dear. Of course, you do. I'm one of the organizers. I can invite whomever I want. Patrick's already promised he'll go. I thought he'd spoken to you."

He'd probably tried. Nevada had spent a good part of the last two days avoiding him, though not because she was angry. She wasn't angry. She was confused. Confused and frightened.

"That's settled then." Great-aunt Leticia placed her napkin on the table next to her empty cereal bowl and stood up. "I have some last-minute arrangements to make this morning and a luncheon meeting at Chez Nous with the other committee members, but perhaps this afternoon you'd like to go through the costume room with me. Patrick's already chosen his, but I haven't quite made up my mind. I'm thinking either Joan of Arc or Marie Antoinette."

Nevada tried to imagine Trick's great-aunt as either of those young Frenchwomen but failed miserably.

"This afternoon then. It's a date," Great-aunt Leticia said just as Trick walked into the breakfast room.

"What's a date?" he asked.

"I have to go, Patrick dear. I'm late," Great-aunt Leticia told him. "Nevada will explain." She ducked out, clip-clopping down the hall in a pair of patent leather pumps.

"How long have you known about the ball?" Nevada asked, flushing when her words came out sounding more accusatory than she'd intended.

"Since last night," Trick said. "Great-aunt Leticia mentioned it during our James Bond marathon, in the lull between *Dr. No* and *Goldfinger*, if memory serves. I take it you don't like the idea."

She frowned. "It's not that I don't like the idea exactly. I mean, what female hasn't dreamed of attending a ball? It's just . . . I'm not sure it would be wise. If you recall, the last time I went out in public, I was nearly apprehended."

"At the Papillon Mall, you mean. But that was Sacramento, which, for reasons I don't understand, seems to be a hot spot. Here in San Francisco, we haven't had any close calls, not at the Harrington mansion—"

"The Smith mansion," she corrected him.

He ignored the interruption. "Not at the jewelry store and not at the park, either."

"There will be more people at the ball," she said.

"Yes," he agreed, "but we'll be in costume. Or had you forgotten? Who's going to recognize you if you're all dressed up as Little Red Riding Hood?"

Just before noon, Trick went looking for Nevada to bring her up to date on the latest information Marcello had unearthed. He finally found her sitting cross-legged on the floor in the nursery upstairs, thoroughly immersed in an old copy of *Black Beauty*.

"You look about twelve years old sitting there like that," he said.

She glanced up with a bemused smile. "I feel about twelve. I remember this book. I've read it before."

He propped himself against the door frame to take the weight off his bad leg. Two flights of stairs were still enough to make his knee ache. "I just got off the phone with Marcello," he said, hating the way her expression changed, the sudden wariness in her eyes.

"Did he learn anything more about the Snowdens?"

"A little," Trick said. "Apparently, my guess that Whitney Snowden freaked out after finding her father's body was correct. According to the newspaper reports, she was hysterical. The police tried to question her but found her answers incoherent. They finally called in a doctor to sedate her."

"But the police never suspected that she was responsible for her father's death?"

"No," Trick said. "Though there were rumors, unsubstantiated for the most part. Marcello did find a somewhat ambiguous statement from an unidentified family member, who claimed Whitney had been emotionally unstable for some time. This anonymous source didn't come right out and say she'd killed her father, but what was said fueled more rumors. Another anonymous source close to the family was quoted as saying that finding her father's body had shoved Whitney over the edge."

"Over the edge of sanity. That's what you're saying."

"No," Trick said. "That's what the unidentified source said."

"What happened to Whitney after that?" Nevada asked tensely.

"She was enrolled at a private girls' school, but she never went back following the funeral. She dropped out of sight completely."

"Because she was institutionalized," Nevada said bitterly.

"Marcello also found an interview someone had done with the Snowdens' housekeeper, Yelena Petrov."

"Yelena?" Nevada looked as if he'd punched her in the gut. "My friend Yelena?"

"The interviewer insinuated that Whitney Snowden had had something to do with her father's death, and Ms. Petrov objected quite strenuously. She claimed she had known Whitney her whole life, that Whitney adored her father and would never have done anything to hurt him. But when the interviewer asked what Whitney was doing now—this was months after her father's death, around the time Whitney's half brother was starting his first campaign for public office—Yelena suddenly became very tight-lipped."

"Yelena," Nevada said again, as if she was having a hard time believing it.

"Marcello believes that interview may have cost Yelena Petrov her job because shortly afterward, Mrs. Snowden hired a new housekeeper."

"After which, Yelena took a job at the Appleton Institute."

Trick nodded. "Quite a coincidence, wouldn't you say?"

"I must be Whitney then."

"Looks like it. Does it feel right to you? What does your gut say?"

"It says yes," she admitted. "I think I must have known the truth the moment I set foot in the study in the Smith mansion. I just didn't want to admit it. But now, after learning that my friend Yelena was the Snowdens' former housekeeper, well, that's too big a coincidence to swallow. I'm Whitney Snowden. I must be."

"But you don't remember."

She shook her head. "The memories are there. I'm sure of it. But something's blocking them."

"Something Dr. Appleton did to you, some drug therapy or brainwashing technique."

"I think so, yes." She frowned. "Yelena's the one who named me Nevada White. She claimed it was a twisted version of Snow White. But maybe she chose it because it was a twisted version of my real name, too. Nevada White. Snow White. Whitney Snowden."

"That makes sense," he said slowly. In a bizarre way.

"Yelena must have taken the job at the Institute so she could keep an eye on me."

"That seems a logical conclusion." Though whether she had done it out of the goodness of her heart or because Regina Snowden was paying her to monitor Whitney's progress was another question altogether.

When Trick's great-aunt had mentioned her costume room, Nevada had envisioned a sort of oversize closet. In reality, the costume room was more like a small dress shop, complete with a wall of mirrors and small but luxuriously appointed changing rooms. Great-aunt Leticia had tried on twenty or more different outfits before finally settling on a Gypsy costume. The rich colors, fringed scarves, and bangles suited her, in Nevada's opinion, much better than the boyish Joan of Arc attire or the towering white Marie Antoinette wig.

Nevada surveyed her own costume in the wall of mirrors and couldn't resist smiling.

"You look radiant, my dear. Positively radiant," Great-aunt Leticia gushed.

She felt radiant. Young and pretty and desirable. She shot a conspiratorial grin at Trick's great-aunt. "Now remember, not a hint to Trick, no matter how hard he tries to weasel the information out of you. My costume is top secret."

"My lips are sealed," Great-aunt Leticia promised, "with superglue."

"Nevada?" Trick called from outside in the hall.

Great-aunt Leticia smirked. "Good thing I remembered to lock the door, huh?"

"Nevada, I need to show you something."

"Just a minute!" She dived into the changing room where she'd left her jeans and T-shirt and slammed the door shut. "You can let him in now," she told Great-aunt Leticia.

Nevada, who was changing as quickly as she could without damaging the fragile fabric of her costume, heard the click of the lock, then Trick saying, "Nevada? Damn it, where are you?"

"Watch your language, Patrick," Great-aunt Leticia scolded. "She's changing her clothes."

"Hurry up," Trick called. "I found something in the paper I think you should read."

Nevada hung her costume on its padded hanger, then draped the garment bag over it and got dressed in her jeans and T-shirt.

Great-aunt Leticia rushed to meet her as soon as she opened the door. "I'll take that." As if she thought Trick might peek if given half a chance.

"Okay," Nevada said to him, "what's so special about this article?"

"It's a follow-up piece on Regina Snowden's disappearance."

"Poor woman vanished on Mother's Day," Great-aunt Leticia said. "How ironic is that?"

Trick handed Nevada a newspaper folded open to the section he wanted her to read. "There's a lot of information. I was hoping something would ring a bell."

Nevada's gaze riveted itself on the photograph of the dead woman.

"Does she look familiar?" Trick asked.

"Yes," Nevada said faintly.

"You remember then?" Excitement edged his voice.

"You know Regina Snowden?" Great-aunt Leticia asked, sounding surprised.

But no more surprised than Nevada felt. "She's the woman from the mall," she said. "The one who stared at me as if she'd seen a ghost."

• • •

Nevada had retreated to her room again. Trick couldn't decide whether to follow her or not. He wasn't sure how long he stood hesitating in the costume room, evidently long enough to irritate Great-aunt Leticia, though. She whapped him on the arm with the newspaper Nevada had left behind. "How would Regina Snowden know Nevada?"

"Let's go sit down somewhere, and I'll fill you in." Something he probably should have done in the first place. With all her Bay Area connections, Great-aunt Leticia was a veritable font of knowledge. He'd held his tongue initially, concerned about Nevada's privacy, but there was no longer any point in reticence.

Great-aunt Leticia patted his arm, as if she'd read his thoughts. "That sounds like an excellent idea."

They ended up on opposite ends of the pink and yellow flowered sofa in her sitting room. Trick tried to decide where to start, but Great-aunt Leticia beat him to the punch. "Nevada's James Snowden's daughter by his second wife, Allison Smith, isn't she?"

"We think so, yes, though Nevada still can't remember. When we visited the Harrington mansion—"

"Smith mansion," she corrected him. "All the old-timers call it the Smith mansion."

"Smith mansion." He frowned. "What can you tell me about the Smiths?"

"Allison, the second Mrs. James Snowden, was the last of them. The house was hers, part of her inheritance. It passed to James when she died."

"Anything funny about her death?"

"If by funny you mean suspicious, then no. She died in childbirth."

"Having Nevada?"

Great-aunt Leticia frowned. "A girl child. I don't remember the name."

"Whitney," Trick said.

Great-aunt Leticia's face cleared. "Whitney. Of course. How did you make the connection?"

"The address to the Har—, that is, the Smith mansion was attached to Nevada's file at the Appleton Institute, where she spent the last five years. It was one of two clues Nevada had linking her to her true identity, the second being an amulet identical to the one that belonged to Blanche Smith, whose ghost haunts the brothel."

"Blanche *Smith*. And you're thinking there's a connection to the Smiths who built the mansion on Broadway."

"Yes."

"I don't know how likely that is. Smith is a very common name."

"I realize that."

"Do you know anything about Blanche Smith, aside from the fact she was a prostitute?"

"Just that she was from San Francisco and was believed to have Gypsy blood."

"You're sure about that?" Great-aunt Leticia asked sharply.

"About what? The San Francisco roots? Or the Gypsy blood?"

"Both, but especially the Gypsy connection."

"Definitely on the first. Fairly certain on the second. I mean, the whole Gypsy curse thing is part of our family history."

"Yes, it is," she agreed, "but Smith is such a common name that I never made the connection. Not until now. The Smith who built the mansion was also rumored to have Gypsy blood. In fact, Allison, the woman we suspect was Nevada's mother, was said to be a clairvoyant."

His excitement stirred. "Nevada's psychic," he said. "She can't control it, but she's definitely gifted."

"So chances are very good that she is, indeed, Whitney Snowden." Great-aunt Leticia nodded thoughtfully. "And chances are only slightly less good that she's related to the Granger ghost as well."

"The question is," Trick said, "who committed her to the Appleton Institute and why?"

"The who seems obvious. The evil stepmother."

"I thought you liked Regina Snowden," he objected.

"She always seemed pleasant enough," Great-aunt Leticia admitted, "but I never really knew her well."

"Why did you immediately think she was the one who'd committed her stepdaughter? Why would she?"

"I can think of several possible reasons," Great-aunt Leticia said. "One, she thought Whitney was insane. Two, she thought Whitney had murdered her father and might murder her, too. Three, Whitney saw something she shouldn't have seen, perhaps something she didn't understand but which might implicate Regina in some wrongdoing."

"Such as her husband's murder," Trick said. "He was wealthy, right? And Regina inherited all his money."

"True," Great-aunt Leticia said, "though of course, Regina was wealthy in her own right long before she married James Snowden."

"So much for that theory then," Trick said.

"No, don't be so quick to reject it," his aunt said. "With some people, greed is a sickness. As far as they're concerned, there's no such thing as enough money."

" 'The love of money . . .' " Trick quoted.

" ' . . . is the root of all evil,' " his great-aunt finished.

Nevada stopped at the corner, squinting up and down the street. Nothing looked familiar in the dark, especially not now that the fog had rolled in. Why had she thought it a good idea to wander around in a city she didn't know?

She peered at the street sign, which reassured her somewhat. This was Pierce Street all right, the street Trick's great-aunt lived on, though how many blocks Nevada was from the house, she didn't know, since she couldn't for the life of her remember the street number.

She shut her eyes, trying to envision the landmarks visible from the Granger house, but all she could see in her mind's eye was the view downhill toward the bay, a view completely obscured now by the fog. She knew she was looking for a large structure, pale gray with white trim and framed by two enormous old trees. The trouble was, the mist cocooning the streetlights distorted colors. Every house she passed seemed to be painted in various shades of gray.

She'd go three more blocks, she decided. If she didn't see anything that looked familiar, she'd backtrack. And if that didn't work, then she'd just have to knock on someone's door and ask to use the phone. Surely Leticia Granger would be listed in the phone book.

But Nevada hadn't gone half a block when she saw a broad, squat pumpkin of a house that triggered her memory. Its big bay windows glowed in the darkness like jack-o'-lantern eyes. Leticia Granger's graceful three-story Edwardian was only two houses down the street.

Nevada didn't bother trying the front door, knowing Rivers would have long since locked up for the night. Instead, she climbed the fence into the back garden, then scrambled up the rose trellis that clung to the rear of the house and onto the balcony beneath the bedroom window she'd left open a crack when she'd slipped out earlier. She shoved the window up and stepped over the sill, ducking her head to squeeze through.

"Don't forget to put the screen back in place," Trick said from somewhere in the darkened room. "Rivers won't be happy if you let bugs in."

Startled, she raised up too fast, bashing her shoulder blade on the window frame. "Ouch! What are you doing here? You frightened me."

"Frightened *you*? Imagine how I felt when I searched the entire house only to find you gone. Where have you been?" He rapped out the last four words, his anger almost palpable.

She heaved herself over the window sill, then with

suddenly trembling fingers, fumbled for the nearest lamp and switched it on. A mistake. Trick looked even angrier than he'd sounded. "I—"

He advanced on her, fists clenched. "Damn it, Nevada, I thought . . . At first, I thought you'd been kidnapped from your bed, that Sarge had somehow figured out where you were and . . . Damn it, how could you just take off like that? You know it isn't safe. Where the hell did you go?"

"To the Smith mansion."

"On foot?"

"It's not that far."

He grabbed her arms. "Are you insane?"

"A question I often ask myself," she said quietly and saw a stricken look wipe the anger from his face.

"I didn't mean—"

"I know." Exhaustion settled on her shoulders like a leaden cloak, but she forced herself to meet Trick's gaze. He deserved an explanation.

"I thought it might help me remember. If I went back, I mean."

"And did it?"

She shook her head. "Maybe if I'd been able to get into the study, but the mansion was locked up tight. No Marvin around to let me in. I stood there forever just staring up at the house, but I couldn't even figure out which windows belonged to the study. I tried to calm my mind, hoping some memories would surface, but"—she shrugged—"nothing happened. I'd even taken a mirror along. I thought maybe if I stared at myself in the mirror with the house reflected behind me, I might be able to trigger a psychic flash."

"But that didn't happen," he guessed.

"Nothing happened, except I got cold. While I was busy trying to reconnect with my memories, the fog crept in. What was worse, I got lost on the way back here. Everything looks different . . . sounds different . . . in the fog."

"You shouldn't have gone on your own. It's not safe, especially at night. Darkness is the vampire's friend."

"So what was I supposed to do?" she said. "Wake you up and ask you to drive me over to the Smith mansion in the middle of the night on the off chance it might jog my memory?"

He scowled at her. "Do you really think I was asleep? How could I sleep with you so close and yet so far out of reach?"

"Trick, I . . ." She didn't know what to say. Yes, she'd closed herself off from him but for good reason. Until she knew for sure that she wasn't a murderer, a monster capable of killing someone close to her, she wasn't going to put anyone at risk, least of all Trick.

"I don't know what you're going through, and I won't pretend that I understand how you feel. I don't. I only know how I feel." He tipped her chin up so she was forced to meet his gaze. "I care about you, Nevada. If something happened to you, I . . ." His jaw tightened. "I've lost enough. I won't lose you, too!" His expression was fierce, his voice harsh.

Nevada knew he was upset. She could see the turmoil in his expression, in his body language, but she couldn't let him harbor any false hopes. "You don't have me to lose, Trick. I'm not a possession. I don't belong to anyone."

"Yes, you do," he said, his voice ragged with suppressed emotion. "We were destined to be together. Don't you get that? When you tumbled out of the cab of the logging truck right in front of me, that was fate. We were meant to meet, meant to join, to bond. I know it, and you know it, even if you are too stubborn to admit it. I belong to you and you to me."

Join. Bond. How careful he was not to say *love*.

And how quick she was to criticize, even though she hadn't been any more forthcoming herself. But damn it, how could she be when she wasn't sure if she was the sort of person deserving of love?

"I don't . . ."

"Feel the same way?" he said, his voice raspy, as if the words were being torn from his throat.

"I can't—"

"Liar."

"I haven't said anything."

He stared down at her, his brow knit, his mouth twisted, his nostrils flared. "Our silence can lie as surely as our words."

Or it could ring with truth. *I love you,* she thought. *I can't tell you. For your own good, I can't tell you, but I love you all the same.*

Trick's expression softened. Had he somehow heard her unspoken words? "Deny this," he said. Wrapping his arms around her, he lowered his mouth to hers in a kiss so sweet and tender that it brought tears to her eyes.

Time lost all meaning. There was only Trick, the clean, spicy scent of him, the warm, hard strength of him, the hot, sweet taste of him. After an eternity, he broke off the kiss, brushed his lips across her cheek, then whispered in her ear. "You can't deny it, can you?" He leaned back, cupping her chin in one hand. "Don't bother trying. I can see the truth in your flushed cheeks." His other hand circled her throat. "Feel it in the thrum of your pulse."

"Kiss me again," she said.

EIGHTEEN

Trick woke spooned up against Nevada's backside, one hand cupping her breast and the other tucked between her legs, all in all, not a bad position to find himself in. Muted daylight—apparently the city was still wrapped in fog—filtered in the unshuttered, and, he suddenly realized, still unscreened window. He'd better remedy that before Rivers noticed. Better dispose of the discarded condoms, too, while he was at it.

He inched backward, trying to ease himself free without disturbing Nevada. But his strategy didn't work.

She muttered something unintelligible, then grabbed his wrists and wrapped his arms around her like a security blanket.

"Nevada?" he whispered.

"Ungh," she said.

"I've got to get up."

"Why?" she said.

"For one thing, I'm starving. It takes a lot of fuel to satisfy a sex fiend like you."

She turned over in his arms and gave him an impish smile. "Who says I'm satisfied?"

"You did," he said, "with all that gasping and moaning."

Her cheeks turned pink. "I gasped and moaned?"

"Yeah, and I was right there with you."

She frowned. "Did I bite your shoulder? I seem to remember . . ."

"A little nip. Didn't even break the skin."

"I'm sorry," she said. "I got carried away."

"Yeah," he said. "I know the feeling."

Someone knocked on the door. "Nevada?" Great-aunt Leticia's voice.

"Yes?" Nevada called.

"May I come in, dear?"

"No," Nevada said, scrambling out of bed. "I'm . . . I'm not dressed."

Trick smiled his approval. Nevada undressed was a sight to stir the blood. In fact, he wasn't sure he needed breakfast after all.

"I wouldn't bother you, dear," Great-aunt Leticia said, "but a man just called for Patrick, a man from McKelvey's. I put him on hold, but I can't find Patrick. I looked in his room. I looked everywhere. I thought perhaps you might know where he's gone."

Nevada, who had by this time managed to pull on some clothes, her jeans and his shirt, motioned for Trick to hide.

He ripped the quilt off the bed with one good jerk, then wrapped it around himself. He considered ducking into the bathroom or the closet, but opted instead to take up a position behind the door where he'd be invisible to anyone peering inside but still be able to hear whatever was said.

Nevada cracked the door open a cautious inch or two and peered out. "Maybe Trick took a walk," she said.

As Nevada spoke, Trick's gaze fell on his discarded cross-trainers lying on the rug next to the bed. *Oh, shit,* he thought, praying that Great-aunt Leticia wouldn't notice.

But evidently God was busy elsewhere.

"Without his shoes?" Great-aunt Leticia said archly.

Nevada wondered again why Trick's Great-aunt Leticia had asked them to meet her here in the formal dining room after lunch. If she was going to give them the boot, wouldn't she just ask them to leave? Though if that were her purpose, she probably would have done it already. The truth was, she hadn't seemed particularly upset or even surprised to find out Trick had spent the night in Nevada's room. Maybe this was going to be a safe-sex lecture.

Rivers propped a large white board against the hutch and set a box of dry-erase markers on the table.

A safe-sex lecture complete with stick drawings.

"Will there be anything else, Miss Granger?" Rivers asked.

"No, thank you, Rivers. You've been a huge help already. The white board is his," she confided to Trick and Nevada. Then as soon as Rivers left, she added with a touch of malicious satisfaction, "He uses it to make lists. Can't see to use paper and pencil anymore, but he's too vain to wear reading glasses." Great-aunt Leticia was looking like a rather pruney Paris Hilton today in jeans, a lavender cashmere sweater, and a blond wig.

Nevada tried to catch Trick's eye, but he was reading an email Marcello had just sent to his gmail account.

Great-aunt Leticia cleared her throat. "Shall we get started then?"

"Of course," Nevada said, "but first, I have a question. What's the purpose of this meeting?"

Great-aunt Leticia looked surprised. "Patrick didn't tell you?"

"No." Nevada frowned at Trick, who still had his nose stuck in the printout of Marcello's email. "He didn't say a word."

Great-aunt Leticia shot him an indulgent look, wasted, as it happened, since he wasn't looking at her, either. "A man of action, our Patrick. Of words? Not so much."

Nevada aimed a kick at his shin but connected instead with a table leg. "Ow," she said.

Great-aunt Leticia raised her penciled brows. "I beg your pardon?"

"It's nothing. I stubbed my toe."

"Serves you right," Trick said under his breath.

"Let's get started then, shall we?" Great-aunt Leticia said brightly. She reached into the box of markers and pulled one out with a little squeal of delight. "Look! A pink one! I didn't know they came in pink, did you?" She was too busy making illegible pink scribbles across the top of the white board to notice that no one answered. "Okay," she said. "Three headings. 'Things We Know,' 'Things We Surmise,' and 'Things We Don't Know.'" She did a little more scribbling.

"What did Marcello have to say?" Nevada asked Trick.

"Nothing happening in Midas Lake. No sign of Sarge since the day he killed Mr. Spinelli at the marina."

"That's good news."

He focused on the papers in his hand. "Um," he murmured, the ultimate in noncommittal communication.

"Isn't it? Good news, I mean."

"Um," he said again, pursing his lips this time.

"Was that all he said?" she persisted. Because that email he was poring over was two pages long, *damn it,* and it didn't take two pages to say 'nothing's happening here.' Even if you were Italian.

Great-aunt Leticia turned around with a big smile. Her gold crowns sparkled under the light of the crystal chandelier. "Things we know," she said. "We know two men have been tracking Nevada ever since she escaped from the Appleton Institute."

"Two vampires," Trick said without glancing up.

"I think the vampire part needs to go under things we surmise," Great-aunt Leticia said.

Trick did look up then. "Surmise hell," he said. "Ethan Faraday and I both watched one turn to dust. The guy took a crossbow bolt through the heart and poof, he was gone."

"Under stress, the mind sometimes—"

"I saw what I saw," Trick said. "Besides, if they weren't

vampires, then why did they rip out all those people's throats?"

"Did you actually see them rip anyone's throat out?"

"I saw one of them sink his fangs in Nevada's neck."

Great-aunt Leticia frowned. "Okay, we'll call them vampires, but I'm going to put a little question mark after it. I mean, maybe there's a logical explanation."

"For some guy turning to dust?" Trick said.

"All this happened in the dark, right?"

"Yes."

"So maybe the man didn't really turn to dust. Maybe he hid behind something."

"I know what I saw," Trick insisted, "but I'm not going to argue with you. Keep the damn question mark if it makes you feel better."

"It's not about my feelings, Patrick dear. It's about accuracy."

"Fine," he snapped.

Nevada wondered if all Great-aunt Leticia's meetings went this way.

"We also know that Nevada looks very much like Blanche Smith, a young woman—"

"Whore," Trick said. "If we're interested in accuracy."

"Whore," Great-aunt Leticia corrected herself, adding a few more bright pink hieroglyphics to the white board. ". . . a young whore, originally from San Francisco, who worked in Midas Lake for our not-so-illustrious ancestor Silas Granger."

"We know that Blanche came from a Romanichal family," Nevada said.

"And we know that the Smiths who built the mansion on Broadway were said to have Gypsy blood." Great-aunt Leticia paused. "Maybe that should go on the 'things we surmise' section of the board, though. We don't know for a fact the Smiths had Gypsy blood."

"We don't know for a fact that Blanche had Gypsy blood, either," Trick said. "Just leave it."

"We know Allison Smith, the last of the Smith mansion Smiths, was a clairvoyant," Great-aunt Leticia said, scribbling some more. "And we know that her daughter, Whitney Snowden, disappeared shortly after her father's supposed suicide in the study of the Smith mansion."

"We know Nevada has psychic flashes," Trick said. "We also know she had the address of the Smith mansion attached to her file at the Appleton Institute. We know she had a powerful negative response upon entering the study at the Smith mansion. From that, we can *surmise* that Nevada has some traumatic associations with that room and that she and Whitney are most likely the same person."

"What we don't know is what specific memories I have of my father's death. We don't know if I killed him or if it was truly a suicide and finding him dead traumatized me."

"Or," Trick said, "maybe what traumatized you was seeing the murderer's reflection."

"Is there a mirror in the study?" Great-aunt Leticia asked.

"Yes," Nevada told her. "A large octagonal one above the fireplace. But . . ."

"What?" Trick asked.

"If I wasn't the one who killed my father, if I wasn't

sent to the Appleton Institute to be 'cured,' if someone else murdered my father and then made it look like a suicide, why didn't the murderer simply eliminate me, too?"

"Two deaths in the same family on the same night?" Trick said. "That would have raised a red flag. Even if it had been set up to look like a murder-suicide, the police would have launched an in-depth investigation, and who knows what dirty little secrets might have come to light?"

"Besides," Great-aunt Leticia said, fussing with her watchband, "there were already rumors about young Whitney's mental instability before the night of her father's so-called suicide. That played right into the murderer's hands. Whatever wild accusations Whitney might make to the police would be discounted because of her prior history. Plus, if it ever did become known that she'd been sent to the Appleton Institute, who would question that decision?"

"Especially now," Nevada said, "with Regina out of the picture."

"The evil stepmother disappears under suspicious circumstances," Great-aunt Leticia muttered, scribbling furiously with her pink marker.

"Better add a question mark after that," Trick said, "in the interest of accuracy."

Great-aunt Leticia scowled at him. "Why? She disappeared."

Trick gave her a superior smile. "No, I was referring to the 'evil' part. We don't know whether or not she was evil."

Great-aunt Leticia snorted, but she added the question mark.

"You know who we haven't considered yet as our potential villain?" Trick said. "Whitney Snowden's half brother, Daniel."

"And for good reason." Great-aunt Leticia glared at Trick. "Representative Daniel Snowden is no villain. Good grief! The man's an environmentalist. He's come down heavily in favor of protecting the clarkia. I ask you, could a man protect wildflowers on the one hand and participate in villainy on the other? Ridiculous!"

"But—" Trick started.

"Ridiculous!" Great-aunt Leticia repeated. Under the "Things We Know" heading, she wrote: Daniel Snowden has an impeccable voting record on environmental issues.

Trick looked as if he were gearing up for an argument, so Nevada quickly said, "If Regina Snowden was the one who murdered James Snowden, that would explain why she sent those monsters after me when I escaped from the Institute. She must have been afraid I'd remembered everything. And that," she added slowly, "also might explain why she's gone into hiding. She's afraid I'm going to expose her."

"So if Sarge and his friend were working for your stepmother, then now that she's gone missing, you should be safe," Trick said.

Daniel, looking suitably somber in black, left the press conference and headed back to his office, where Sarge Collier waited for him. Daniel thought he'd struck the right note, with his brave announcement that, despite Regina's disappearance, he was still contemplating a run for governor. It had been his beloved stepmother's dearest wish, he'd told the press, to see him in the governor's mansion.

As he entered the outer office, Ms. Grimshaw glanced up, a worried expression on her face. "Sir, there's a man in your office. I tried to stop him, but he said—"

"That's quite all right," Daniel told her. "I was expecting him."

As Daniel walked into his office, Sarge glanced up guiltily, his big hand stuffed in Daniel's crystal candy jar.

"Chocopologie truffles by Knipschildt. Two hundred fifty dollars a piece. Two thousand, six hundred dollars a pound. By all means, help yourself."

With a sheepish grin, Sarge pulled out a truffle, unwrapped it, and then shoved it into his mouth.

"Still no sign of my sister?"

"Zippo," Sarge mumbled around a mouthful of chocolate. "It's like she's disappeared off the face of the earth."

"She doesn't remember," Daniel said.

"How can you be sure?"

"If she remembered what happened, she'd have gone to the authorities by now. Ergo, she doesn't remember."

"So . . ." Sarge frowned. "Does that mean we're not going to look for her anymore?"

"We can keep our eyes open, of course, but since she poses no immediate threat, we may as well focus on more important things."

"The campaign," Sarge guessed.

"Bravo," Daniel said. "Apparently there's something to the story about chocolate being brain food."

"So you have no further need of my . . . services?"

Daniel smiled, the same charming, confident smile that had been wowing voters for the last five years. "No, I'd like you to stay close, at least until after the election. In fact, I'm making you an official member of my security team. We'll be leaving for San Francisco aboard my private jet in a little over an hour. Don't be late."

"Okay." Sarge stuffed another two hundred fifty dollars' worth of chocolate into his mouth.

"Da-da-da-DA-da-DA!" Great-aunt Leticia sang in her crackly voice.

Trick glanced up to see her descending the grand staircase of her Pierce Street home in a short fuchsia flapper dress and enough glitzy jewelry to blind anyone foolish enough to look directly at her.

"What do you think, Patrick?" She paused at the foot of the stairs, then did a slow-motion pirouette to show off her costume.

"I think you'd have made one hell of a flapper."

"A bit before my time, dear boy, but yes, I agree." She adjusted the fringe along her hem. "I would have made one hell of a flapper. You're looking pretty spiffy yourself."

Trick laughed. "Spiffy?"

"Dashing then," she said with a fond smile. "With the boots, the scarf, the cutlass—"

"The eye patch."

"The eye patch goes without saying, of course, but my favorite part of your costume is that shirt. Voluminous sleeves, the open V at the neck showing just a hint of muscular pecs. Very sexy. Pirate's a good look on you, though personally, I'd lose the parrot."

"Argh. A pox on you, woman. What pirate worth his salt would venture forth without his faithful feathered friend?"

"One who wanted to be able to dance without worrying about his partner's eyes being pecked out."

"It's a fake parrot," Trick pointed out, but Great-aunt Leticia still made a valid point. The parrot would definitely be in the way on the dance floor.

Trick was removing the bird when he heard Great-aunt Leticia give a gasp of excitement. He glanced up to see what had prompted her reaction and caught his first glimpse of Nevada as she came floating down the stairs like a fairy princess. The stuffed parrot hit the checkerboard tiles of the entry with a thunk. Trick wouldn't have been in the least surprised if his jaw had done the same.

Nevada glanced at Trick and his great-aunt, then frowned. "What's wrong? Do I look stupid? I look stupid. I'll go—"

"Stop," Trick said when she turned and started back up the staircase.

She hesitated.

"Don't change. You don't look stupid; you look fantastic." And she did, in a glistening beaded white gown with a low neckline and a long, full skirt. "Who are you? Cinderella?"

"I'm supposed to be Snow White, not the early-in-the-story version, who lived in the forest with the seven dwarfs, but the happily-ever-after version, who lived with the prince in the castle."

Great-aunt Leticia heaved a sigh. "Perfect, my dear. You look absolutely perfect. Without a doubt, you'll be the fairest of them all."

"Without a doubt," Trick said.

"Of course," Great-aunt Leticia added with a frown, "most of your competition falls into the over-forty category. Still"—she brightened—"you really do look fabulous."

"So do you," Nevada told her. "Though I thought you'd decided to go as a Gypsy."

"It's a lady's prerogative to change her mind."

"How about my costume? Very fitting, wouldn't you say?" Trick asked.

Nevada smiled, then trailed her fingers along his jaw. "You, me hearty, belong on the cover of a romance novel."

"That good, huh?"

"Better," Nevada and his great-aunt said in chorus.

"Well then," he said and swaggered out to the car, a lady on each arm.

NINETEEN

Nevada had expected to feel out of place rubbing shoulders with San Francisco's elite. Instead, the situation felt both comfortable and oddly familiar. Or maybe not so oddly if she was, indeed, the missing heiress, Whitney Snowden.

"You seem to be having a good time," Great-aunt Leticia observed in one of the lulls between dances.

Nevada smiled. "I am," she said, surprised to realize it was true. "I can't remember the last time I felt this relaxed, this happy." Of course, those ten stolen minutes she and Trick had just spent in a darkened alcove off the short hall that separated the main ballroom from the buffet were probably responsible for at least some of those happy feelings. She waved at Trick, currently working his way through the crowd toward them while juggling three champagne flutes. He smiled, looking every bit as happy as she felt.

I love you, she thought.

Then someone tapped her on the shoulder. "May I have this dance?"

She turned, still smiling, but when she saw the handsome cowboy gazing down at her, her heart did a cartwheel, and for a second or two, she couldn't catch her breath. "Mr. Faraday? What are you doing here?"

He tilted his head and extended one big hand. "Well, miss, I'm fixing to dance with the prettiest girl in the room. That's what I'm doing."

Next to Nevada, Great-aunt Leticia heaved a sigh, fanning herself with one wrinkled hand. "John Wayne couldn't have delivered that line with any more sincerity. Dance with the boy, Nevada. He's earned it."

"But Trick—"

"A little healthy competition never hurt anybody," Great-aunt Leticia said. "Now go. Dance."

But Great-aunt Leticia didn't understand. She didn't realize Ethan Faraday was a demon hunter, and that where there were demon hunters, there were bound to be demons.

Not sure what else to do, Nevada placed her hand in Faraday's and let him lead her onto the crowded dance floor, where he pulled her into his arms, not a body-to-body embrace but rather a formal waltz position. Even so, she knew he must be able to feel her trembling. The only saving grace was that her trembling was only partly fear. Another, almost equal part, was anger. She'd been having such a good time, a fairy-tale evening, and now here was Faraday, a flesh-and-blood reminder that no one got a happy ending without earning it, that monsters lurked in the dark, and that at least some of them were waiting for her. "How did you recognize me? I thought between the mask and the costume, I was pretty well disguised."

"You are." He gave her hand a reassuring squeeze. "If I hadn't seen you dancing with Granger, I wouldn't have made the connection. Who's the old lady?"

"Trick's great-aunt. She helped plan the event. She's why we're here. How about you? Why are you here? Did you follow Sarge?"

Faraday missed a step. "No. He's here, too?"

"I haven't seen him. I just assumed . . . What do you mean 'too'?"

"I'm chasing more dangerous prey tonight."

"More dangerous than Sarge?"

"A hell of a lot more dangerous. Older, richer, smarter. We don't know his real identity or what he looks like, but—crazy as it sounds—we think he's trying to take over the world, manipulate financial markets, control governments, heavy-duty stuff like that. Apparently, blood's not enough to satisfy him anymore."

"And he's here?" she said. "Why?"

Faraday shrugged. "Lots of rich, powerful people in attendance. Maybe he's planning to make a deal with one of them."

Nevada glanced around the crowded ballroom full of costumed guests. "How will you recognize him?"

Faraday shrugged again. "No saying I will, but hell, I figured it was worth a shot. Not every day a guy gets the opportunity to take down royalty."

"Royalty?"

"That's a joke," he said. "The guy's code name is King. All I know for sure is that he's English. You haven't heard any British accents this evening, have you?"

"A couple," she told him. "That actor, Hugh Sterling, for one."

Faraday shook his head. "Hollywood's full of blood-suckers, but I can't see a centuries-old vampire making romantic comedies."

Trick tapped Faraday on the shoulder. "May I cut in?" he asked.

"Music's finished," Faraday told him with a grin.

"Bad timing on my part," Trick said. "I didn't expect to see you here, Faraday."

"Yeah, I'm not much for these fancy shindigs, but I got word that Number One on our Ten Most Wanted list was going to be here. Couldn't pass up an opportunity like that."

"Not Sarge then?" Trick asked.

Faraday shook his head. "Lost him in Sacramento a couple days back."

"Sacramento," Trick said. "Wish I knew what it was with vampires and Sacramento."

Trick noticed that it took a while for Nevada to regain her spirits after the run-in with Faraday, but for the last half hour or so, she'd been glowing, and *damn,* he thought, Nevada in jeans and a T-shirt was sexy as hell, but Nevada in silk with her glow on outshone Hollywood's loveliest young starlets, several of whom were scattered around the ballroom.

"I still can't believe it," Nevada said. "Your great-aunt introduced me to the governor!"

"I met him, too."

"Wasn't he charming? Not nearly as intimidating as I would have expected him to be."

"Charm is political currency," Trick said dryly, "and readily doled out." Especially when the recipient of said charm was as young and beautiful as Nevada.

"I was introduced to one of the Silicon Valley geniuses, too, but I have to admit I didn't understand a single word she said after 'how do you do.'"

"Geek speak is a whole different language," Trick said. "Marcello's fairly fluent, but I only know a smattering myself." Out of the corner of his eye, he caught a glimpse of Faraday. With a tall, curvy Wonder Woman in tow, he was headed in their direction. "Let's get out of here," Trick whispered in Nevada's ear.

"Your great-aunt won't mind?"

Trick nodded toward the fringe of the crowd where Great-aunt Leticia was involved in a lively discussion with a tall, paunchy Abraham Lincoln. "I doubt she'll miss us."

"All right," Nevada agreed, giving him an impish smile that set his heart thumping so loudly, he could scarcely hear the music.

"Let's go make our excuses to Great-aunt Leticia."

"You go," Nevada said. "I'll meet you at the entrance. I need to freshen up."

One minute Nevada was working her way through the crowded bar and buffet area, heading for the ladies' room. The next, she heard a man laughing and stopped dead in her tracks, chills running up and down her spine. She knew that laugh.

In an instant, all her missing memories came rushing back: her father's body slumped in a chair beside the fireplace, her screams, footsteps pounding down the hall, then the murderer's reflection looming up behind her in the octagonal mirror.

The flash had been unbearably painful, much worse than normal, perhaps because the crime had been so fresh. "Dead," she'd managed to say in the split-second before she'd lost consciousness.

Nevada's anger flared white hot. She whirled around to face the man who'd taken her father's life, then done his best to destroy hers. He had his back to her, but once again, she saw the truth, reflected this time in the mirror behind the bar. A dark-haired man in a Zorro costume sat chatting with a distinguished-looking older gentleman dressed as Julius Caesar. "A pox on the Republicans!" Caesar said, speaking with an upper-crust British accent.

Another memory nagged at Nevada, but before she could extract it from the depths of her still-clouded mind, her half brother Daniel glanced up and saw her reflection. He stared intently. Caesar murmured something to him, but he didn't respond.

Surely he couldn't see through her disguise, not with half her face covered by the sequined mask. *Move,* she told herself. *Just turn and move away. Casually.* But she remained frozen in place.

She knew the instant he made the connection. His eyes narrowed even before he leaped to his feet.

A surge of adrenaline sent her racing. Even so, she seemed to be moving in slow motion. She dodged around guests heading to and from the bar, the voluminous skirt of her costume slowing her down as she made her way toward the exit sign. She didn't dare look back to see if Daniel was following her. If she could just make it to the women's restroom . . .

Halfway along the deserted hallway, he grabbed her roughly from behind and spun her around. "Spying on me again, Whitney?" He shook her as if she had no more substance than one of Great-aunt Leticia's rag dolls.

Nevada didn't waste time with pointless denials. She just screamed. Or started to. She'd barely sucked in a breath when Daniel clamped his hand across her mouth.

Ignoring the elevators, he dragged her toward the stairwell, forcing her inside.

The instant he removed his hand, she screamed, the sound echoing in the enclosed space.

His fingers tightened viciously on her arm. "Shut up."

But she didn't. She couldn't. Someone might hear. Someone might come to investigate.

"Shut the hell up!" Daniel slammed her against the cinder block wall, then slapped her repeatedly across the face, knocking her mask askew.

She couldn't see, couldn't breathe, couldn't do anything but gasp for air as tears ran down her face.

Daniel ripped her mask off and tossed it to the floor. "Thought you could hide from me, did you?"

"I wasn't hiding. I didn't know you were here."

"Just like you didn't know I was at the mall that day in Sacramento." He gave a harsh laugh. "How much did that bitch, Yelena, tell you?"

"Nothing, I swear."

"Liar!" he said. "I paid her to keep an eye on you, and she betrayed me."

"I'm not going back to the Appleton Institute."

"No," he agreed. "That would be pointless. I only allowed it the first time because Regina was dead set against silencing you more . . . permanently."

"You mean by killing me?"

"I don't like loose ends, and that's what you are, Whitney. I think it's time for you to disappear again, for good this time, just as our dear stepmother did."

"You killed Regina? But why? I thought you two were in this together."

"She grew tiresome."

"But you killed Dad because he found out what you and Regina were doing behind his back."

"No, Whitney." Daniel's smile chilled her blood. "I killed Dad because he threatened me, threatened my career. And it had nothing to do with Regina. Dad was no fool; he suspected what I was doing to you."

"Doing . . . to me?" she faltered.

"While you were sleeping. Drugged, actually. I was careful, too, not to leave any obvious marks. You never suspected a thing, did you?"

Nevada shuddered uncontrollably. She stared at

Daniel's handsome face, but all she could see was the monster who lived inside his skin. To think this foulness had touched her, had . . .

"Don't look like that. It wasn't as if I had a choice," he explained reasonably. "Regina was willing, of course, but I needed more than she had to offer. I've always been cursed with a voracious appetite."

Wave after wave of horror and disgust rippled through her. "You raped me? Your own sister? You drugged and raped me?"

"That's half sister," he corrected her. "And don't be ridiculous. Of course, I didn't rape you. Rape implies forcible entry, and I was always very careful, very gentle. It was never sex for its own sake anyway. Arousal increases blood flow, you see." He paused, but she was too horror-struck to say a word. "Greed was my downfall. Everyone started to comment on how pale and anemic you looked."

Pale and anemic?

"Then Dad caught me in your room at one in the morning with blood on my chin and my hand in the cookie jar, so to speak."

A horrible possibility occurred to her. "You were feeding more than your sexual appetite," she said faintly.

He showed his fangs in a travesty of a smile. "Yes, I *am* a vampire, though I'd appreciate it if you didn't spread it around. Oh, wait. I forgot." The vicious expression twisting his handsome face made her blood run cold. "You aren't going to have that option, are you, Whitney? You're about to disappear."

• • •

Trick glanced at his watch. What was keeping Nevada? He scanned the crowd in the ballroom, but there was no sign of her anywhere.

"Problem?"

He turned to find Ethan Faraday at his side. "Nevada went to the ladies' room, but she's been gone longer than expected. I'm probably overreacting."

"Or not," Faraday said. "If Nevada accidentally stumbled across that vamp I told you about . . ."

And had one of her unpredictable psychic flashes . . . Trick's heartbeat kicked up. "What does this vamp look like?"

Faraday shrugged. "See, that's the thing. Nobody seems to know. Or if they do, they're not talking. I did spot another mutual 'friend' of ours about five minutes ago, though."

The only candidate for that role was . . . "Sarge?" Trick's alarm level jumped from concerned to panicky. "Sarge is here?"

"Yeah," Faraday said. "Dressed as a clown. How's that for irony? Right now he's hovering near the elevators just outside this entrance."

"Shit," Trick swore. "Where he can't miss seeing us leave."

"There's a second bank of elevators in the hall beyond the bar," Faraday said.

"Where the restrooms are," Trick said. "I'll go wait for Nevada there. We'll have to leave the back way."

"Just in case," Faraday said, "you might want to keep

this handy." He passed Trick a pointed wooden stake. "Takes more muscle than a crossbow but works just as well. Keep an eye peeled for my badass, too. King's a major threat."

Trick slipped the stake into his pocket. "More dangerous than Sarge?"

"A thousand times more dangerous."

Dangerous. Nevada's father had died, and her stepmother had disappeared. What if . . . ? Fear made Trick's voice hoarse. "How much do you know about Daniel Snowden?"

Faraday shot him a speculative look. "Why?"

"He's Nevada's half brother, damn it. Any chance *he*'s your badass?"

Faraday seemed surprised at the suggestion. "No way. He's not British, not old enough, and as far as I know, not a vampire. Doubt he's here anyway. Didn't his stepmother just go missing?"

Yes, Trick thought, but if Snowden was responsible for his stepmother's disappearance . . . Fear threatened to choke him. "I'm going to find Nevada," he told Faraday, then took off across the ballroom at a run.

No sign of her in the room where the buffet was laid out. No sign of her in the crowded bar, either.

"You see a dark-haired young woman in a beaded white gown?" he asked one of the bartenders.

The guy shrugged. "Sorry, buddy. Can't help you. I've been too busy to do any people-watching. Any of you notice a dark-haired girl in a white dress?" he asked the other bartenders. No one had.

More worried by the second, Trick headed down the hall to the women's restroom, where he knocked on the door.

No answer.

He knocked again, harder this time. "Nevada? You in there?"

He heard a muffled scream but not from the ladies' room. He listened hard and heard another, even louder wail. The sound terminated abruptly, but not before he'd identified its source. The stairwell.

Trick burst through the door onto the landing, colliding with a man in a Zorro costume.

"Where is she?" Trick demanded.

"I don't know what you're talking about," Zorro said.

"I heard her scream. Where is she?" Trick grabbed the man, spun him around, and shoved him face-first against the wall. "Where's Nevada, damn it?"

"Don't know anyone named Nevada," the man said. "You've obviously mistaken me for someone else. For your information, I'm State Representative Daniel Snowden, and if you know what's good for you, you'll take your hands off me this minute."

"What did you do with her?" Trick, who'd been punctuating his interrogation by slamming Snowden repeatedly against the wall, suddenly caught a glimpse of Nevada lying motionless at the bottom of the stairs.

Snowden took advantage of Trick's distraction, twisting around and using the wall at his back as leverage to shove Trick off balance.

Trick stumbled sideways and teetered on the edge of the first step as Snowden lunged for the door.

"No, you don't!" Trick, flailing his arms in an attempt to regain his balance, connected with the railing, which he used to propel himself forward like a human projectile. He head-butted Snowden in the back, then sandwiched the bastard between the door and his own body, punching and pummeling. "Not so much fun, is it," Trick panted, "when you're the one on the receiving end of the punishment."

"To hell with you," Snowden said. "The little bitch deserved what she got."

"She didn't . . ." Trick slammed the other man's face against the heavy metal fire door and heard the crunch of breaking bone. ". . . deserve to die." Again he smashed Snowden's face into the door. "But you do."

Snowden shook his head and blood sprayed across the door. "My kind's hard to kill."

His kind? Meaning vampires? Trick suddenly remembered the stake Faraday had given him. Wedging Snowden against the door with his left hand and his good knee, he fumbled in the pocket of his trousers with his right hand.

Snowden, his face a pulverized mess, twisted his neck to peer over his shoulder. "What are you doing?" His voice had gone shrill with fear.

Trick brandished the stake. "Ending it."

Snowden moved faster than Trick would have believed possible. Bracing his hands against the door, he arched his back and shoved. Trick felt his bad knee start to go and staggered backward several feet, managing to anchor himself with his good leg before the impetus of the shove could send him toppling down the stairs.

Unfortunately, by the time he got his feet firmly under him, it was already too late. Snowden had his hand on the doorknob. In another instant, he would be gone.

Time slowed to a crawl. Snowden turned to face Trick. A triumphant smirk spread across his battered, blood-smeared face.

"You son of a bitch!" Trick yelled. Each word echoed eerily off the walls of the stairwell. "You-you-you-you son-son-son-son . . ."

Something slammed against the door from the other side with a solid blam. The door swung open, and Snowden was thrown forward onto Trick with tremendous force. It wasn't until he felt the force of the impact reverberating up his arm that he realized what had happened. The stake Trick still gripped tightly in his right hand had buried itself in Snowden's chest.

"Fu—" Snowden started, then exploded into dust.

Trick closed his eyes to protect them from the cloud of fine particulate matter, but he couldn't close his nose to the odor. The rotten stench of evil, he thought.

Then Ethan Faraday and two uniformed hotel security guards rammed through the door, and time once again resumed its normal pace.

Quickly pocketing the bloody stake, Trick blinked at the others through the dusty haze that was all that remained of Snowden.

"What's going on in here?" one of the guards demanded.

"A man attacked me and my date," Trick said.

"There he goes!" Faraday shouted and took off up the stairs. The security guards followed.

Slowly, the dust settled. Trick brushed himself off, then sick with rage—rage at Snowden for killing the only woman he'd ever loved and rage at himself for showing up seconds too late to save her—he stumbled down to the landing below, knelt, and gathered Nevada's body close, cradling it in his arms.

She'd never have her happy ending now.

He wasn't sure how long he crouched there, just holding her limp body and trying not to think. But there was no stemming the flood of recriminations. If only he'd been a few seconds earlier. If only he hadn't wasted so much time talking to Faraday. If only he hadn't stopped to question the bartender. If only . . .

Feeling like the worst sort of failure, he gazed down at her pale cheeks, glistening now with tears. His tears. He pressed a kiss to her lips, one last kiss good-bye, then nearly dropped her when he felt her return the pressure, kissing him back.

"Nevada?" He wiped his eyes on his shirtsleeve. "Nevada, can you hear me?"

"Trick?" Her eyelashes fluttered open.

"You're not dead."

"Are you sure?" she said with a grimace.

"Very sure." He smiled so hard his cheek muscles hurt. "The fall must have knocked you unconscious for a few minutes."

She frowned. "I fell?"

"I didn't see it happen, but I suspect Snowden pushed you."

"Daniel. My half brother." Her frown deepened. "I remember now. I remember everything." Suddenly her frown morphed into a look of sheer panic. "Where is he?"

"Gone," Trick told her. "And he won't be coming back. I staked him, or, to be precise, he accidentally staked himself."

Surprise supplanted panic. "You know about him then?"

"That he was a vampire? Yes, he told me."

"Something Daniel said made me think my step-mother was a vampire, too."

"So she wasn't kidnapped, and she didn't just take off."

"I don't think so, no. I think Daniel killed her. He killed my father, too. He admitted it."

"So it was his reflection that triggered your psychic flash," Trick guessed.

"More like a psychic meltdown."

"He and your stepmother must have been fooling around behind your father's back," Trick said. "Your father figured out what was going on, confronted Daniel, and Daniel killed him, then made it look like sui-cide. Only you, with your psychic flash, nearly ruined everything. That's why you ended up at the Appleton Institute."

"Daniel wanted to kill me, too, but Regina wouldn't let him."

"So the evil stepmother wasn't quite as evil as we thought."

"No," Nevada said, struggling to a sitting position. "And my guardian angel wasn't quite as good as we thought, either."

"Yelena, you mean?"

"Daniel admitted that he sent her to the Institute to keep an eye on me. He paid her over and above what she earned there. Blood money," she said. "I should have known. The minute I set foot in her town house, I should have realized no one could afford a place like that on a cleaning woman's wages. I was so stupid, so gullible."

"And yet, Yelena was the one who freed you in the end," he reminded her.

Nevada's lower lip quivered. "I guess her guilty conscience finally got the better of her."

"Or her love for you."

"How could she love me and be a party to the torture they put me through?" Her voice shook with strain.

"People aren't all good or all bad. We're a mix of the two. Yelena may have allowed herself to be ruled by greed for a while, but in the end love won out. She double-crossed Daniel to save you."

"And ended up dead." Tears welled up and slid silently down her cheeks.

He held her close and let her cry.

When at last the tears subsided, he pressed a quick kiss to her forehead.

Faraday came clattering down the stairs at that moment sans security guards. "Oh, hey. You're all right," he said to Nevada.

"We need to get her to a doctor," Trick said, "have her checked out."

"Sure thing." Faraday shot her an encouraging smile.

"While I'm thinking of it . . ." Trick returned Faraday's stake.

The demon hunter eyed the bloodstains. "Glad I could help."

"You knew my half brother was a vampire?" Nevada asked.

"Didn't have a clue," Faraday said. "The spike was for Sarge."

Nevada's eyes widened. "Sarge is here?"

"Not anymore," Faraday said.

Trick lifted Nevada into his arms and carried her up the stairs. "You staked him?" he asked.

"No such luck. Tricky bastard gave me the slip," Faraday said. "Again."

"And the security guards?"

"Heard a chopper on the roof and figured your so-called attacker was getting away." He grinned. "I might have planted the suggestion. Anyway, once they were focused on the chopper, I headed back down, figured you might need some help."

"Thanks, Faraday," Trick said, meaning it. "Thanks for everything."

TWENTY

Nevada didn't say much on the drive back to Midas Lake. She spent half the time pretending to doze, the other half staring at the dashboard.

"Do you have a headache?" Trick asked finally.

"No. Why?"

"You're frowning."

She gave him a halfhearted smile. "I'm thinking. It's hard work."

"Thinking about what?"

"The future," she said.

"When I talked to Marcello this morning, he said the Realtor got a bite on the house. Prospective buyer didn't even try to dicker."

"All your hard work paid off."

"*Our* hard work," he said.

She didn't respond to that. "Where will you go?" she asked some time later, carefully not looking at him.

"Somewhere in the South Seas. Aside from Hawaii,

I've never been anywhere in the Pacific, though it might be fun to try Tahiti or maybe Samoa for a while. What do you think?"

"I think . . ." She paused for so long he thought she wasn't going to respond at all. "I think," she said finally, "it's your decision, not mine. How about Marcello? What does he have to say about your plan?"

"Marcello's been making his own plans."

"Really?" She seemed to perk up a little at that. "Is he . . . I mean, do you think he and Britt . . ."

"Are planning their future?" he asked, raising an eyebrow.

"Well, yes, I definitely think there's something going on there."

"If you mean, Marcello has feelings for Britt and vice versa, you're right. But if you're thinking Marcello's going to do anything about it, then you don't really know him. He's married, Nevada, and he takes those vows seriously."

"In sickness and in health," she said.

"He's already made arrangements for his future, and they don't include breaking Britt's heart."

"Too late," she muttered.

"He's joining the organization Faraday works for."

She whirled around to face him. "As a demon hunter?"

"Don't sound so surprised."

"But a demon hunter? Marcello?"

"Actually, he's going to be working in the office. At least until he learns the ropes," Trick said. "And face it, who better? The man's a computer whiz."

"Geek," she said. "The word you're searching for is *geek*."

Nevada took one last look at the shabby little apartment over the stables. She was going to miss this place—the rusty shower, the saggy couch, the ugly brown box of an oil heater that took up half the living room.

Okay, damn it, the apartment wasn't what she'd miss. Seeing Patrick Donatelli Granger. That's what she'd miss.

She'd arranged for the taxi to pick her up at the end of the driveway in ten minutes. Time to start hauling her stuff down. How had she accumulated so much in so little time? She'd arrived with the clothes on her back. She'd be leaving with enough to fill one of those oversize wheeled suitcases. Only of course, she didn't have an oversize wheeled suitcase. All she had was the chic little overnight case Trick had bought her at the Papillon Mall, a bulging backpack, and a stuffed-to-the-gills army surplus duffel bag.

With the backpack slung over her left shoulder and the overnight case hanging from its strap over her right, she dragged the duffel bag two-handed as she backed out the door onto the rickety wooden landing. She dropped the bag with a thunk and made a grab for the door, trying to catch it before it slammed shut.

"Going somewhere?" Trick asked from behind her, startling her so badly that her heart skipped a beat.

"Yes," she said, sounding much calmer than she felt.

"In the middle of the night?" Trick didn't sound calm, though. In fact, he sounded totally pissed.

"Bus leaves for Reno in an hour."

He stared at her, his face starkly angular in the moonlight, brows knit, jaw squared, mouth a tight line. "All you had to do was ask," he said mildly. "I'd have given you a ride."

She closed her eyes against the sudden pain. "Don't."

"Don't what?" He paused, continuing when she didn't respond. "You were planning to run away again, weren't you?"

"Trick, I—"

"At least, read this first before you go." He held out a sheet of parchment.

"What is it?"

"A letter Jonathan Calhoun thought might interest you."

She set down her luggage and took the letter, tilting it so the security light illuminated the words.

My darling Blanche,

Your death lies heavy on my heart. Many in this town believe I murdered you. You know that isn't true, and yet, the guilt is mine. I was so obsessed with you that I underestimated the depth of Opal's jealousy. I should have realized the danger she posed. Rest easy, my love. Opal has paid for her sins as I, too, shall pay for mine.

All my love,
Silas

Nevada frowned. "Opal killed Blanche?"

"And Silas killed Opal."

"But what did he mean when he said 'as I, too, shall pay for mine'?"

"You never heard that part of the story?" he said. "The same day Silas wrote this note, he hanged himself in Blanche's room."

"That's why she cries—not because he killed her, but because he killed himself. She loved him."

"And I love you," he said. "Marry me."

Her chest constricted. She tried to make sense of Trick's words, but she couldn't breathe, let alone think. "What?" she finally managed. "No, I can't."

"I didn't plan to do it this way, you know." He dug a small jewelry box from his pocket. "I'd thought we'd go the romance route, flowers and dinner and me down on one knee. In fact, I intended to ask you after the ball, only then you got hurt, and the ER didn't really have the right ambiance."

"Trick, no. Don't do this."

He opened the box and pulled out a ring. "I bought this at McKelvey Fine Jewelry. Seemed fitting somehow. Remember the call I received the morning Great-aunt Leticia caught us in bed together? That was the salesman telling me the ring was ready. I had it specially engraved. 'Happily ever after . . .' "

"I . . . no . . . Trick," she stammered.

He held the ring, tilting it until it caught the light. A narrow band with a large stone. Not a diamond, something darker. "An emerald," he said, as if in answer to her unspoken question. "To match your eyes."

"It's beautiful, and I'm touched by your offer, more than I can say, but—"

"No buts." He took her left hand in his and slid the ring on her finger. "A little too big, but we can have it sized to fit."

Oh God, why wouldn't he listen? "I can't marry you, Trick."

"Why not? And don't try to convince me that you don't love me, because I'm not buying it."

"Don't ask me why. I just can't."

He eyed her closely. "You've been acting strange ever since your run-in with Snowden. This has something to do with your half brother, doesn't it? He said something to you, something that frightened you."

Yes, she thought, but, "No," she said.

"Whatever he told you, don't believe a word of it. What did he say? That you were the one who'd killed your father? That he'd arranged your father's murder to look like a suicide to protect you?"

"I know better than that. I 'saw' what he did."

"Then what's the problem? What other lies did he tell you?" Trick stared at her face for an endless moment. Then he groaned. "No, he didn't."

Oh God. He knew.

"He told you that you were a vampire, too. And you believed him?"

"How could I not? The clues were there all along. I just refused to see them. All Daniel did was open my eyes."

"Snowden didn't open your eyes, Nevada. He poisoned your mind."

"I know it's a shock, finding out this way. Imagine how I feel."

"I am imagining," he said grimly. "I swear, if I could bring that slimy bastard back to life, I would, just for the satisfaction of staking him a second time."

"I'm a vampire," she said, "but I didn't choose that path. I wouldn't. I didn't even know what he'd done, not until he told me. I was drugged so I wouldn't remember. Only my father noticed how pale I was, and started to get suspicious."

"Snowden was drinking your blood."

"I don't think my father knew exactly what Daniel was up to, but when he caught Daniel in my room in the middle of the night, there was an ugly confrontation. Daniel killed my father to protect himself and his secret. Then he convinced Regina to send me to the Appleton Institute to protect mine. I wasn't locked away because of my random psychic flashes or because they believed I was mentally unstable. Dr. Appleton was trying to cure my vampirism."

Silence stretched between them—cold and bleak.

Trick was the first to break it. "Snowden lied, Nevada. The bastard lied. He was trying to hurt you, destroy you. You're not a vampire."

"But it all makes sense," she said.

"In what alternate universe?"

"No, Trick, listen. I bit you. Remember? When we had sex, I bit you."

He dismissed her words with an impatient flip of his hand. "You nipped at me, didn't even break the skin. Haven't noticed yourself craving blood, have you?"

"No, but"—she held out a hand—"look how pale I am."

"Lots of people have fair skin."

"But I'm part Gypsy. Shouldn't I be darker? And what about my sensitivity to the sun? If I don't slather on sunscreen, I burn within minutes of exposure."

"Burn, yes, but that's not the same as burning up, bursting into flames."

"What about those pills, the ones Yelena insisted I take, one a day, every day? I've been thinking about that. She was so insistent. I think she knew I needed the pills to suppress the worst of my symptoms."

"That's bullshit."

"You don't know that."

"Actually, I do. Marcello already had a pharmacist check out your pills."

"He thought I was a vampire?"

"What can I say? The man has a suspicious streak a mile wide. Imagine his embarrassment when he found out your 'antivampire pills' were actually prescription allergy medicine," Trick said.

"Allergy medicine?" she repeated, thinking she must have misunderstood.

"Fexofenadine. A cheap generic."

"Okay, so maybe the pills aren't bloodlust suppressants, but Daniel drank my blood. He admitted it. He bragged about it."

"And I believe that part of the sick son of a bitch's story. He drank your blood. Hell, he probably did his best to suck you dry. Only there was no reciprocal bloodsucking. Think about it. How could you have drunk his blood if you were unconscious? And since according to Faraday, vampirism is caused by a rare blood-borne parasite, there's no way you could have been infected because you didn't ingest any of his infected blood."

Nevada's heart gave a wild leap. "Oh God."

"What's wrong?" A worried expression crossed Trick's face. "Why are you crying?"

"Relief, I guess. I'm not a vampire."

"I already said that. And if I remember correctly, I also asked you to marry me."

She moved closer, wrapping her arms around his neck. "And I said no." She kissed him, a long, lingering kiss that only made her hungry for more.

"Does that mean you've changed your mind?" Trick's voice was unsteady. "You *are* going to marry me?"

"Yes," she said, her voice just as shaky as his. "Definitely yes."

"You'll never have to run away again," Trick promised.

"Never," she agreed.

"Because this"—he kissed her—"is the official beginning of the happily-ever-after part."

And it was.

Discover the darker side of desire.

Discover the darker side of passion with these bestselling paranormal romances from Pocket Books!

Kresley Cole
Wicked Deed on a Winter's Night
Immortal enemies…forbidden temptation.

Alexis Morgan
Redeemed in Darkness
She vowed to protect her world from the enemy—
until her enemy turned her world upside down.

Katie MacAlister
Ain't Myth-Behaving
He's a God. A legend. A man of mythic proportions…
And he'll make you long to myth-behave.

Melissa Mayhue
Highland Guardian
For mortals caught in Faeire schemes,
passion can be dangerous…